THE HOLLOW ONE

CORINNE WESTBROOK

A PERMUTED PRESS BOOK
ISBN: 979-8-89565-599-3
ISBN (eBook): 979-8-89565-600-6

Cover art by Jim Villaflores

Permuted Press
New York • Nashville
permutedpress.com

Published in the United States of America
1 2 3 4 5 6 7 8 9 10

CONTENTS

AFTER SCHOOL

Ellie white-knuckled the pink straps of her backpack as she walked home. The sun was slanting low behind the school, dragging stretched fingers of dusk over the sidewalk. Her dingy sneakers scuffed against the cracked concrete with a *shff-shff-shff*, a sound Mom said made her teeth hurt. "Pick up your feet, Ellie, you're going to ruin your shoes." But Ellie wasn't thinking about that now.

"One, two, three..." she whispered, eyes on the sidewalk, her blond hair hanging in her face. Usually, she skipped over every crack she counted, a game to occupy her mind on the walk home. One misstep and she'd break her mother's back. But today, she stepped across them with purpose. No skipping. No pretending. No time for games. The risk felt small. Her mother's back would be just fine under the blanket she liked to pull over her head. If she was even home at all.

No, there was no time for games. Not when Sam was most likely alone.

Her little brother was just a baby, barely past the stage of holding up his own head, and not past the stage of crying himself hoarse if he was hungry or cold or scared. Ellie's fingers clenched around the fabric of her bag. Had Sam eaten today? Had he been changed?

Mrs. Rieke had tried to stop her as she left the classroom, holding out a plastic cup of orange slices and saying her name in that slow, careful voice teachers used when they know something isn't right. "Ellie, do you want to sit with me for a snack? Just for a little bit?"

But Ellie had just shimmied on her backpack and said "My mom said I gotta go straight home."

Mrs. Rieke tried to press the paper cup into her hand. "For later," she said, but Ellie was already rushing out of the classroom.

Ellie had lied. Her mom hadn't said anything this morning. Not *good morning*. Not *don't forget your coat*. Not *have a good day at school*. Ellie had just started first grade the month before, and her mother never asked her about Mrs. Rieke, about what she was learning, about how she did on her spelling tests. If she was home, she just laid there, curled toward the wall with her face hidden, the bottle on the floor half hidden by a crumpled T-shirt.

"Four, five, six…" Ellie kept counting the cracks, eyes down, jaw clenched. Her stomach gave a low, watery growl, loud against the *shff-shff-shff* of her feet. She hadn't eaten since lunch, and barely then. Overcooked chicken nuggets and canned fruit. She'd tucked her carton of milk into her backpack for Sam's bottle, just in case there was no formula in the house.

It was still October and the kind of Oregon fall that felt like a warning. The sun looked colder than it used to, and the trees had started to shake off their leaves in a cascade of yellow, orange, and red. The wind that came around the corners of buildings had teeth in it now—baby teeth for the moment—but sharp enough to make Ellie button her jacket up to her chin.

The Hollow One

She passed the old tire swing with the fraying rope in the neighbor's yard without an upward glance. Its shadow swayed in the breeze. A few more houses down, a dog barked at her and continued barking at nothing behind her. The dog stared into the empty street, ears stiff and body frozen. Ellie's skin prickled. She didn't slow down. Just a few more houses farther and the sidewalk ended, giving way to gravel, the neat shape of the town stretching behind her.

Ellie stayed on the edge of the road where the gravel met the grass. Her legs were tired, and the uneven ground hurt her feet, but she didn't want to walk in the road—not this far out. Cars didn't pass through here often, but when they did, they came fast.

She could see her house just ahead. It was small, the paint peeling, the screen door hanging on one hinge. One gutter hung low and bent in a crooked smile. The yard was patchy and wild with weeds. A small, broken windmill lay on its side by the front porch, half-buried in the brush.

She reached the front porch and stopped. The porch light was off. No car in the driveway. Her mom's car was rarely there at night, but Ellie had still hoped. Sometimes the grind of the tires on gravel would fill the quiet of the house, the headlights slanting across the windows in a sharp, searching sweep.

The front steps let out a creak as she climbed them. The third one would squish even under her small frame; she stepped over it. The door was locked, like it always was. Ellie crouched and reached under the flowerpot filled with crumbling stems for the spare key, grime sticking to her hands. She wiped them on her jeans and tried to remember if they had laundry soap.

Inside, the house wasn't quiet. A keening wail came from the back room. Sam was crying. No, not just crying—he was screaming that hoarse, frantic kind of cry that meant he'd been doing it for a while.

Ellie flinched then hurried inside, locking the door behind her with a soft click. The crying kept going, steady and wild. She dropped her backpack on the floor. *I shouldn't have gone to school,* she thought. *I know better.*

It's always up to me, she thought.

Then, softer, meaner: *It's not fair.*

But Sam was still crying.

The air in the house smelled like mildew, dust, and sour milk with the faintest hint of baby powder. The blinds were half closed; some of the slats were bent out of shape. Lines of pale light striped the floor and furniture like a cage.

"Mama?" she called out, even though she already knew. No answer.

She kicked off her sneakers and stretched her toes. They ached. Her socks whispered over the worn carpet as she hurried down the hallway, her heart in her stomach at the sound of Sam's cries. She walked straight to the room she shared with Sam.

The door was cracked open, and the soft glow of their nightlight spilled out in a thin line across the floor. It was the only light in the hallway. It made the air feel slowed, like everything was underwater. The crying grew louder as she moved toward the door, echoing off the narrow walls. Her stomach twisted into a knot, drawn and hot and guilty.

Ellie pushed the door open with her small hand, her breath catching.

Sam was bright red, his face blotchy and wet with tears and snot, his little fists clamped to the railing of his crib like a vise. His knuckles were as white as Ellie's after gripping the straps of her backpack for the whole walk home. His blanket was tangled around his legs. His bottle lay on the floor near the dresser, tipped on its side, empty. His diaper sagged low, swollen and dark. The sour smell made her eyes and nose sting.

"It's okay," Ellie whispered, stepping into the room. She stretched her hands up to frame his face, the railing of the crib just as high as the top of her head. Her voice was soft but steady. "I got you, okay? I'm here."

Ellie reached for the little white step ladder folded against the wall. It was old and shaky, but it worked. She climbed up carefully, one hand braced on the crib's wooden railing for balance. She leaned over the bars and gently scooped her arms under him. She wobbled a little from the stretch, but she held on tight. He clung to her shirt, his cries breaking into hiccups, his body hot and desperate.

She laid Sam down on a towel and peeled off the soaked diaper. The wipes were almost gone, only two left, and she didn't want to waste them. He needed a bath anyway; he already had the start of a rash. She'd been gone too long. She wiped him down just enough to keep things from getting worse, then bundled him in the towel and carried him to the bathroom.

The bathroom was small and everything inside was just a little off. The linoleum peeled up in the corners, the towel rack hung lower on the left than the right, and one corner of the mirror had turned black. The cabinet under the sink was long warped from water damage and never closed all the way.

The old fiberglass tub was scratched and peeling from the walls, dulled by years of scrubbing and shampoo. A long gray streak ran from the drain to the back, and dull rings discolored the floor of the tub where the water pooled. These were the kinds of stains that don't come from dirt, but from time. Ellie didn't bother trying to scrub them away anymore.

She turned on the tap. The faucet gurgled, then let out a cough of cold water before the warmth caught up. The water came out cloudy at first, full of air bubbles from the old pipes. She kept her hand under the chugging flow of water, testing and adjusting until it felt just right. Warm, not hot.

She watched the tub fill, the water rising above the stains until it looked like something better than it was. Then she turned off the faucet, scooped up Sam, and settled him gently in the warm water. His cries stopped and he blinked at her, wide-eyed, the warmth lapping at his skin. He started to kick his legs with a giggle, splashing and saying something in that language only babies understand.

Ellie smiled and poured water over his belly with her hand, washing away the sour smell. The scratches on the side of the tub caught the light as she leaned over to grab the bar of soap. She avoided looking at them. She didn't want to think about how many things in this house were broken in places nobody bothered to see.

In the kitchen, the overhead light flickered once with the click of the switch, then steadied, casting everything in a dim yellow wash. Ellie set Sam on the floor as she popped the bottle into the microwave. Filled with the milk from her lunch, it spun slowly behind the smudged glass, the machine buzzing like it might give up any second.

Sam was clean now, his skin warm and pink from the bath. His fresh diaper crinkled when he scooted across the floor. His curly hair was damp and clung to his head, smelling faintly like the green bar of soap.

She bundled him in a onesie that was too small to snap and pants that stretched over his legs. The little blue socks on his feet would be lucky to stay on all night. It felt good to have him clean and dry and safe, even if only for a little while.

While the bottle warmed, Ellie grabbed a slice of bread and dropped it in the toaster. Just one—there was only enough for tonight and maybe breakfast. She leaned against the counter waiting for both things to finish. The kitchen was filled with the hum of the microwave, the slow *click-click* of the toaster coils warming, and the babbling of the baby at her feet.

When the microwave beeped, she took the bottle out and tested it on her hand. Warm, not hot. Just right.

Sam latched onto the bottle the moment it touched his lips, his breath hitching in that desperate little way. Ellie brushed her hand over his damp hair and watched him drink his milk, her own body slowly unwinding and settling into the evening.

The toast popped up and Ellie started. She had forgotten. She got up quietly, taking the warm bread in her hand. She scraped down the sides of a jar of peanut butter, spreading a thin layer on the crusty bread. She took a few slow bites, savoring her dinner.

When Sam had finished his bottle, he rubbed his eyes and made a soft sound of contentment, more of a yawn than a cry. Ellie wiped the dribbles of milk from his face with the corner of her sleeve, then lifted him gently from the floor, carrying him to the living room.

The worn blue blanket with faded stars was draped across the couch cushions. Ellie sat down with her brother, pulling the blanket over both of them and, as she leaned back, letting out a long, quiet breath. The blanket used to smell like her dad. He'd wrap it around them both when the house was dark. He'd turn on cartoons and say it was a special night, just for fun. His voice was always loud and excited on those nights. She tried to laugh with him, but her eyes kept closing. He would give her cookies and tell her not to tell Mom. Her mother never came out of the bedroom on those nights. The door stayed shut, even when the TV was too loud. Now, the blanket mostly smelled like her. Soap. Baby spit. Toast.

Ellie clicked on the TV, but neither of them watched it. Old cartoons danced across the screen. Sam's thumb was in his mouth now, the other hand resting lightly on her leg; he needed to make sure she wasn't going anywhere. She stayed like that until his body grew slack with sleep. A calm settled over his lungs. His fingers twitched.

When she finally carried Sam back to their bedroom, her arms hurt from holding him. She didn't mind the ache. It was the kind of ache that made her feel useful.

She nudged the bedroom door open with her foot and crossed the creaky floorboards, careful, shifting Sam's weight so he didn't wake and so she didn't drop him. The rickety, white step ladder sat where she had left it, standing at the ready next to the crib. She climbed up, knees wobbling slightly beneath her.

Getting Sam into the crib without waking him took patience and precision. She lowered him slowly, arms stretching deep over the railing, standing on her tiptoes to reach, her muscles shaking. He gave a tiny sigh when his back met the mattress of the crib, but his eyes didn't open. His lashes simply fluttered once and then settled.

She stood there watching him. She adjusted his blanket, pale green with a stitched bear in the middle. She smoothed it carefully, covering him from his shoulders to his toes, tucking the edges underneath his small body. As the house settled into the night, the room was filled with the scent of dust and quiet.

She stepped down from the stool and dragged it back to its resting place. Then she turned to her own bed across the room.

It was narrow, with a mattress likely older than the children's mother. It dipped in the middle like a spoon. It was in that dip that Ellie would fold herself. The sheets and pillowcase didn't match, and the pillow had gone flat a long time ago. Ellie would fold it in half to make it feel like more.

When Sam first came home, she'd hated sharing a room with him. He was noisy and her things started to smell like his. But now it felt safer, being together. The quiet couldn't get as big if you split it between two people.

She climbed into bed and pulled the blanket close around her, covering her head, but not her face. She was balled up on her side facing the crib. She liked being able to see Sam while he slept. It made her feel like the world couldn't quite tip over as long as she was looking.

Moonlight seeped in through the blinds in thin silver streaks, striping the floor with soft bars. The light shifted with every breeze that passed through the trees outside. The shadows of the leaves moved gently, like they were dancing slowly, like they knew something she didn't.

She watched the stripes on the floor for a long time, breathing slowly. Counting her breaths to calm her mind.

One. Two. Three.

Back again.

One. Two....

She balled her fists around the edges of her blanket, knotting it beneath her chin. Her eyes burned, but she didn't cry. She didn't want to cry.

"Goodnight, Daddy," she whispered, her lips barely moving.

Her voice didn't carry, but the words felt weighted, like stones pressed deep into the earth in a place no one visited anymore. She whispered it like she had every night since he left.

Since the door slammed behind him.

But she didn't want to think about that. Not now. Not tonight.

He used to stand in her bedroom doorway and say it back. *G'night, baby girl.*

He used to leave the hall light on for her.

She turned onto her other side and stared at the wall, tracing the cracks in the old paint with her eyes. The wind picked up outside, and she could hear faint groaning in the distance. Maybe the porch. Maybe the trees.

She tried not to think about the woods. About the way the trees creaked. About the branches that looked like arms reaching out.

She closed her eyes. And tried very hard not to think about any of it.

TAPS

At first, Ellie didn't know what had woken her.

The world felt soft around the edges, and nothing held a definite shape. She might have twisted and turned, or maybe she hadn't moved at all. The only thing she knew was something was…off.

Tap, tap, tap.

And there it was. The sound that had woken her.

Her lashes fluttered. Her limbs felt leaden, too heavy to move. She was warm, cocooned under the blanket, but the air on her face was cold. It clung to her skin, thin and biting, the kind of cold that slipped in unnoticed until it filled the room. The kind that reminded her of forgotten stairways in school buildings—the kind about which kids told stories and dared each other to walk down.

Again. *Tap, tap, tap.*

This time, the tapping was sharper, more insistent. It didn't sound like it belonged to the world inside the room. Ellie blinked up at the ceiling, confused, still half lost in sleep. She kept her body still. Not from fear, at least not yet, but from instinct. The deep-rooted animal instinct to hunker down before a storm. The kind of stillness that came when you suddenly felt eyes on you, when you knew you weren't alone anymore but couldn't prove it.

Tap, tap, tap.

She didn't sit up right away. She lay there, her chest barely moving with each inhale, eyes half open, attuned the quiet pulse of the night outside. The shadows of the leaves outside danced gently along the wall. They looked like they were moving with purpose rather than their typical slow, lazy dance. They looked like they were listening.

Tap.

This time, she felt it in the pit of her stomach. A thin, brittle sound that definitely did not belong in the room.

Ellie sat up, her blanket slipping down around her waist. The air hit her skin and sent goose-prickles across her arms, legs, and down her back. Her heart was racing, fluttering quick and light like a trapped moth beating its wings inside her ribs, begging for her mind to catch up. Her ears rang with the quiet.

She quickly looked toward the crib across the room. She found it before anything else. Sam was asleep, curled and tiny under his blanket, his fingers tucked near his face. His breathing came in soft, steady puffs. He needed another blanket, but he was safe.

Tap, tap, tap. It was coming from the window.

Ellie stayed where she was, her legs huddled beneath the blanket and her back straight and trembling, the hairs on the back of her neck standing straight up. The sound stopped again. The quiet felt worse than the tapping. She turned her head, straining to listen—the kind of listening you did with your whole body.

The trees outside weren't creaking. The weathered boards of the porch didn't groan. The leaves danced, but the breeze was indistinguishable. There was no humming from the refrigerator down the hall. No rustling or movement from her mother's room, no shifting of the pipes or settling of the house. Just the fair, constant buzz that lived in the corners of silence. Ellie realized she was holding her breath. She let it out slowly, so slowly as to not make a sound.

She wrapped her fingers around the blanket bunched at her waist. Her eyes darted to the door. Back to Sam. Still breathing. Still asleep. Still safe. Back to the shadows on the wall, studying them for any movement not of the leaves. She studied the lines of moonlight cast on the wall through the narrow slats of aluminum that never closed quite right. The streaks moved, like something outside had passed in front of the light. She told herself it was a branch. She told herself a lot of things all at once.

Tap, tap. Closer. Firmer. Right against the glass.

Ellie turned toward the window.

She slipped out of bed, her bare feet pressing quietly into the carpet. *Tap.* It came quick and deliberate, not loud but splintering, cutting through the hush of the house. She crept toward the window, careful not to breathe too hard, careful not to step too hard. Everything around her felt like it was holding its breath. The walls, the furniture, even the air, suspended in stillness, waiting.

She reached out and slid her fingers through the bent aluminum, nudging the slats apart to peek through. For a second, all she saw was herself, her face ghostly as it reflected faintly back at her from the glass, hair wild and tangled, her eyes wide. She flinched, not recognizing the shape of herself in the dark. Her own reflection shimmered back at her like someone watching from the other side. But it was just her.

She leaned in closer, squinting past the glare, pressing her forehead gently to the cool glass. The backyard unfolded on the other side of the window, still and silver in the night. The yard was patchy and untamed, like the front, glinting faintly where the moonlight touched it. Weeds crept along the base of the fence line, and a broken lawn chair sat tipped on its side near the edge of the porch, legs splayed. The trees pressed close behind the yard, beyond the fence, dense and dark and hunched, their branches tangled against the sky.

And there, just beyond the window, standing where the moonlight fell in uneven patches, was a figure. He was far enough back that she couldn't see every detail, not at once, but close enough that she knew he was watching. His shape was loose, shoulders huddled inward as if to make himself seem smaller.

Ellie's heart paused, then kicked against her ribs like it was trying to crawl higher in her chest. She stared, not sure yet if what she was seeing was real or just the kind of not-real thing that sometimes crept into the world when you woke up too fast in the dark.

The figure wasn't moving. He just stood there, almost blending into the stillness of the night around him, almost swallowed up by it. But the moonlight touched part of his face, enough for her to see and her mind to catch up to what her eyes already knew.

Her father.

He stood as if he had been waiting there for a long time. His clothes hung strangely, loose, like they didn't belong to him anymore. Like someone else's shape had stretched them out before they were handed down. His face was pale, paler than she remembered, his skin pulled thin across his cheekbones. The shadows under his eyes were deep, his frame slumped.

He stepped forward, hand raised, slow and careful, reaching toward the window. He didn't press his palm to the glass. He stayed an arm's length away and extended his fingers to drum them against the pane.

Tap, tap, tap.

That was the sound that had pulled her from sleep. That soft, bare touch of his nails against the window. Not a knock. Not a demand. A request.

The atmosphere pressed down, suffocating and still. She didn't speak. Didn't call out. Didn't move away from the window. Some part of her knew she should. She should run to her bed and bury her face in the covers, should try to find her mom, should shut the blinds and never look again, but her body wouldn't listen.

His eyes found hers through the slats. They didn't search, didn't get lost in their own reflection as hers had. It was like they knew exactly where she would be, as if he'd been looking at that spot for a long time, just waiting for her eyes to appear. Even from where he stood, just beyond the glass, bathed in a spill of moonlight, she could feel his attention wrap around her, steady and focused, the way he used to look at her.

He didn't smile, but the more she looked, the more his face felt soft…inviting. There was a weariness in the way he held himself, but he was warm, familiar. He looked like he had walked a long way to get there, and she thought she could see something behind his eyes. Something careful. Something a little sad. It made her stomach ache.

"Baby girl," he said.

The words opened something in her heart. She let out the breath she had been holding, and her eyes stung for reasons she didn't understand all at once. It was the way he said it. Like no time had passed at all. Like he had never left. She was always *baby girl.* And hearing those words now, whispered just for her, made the world feel smaller. Simpler. She leaned a little closer to the window, not even thinking about it, drawn by something comforting and known. Her fingers pulled down on the slats of the blinds, opening them wider.

He spoke again. Slower this time. Gentle.

"Baby girl," he repeated. "Let me in."

She heard it. Not just the sound of it, but the way it folded around her. A blanket being pulled up. There was no harshness in his voice, no demand. Just something soft. Careful. He didn't move. Didn't knock again. He just stood there, waiting.

Her hand cinched slightly on the blinds. Her other hand hung at her side, trembling. She didn't notice her toes balled up in the carpet. She didn't notice the chill in the room. All she noticed was the way his voice settled in her ribs, the way her body remembered the feel of his arms lifting her up, the smell of his coat, the rhythm of his voice in the hallway light.

The house was quiet.

She didn't speak.

She didn't blink.

She didn't move.

She stood staring through the narrow gap, trying to memorize the way he looked. The distance between them felt so small. So easy to cross.

She didn't know how long she had been standing there, watching him on the back porch. He stood, waiting. His face didn't change, but there was something in the way he held himself, quiet, patient, like he didn't want to scare her. He wasn't trying to force anything. He was just...asking. Like he was tired of being outside in the cold. Like he wanted to come home.

She loosened her grip on the blinds and let them fall back into place, the slats giving a soft metallic click as they settled. The world behind her grew brighter as she pulled the cord to raise the blinds fully, light pouring in from outside. Her fingers hovered over the window latch, uncertain. Her heart was still fluttering, but it didn't feel like fear anymore. It felt like excitement.

“I need to come inside,” he said. His voice was low, even, the same voice she remembered from stories at bedtime, from scraped knees and quiet mornings before school. “Let me in.”

She slid the lock aside with her thumb, then pushed the frame up just a few inches. The cold air slipped in, carrying with it the smell of damp grass, the trees at the edge of the yard, and something else, something she couldn’t quite name.

“Daddy?”

He put his hand on the windowsill. His face came clearer now. The shadows softened around his features. His eyes were burdened with something deep and sad. They searched hers, hoping. His eyebrows were furrowed in quiet concern. Like he was afraid she’d turn away.

“Can I come inside, baby girl?” he asked.

His other hand came to rest beside the first, and now he was close enough that she could see the lines around his eyes, the curve of his jaw, the way his lips pressed together like he was trying hard not to cry. Or not to smile. Or maybe both.

Ellie pushed the window open the rest of the way. The frame scraped, cool air rushing in to meet her, laced with the smell of wet dirt and bark, and something stinging that clung to her father’s skin. It curled in her nose. She breathed it in anyway.

“Thank you,” he said, just above a whisper.

Ellie stepped back to give him space, and he pulled himself through the window, one leg swinging through, then the other. He moved stiffly, but he made it over the sill and onto the carpet without a sound.

The moonlight stretched across his face now, blurring the sharpness of his features. Standing there in her room with the wind brushing through the open window behind him, he looked almost exactly like she remembered.

Almost.

Ellie's throat closed, and her arms folded across her stomach like she had to hold something in. She hadn't known she missed him this much.

"I missed you," she said, her voice barely rising above a whisper. The words felt strange coming out of her mouth, small and fragile. She hadn't planned to say them. They slipped out on their own, straight from the soft part of her that still remembered how things used to be, back when the nights weren't so long and quiet. Her eyes burned, but she pushed the sting away. She wasn't crying. She was just…remembering too hard.

His smile widened, just a little, the corners of his mouth pulling up with visible strain. His shoulders lowered, like a weight had been loosened inside him.

"I missed you too, baby girl," he said, his voice low and steady. "So much." And the way he said it made her heart turn inward on itself. There was something about the way he said "baby girl" that made the world feel smaller. Safer. Like nothing bad could reach her while he stood in the room.

He reached out then, slowly, one hand extended, palm open. Not grabbing. Not urgent. Just offering. He was giving her the choice. Letting her decide. His fingers were long and still, and the space between them trembled slightly. His hand hovered in the quiet, as if crossing the last few inches might break something delicate between them. And Ellie, who still remembered the weight of his arms lifting her with ease, the scent of his leather jacket that always carried a whisper of cigarette smoke, the warm thunder of his laugh bouncing off the kitchen ceiling, stepped forward.

Just a little.

Enough to be close.

Behind her, Sam lay still in the crib, his breath rising and falling in gentle waves. The soft shushing sound of it filled the room, a steady reminder that this moment was real, or at least real enough. Ellie didn't look back at her brother, but she felt his nearness, the safety of his proximity. It gave her courage, or maybe something that only felt like courage.

Her father reached forward and lowered his hand onto her head. His palm rested lightly against her hair, fingers slipped gently behind her ear. His touch was cool, not cold, but like he'd been standing outside for a long time. His touch was careful. Soft in that particular way only someone who loves you could be. He brushed a strand of her hair away from her face, the movement slow and deliberate, like he was trying to remember how.

Then he began to hum.

It was the same song.

The one with no words, only notes. Just the low, slow melody he used to hum when she was small and curled against him on the couch, or during long car rides after dusk, or when thunder rolled close, and her hands trembled in her lap. The tune was part lullaby, part memory. It didn't belong to anyone except them. And hearing it now, wrapped in the cold quiet of her bedroom, made her muscles ache.

She didn't speak for a long time. She just stood there, her forehead leaning gently into the edge of his coat. It didn't smell quite right. It was close, but not exact. The scent had faded and something else had crept in behind it. Still, her father had come home.

He bent his head toward hers, his voice slipping into her ear like it didn't want to wake the walls.

"We can't tell Mom I was here," he murmured. "We have to keep this a secret, baby girl. Or she won't let me come back."

Ellie's brow furrowed in understanding. That made sense. Of course it did. Her mom didn't talk about him. Didn't even say his name. She told him to never come back and slammed the door behind him. That had been not long after Sam came home from the hospital. After the arguing turned into yelling, and the yelling turned into slammed fists on the walls and, "Liar! It's not mine. You were gone for days!" echoed through the house.

He'd left before. Lots of times. Disappeared for a night, sometimes a weekend. Sometimes he'd come home smiling and spinning her in circles. Others he came back smelling like something bitter and sour. It made Ellie wrinkle her nose when he tucked her in. Ellie learned not to trust the weather in her own house. But this last time had been different. This time he didn't come back. Not even to say goodbye. It had been six months since Ellie had seen him.

Of course her mother wouldn't let him back in now. It felt like something important, something serious. It felt like the kind of thing grownups said when they needed you to be quiet and understand that if you spoke up, something bad would happen.

But where had he been? Why did he look so thin? Why was his voice just a touch too low, like it had been stretched out in the dark? Would he stay this time?

Her eyes were heavy now, her body leaning into his side, a reflex—it remembered what it was like to rest there. Her limbs softened, and the room wrapped itself around her.

She meant to ask.

But she was already falling asleep.

His hum had grown quieter, just a thread of sound now, weaving through the hush like smoke. Ellie leaned into his side, slack with sleep, her cheek resting against the curve of his ribs. He shifted carefully, one arm beneath her knees, the other cradling her back, and lifted her into bed the way he used to when she would fall asleep on the couch before bedtime. She didn't open her eyes, didn't resist. She let herself be carried, her small hands resting under his jacket, against the worn fabric of his shirt. His chest was cold.

He laid her down on the narrow bed, the one with the whining frame and the mattress that dipped in the middle. She sank into it, tucking herself in slightly on her side as the blanket was pulled up over her. The sheets were cool, the pillow flat beneath her head, but she didn't care. She was too tired to care.

He settled in beside her. Not watching from the doorway like he used to, but there, on the bed beside her. His body stretched along the edge, quiet and still, like he belonged there. One arm curved over her, not quite touching but near enough that she could feel the shape of him, where his warmth ought to have been.

Ellie drifted down into the dark, her head against something that used to be safe, and her hands hung loosely at her sides, empty.

And she slept. With her father beside her, quiet as the dark.

THE MORNING AFTER

Ellie stirred herself awake, her eyes sticky with sleep, lashes glued together. She squinted in the early morning sunlight filling the room. It was too invasive for this early, much too loud. The air was cold against her shoulders where the blanket had slipped down in the night.

She lay there, her body sluggish and tangled in the blankets, her mind wading through the fog of half-sleep. Her limbs were stiff, like she hadn't shifted all night. The familiar divot in the middle of the bed was still there. The room looked the same, with the step ladder resting against the wall and the worn carpet between her bed and the crib. Dust wandered lazily in the sunlight, floating like slow, golden insects or like ash.

The space beside her was empty. No dent in the mattress, no wrinkled blanket, no warmth, just flat, cold sheets. A knot rose in her throat as she sat up slowly. The air felt as if it was being sucked out of the room. She slid her legs over the side of the bed and touched the floor, and the familiar squeaking of the frame sounded too loud in the silence.

The window was open. Not just unlatched. Not cracked an inch like she sometimes left it when the room got too stuffy. It was pushed all the way up. The blinds swayed slightly, clicking against the frame. Outside air poured into the room—cool, damp, and edged with the scent of wet grass and wood and something else. Something faintly sour. Like metal. Or old breath.

Sam stirred in his crib, letting out a quiet whimper, then a sigh. Her eyes darted over. He was fine. Curled up like always, his tiny hands bunched into fists, the corner of his blanket pulled up over his nose. His breathing was soft and even. Her eyes returned to the window, the blinds tapping gently, rhythmically in the breeze.

She knew she had closed the window. Hadn't she? She was sure of it. She watched as the blinds made their cadenced *tap, tap, tap* on the window frame.

Memory caught her suddenly. The humming. That voice. His hands brushing the hair from her face. The smell of his leather jacket.

Her father.

The thought sat uneasy inside her mind, unfolding strangely. Had he really been there? Or had she only dreamed it so deeply and vividly that it had followed her into the morning? Sometimes dreams felt like that. They wrapped themselves around your thoughts and held on.

She rubbed her eyes with her fists, pressing firmly, trying to wake herself up all the way. Her hands came away smeared with tears, her vision blurry at the edges. She stared at the open window again, its wide mouth drawing in the morning air and light. The blinds clacked against the frame with persistence. *Tap, tap, tap....*

She remembered the sound of his nails drumming the glass. Was it just the blinds? Had she dreamed the rest? Maybe. Maybe not. The room hadn't quite made up its mind about what belonged to memory and what belonged to now.

Ellie didn't know if it was really him or just her own hope pulling at the seams of her sleep. She didn't know if the weight she was carrying was truly his arm or just the echo of a memory. She didn't know if he had stood at her window at all. But the one thing she did know was that she *wanted* it to be real. That much she knew without question. She wanted it in that deep, desperate way that made your stomach hurt a little. The way that made you want to hold still so nothing would shift and prove you wrong.

She didn't close the window.

Across the hall, Ellie heard the shift of a mattress, a muffled cough, and the soft thud of something being knocked off a nightstand. Her mother had come home during the night and was awake, barely. Ellie held her breath, waiting to hear if her mother would come to the room or just stay behind her closed door.

Her mother's bedroom door scraped open across the hall. Ellie didn't need to see her to know how the morning would begin. The familiar thump of footsteps followed, weighty and uneven, and then the scrape of a cabinet opening in the kitchen. A drawer slammed shut. Something hit the counter with a hollow clatter, maybe a mug or a plate.

"God, I can't deal with this today." Her mother's voice was dry and brittle as it drifted up from the kitchen.

Ellie imagined the clang of a pan on the stove, the scent of butter melting in a skillet. She pictured her mother at the counter, hair tied up messily, humming something half-familiar as she cracked eggs into a bowl. She remembered a morning from two winters ago, when she'd been sick, burning with fever, legs too shaky to stand. Her mother had carried her in both arms, barefoot across the floor, whispering, "My poor bug. Let's get you back to bed." Her robe had smelled like dryer sheets and old lotion.

Down the hall, a cabinet slammed. The memory flickered and faded, drowned beneath the clatter and the thud of footsteps.

Sam let out a sound from his crib, half yawn, half whimper. Ellie pushed herself up, crossed the room, and peered in through the railing. He was lying on his side, legs drawn up, fingers in his mouth. He peered up at her with pink-rimmed eyes and reached for her with both hands. Climbing up her step ladder, she reached down, sliding her arms carefully under his body and lifting him close. His head fell onto her shoulder immediately, and he burrowed against her without a sound. Ellie pressed her cheek to the top of his head and held him there a moment.

The floorboards complained as she walked, loud enough to make her feel watched.

She carried Sam into the kitchen. Her mother was hunched at the table with both hands wrapped around a chipped mug. She wasn't drinking—she was just holding it like it might keep her upright. Her eyes were rimmed in red and glassy with sleep…or something meaner.

"You're gonna have to be quiet this morning," she snapped without looking up. Her voice was scratchy, brittle at the edges.

Ellie paused by the cupboards, shifting Sam in her arms. He stirred, sighing into her neck. She rocked him back and forth.

"I wasn't trying to be loud," Ellie said. "He just woke up. I was making his bottle."

Her mother didn't answer. She muttered under her breath, "Shut up, shut up, just five more minutes." Ellie turned toward the counter, setting Sam down on the floor by her feet. He rubbed at his eyes. She stretched as high as she could, reaching for the formula, then measured out the scoops with practiced motions. She stood up on her toes as she went to put it back.

As she reached up with both hands, awkward and unbalanced, the can wobbled.

Her mother stood abruptly and slammed the cabinet shut. The bang echoed through the kitchen. "I said quiet!" she snarled. "My head's splitting in half!"

Ellie flinched, almost dropping the bottle. Sam started at the sound.

"I wasn't trying to make noise," Ellie said, her voice barely above a whisper. "I was just…"

Ellie stared at the floor, her lips pressed together. Her chest felt like it was too small for her heart. "I didn't mean anything," she said. "I was just putting it away."

She twisted the faucet on with a shaky hand, filled the bottle to the line, and screwed the cap tight. She slipped it into the microwave, hit the button, and waited through the low hum until the timer beeped. Pulling it out, she tested a drop on her wrist before turning back toward the table.

Her mother sighed, long and low. She reached for Ellie, putting her arms on her shoulders. "Look, I didn't mean it." Her mother's face softened. "You just…sometimes you go on and on, and my head's a mess today. I'm sorry, okay?"

Ellie nodded and gave the bottle to Sam, watching him latch onto it with slow, sleepy determination. The mug of coffee sat on the table, cooling. Her mother sat back down. She was coated in the dull haze of someone trying not to feel anything at all.

The rest of the morning passed in the quiet rhythm of routine. Ellie cleaned Sam's face with a damp cloth. Changed his diaper. Found a clean onesie. Her mother had folded herself onto the couch again, a blanket pulled over her head, her body disappearing into the cushions. One arm hung limp off the edge.

Ellie settled Sam next to her with a few soft toys in his lap and went back to the bedroom to change for school. As she pulled a fresh shirt over her head and turned to grab her socks from the floor, she froze. There, beside the crib, sunk into the carpet, was a footprint.

Not hers.

Not Sam's.

Not her mother's.

The shape was long, the heel deep, the edge of the sole clearly visible. Dirt clung to the fibers of the rug, dark and dry, like it had been there a few hours at least. Around the edge, it had started to crumble into the carpet. Ellie stared at it, her whole body still, her fingers winding around the socks in her hand.

She crouched slightly, moving closer, but not too close. Her eyes scanned the floor and then she saw something else, just a few feet away, tucked under the crib. It gleamed faintly when the sun hit it. A watch.

She reached for it slowly, cautiously. The leather strap was worn soft, the face scratched, a hairline crack along the glass from being knocked on corners and walls. She didn't have to guess. It was his. She had seen it a hundred times on her father's wrist, peeking out from under his sleeves, catching the sun when he bent over to tie her shoes.

She held it in her palm. She wrapped her fingers around it and squeezed, the cool metal warming against her skin. It was real.

She wouldn't tell her mother. The thought rose and fell in her mind like a wave—she'd made a promise. Instead, she slid the watch into her pillowcase. Then she smoothed the pillowcase down with both hands and stared at it for a second longer, her heart beating somewhere high and fluttery in the space beneath her collarbones.

The school day passed around her in soft, echoing shapes. She couldn't remember what she learned. She stared through the numbers on the board, through the windows. At lunch, she picked apart her sandwich without eating it. At recess, Ellie simply sat at a picnic table on the playground as the other children squealed and ran around her. When the bell rang signaling it was time to go inside, it startled her.

She walked home even more quickly than she had yesterday, the sidewalk and gravel uneven beneath her feet. Each drag of her heel scraped beneath her, until the house came back into view. The door was still unlocked. Her mother didn't say anything when Ellie walked in.

She was in the kitchen, moving fast; much faster than usual. A pan hissed on the stove, smoke rising from its edges as she scraped at it with a wooden spoon. The baby was on her hip, one leg bouncing against her side. Her cigarette hung from the corner of her mouth, the ash long and trembling, but she didn't seem to notice. Her eyes looked shiny and too wide, like she hadn't blinked in a long time. Her foot tapped against the floor without music, her shoulders twitching with each tap. Ellie could hear her muttering, but the words didn't make sense, like she was talking to someone who wasn't really there.

Sometimes her mother got like this. Fast and shrill, like everything inside was buzzing. She didn't sit down, didn't slow down, and she wouldn't fall asleep either.

"You just get home?" her mother said without turning. Her voice was high and clipped. "You better not be tracking dirt through here, Ellie. I just cleaned." Rags were strewn across the floor, and the kitchen smelled faintly of bleach. Patches of paint on the walls had been scrubbed off.

Ellie paused, her fingers gripping the strap of her backpack.

"I'm not," she said.

The kitchen looked like the "project nights." Her father would tap her shoulder at 2:00 a.m. and say "Race you," flicking on the lights. He scrubbed baseboards with a toothbrush and took the toaster apart. He timed her with his phone while she polished the doorknobs to a squeak, his jaw clicking constantly as he chewed gum. Cartoons murmured on the TV. When everything gleamed, he pressed a candy into her palm. "Winners get prizes," he said. She sucked the sugar, and her eyes watered from being so tired.

"Mm-hmm," her mother muttered. "Always something with you." She turned briefly, eyes darting, a smile that didn't reach them. "You hungry? I made noodles. They're good. You like noodles!" Her mother's eyes lit up suddenly, too bright, too eager, her voice speeding up like she'd just remembered how to be cheerful. She turned quickly, grabbed a bowl from the cupboard and scooped a tangled heap of noodles into it, steam rising in small curls. "Here!"

Ellie hesitated, shifting her weight. Her stomach was in a knot, coiled and nervous, but empty too. "Okay," she said.

Her mother beamed. She pressed the bowl into Ellie's hands with too much force. It was Ellie's favorite bowl. The blue one. "See? Told you they're good. Sit down, come on. Sit, sit, sit. Don't let it get cold." The words came fast and frantic.

Ellie crossed the room and slid onto one of the kitchen chairs, its legs uneven and scraping faintly on the linoleum. She folded her hands in her lap and stared down at the mess of noodles slowly congealing in the bowl.

"Eat," her mother said, already turning back to the stove, bouncing the baby on her hip. "You're getting skinny."

Ellie picked up the fork. The noodles were tangy, buttery, too salty, but warm. She took a bite, then another, chewing slowly, careful not to slurp. Her mother didn't look at her again, already humming to herself, walking fast in a slow room.

Ellie ate until the bowl was nearly empty, her head bowed, eyes fixed on the noodles. She didn't say thank you. She didn't say anything at all. When she was done, she placed the bowl in the sink, stood up, and walked out of the kitchen as quietly as she could.

Then Ellie went to her room.

The muddy footprint was gone. Not a smear left behind. But she remembered. Her eyes locked on that empty patch, and she stood there for a long time, barely breathing. It had been there. She hadn't imagined that. She knew the shape of it.

She crossed the room slowly and climbed onto her bed, the mattress giving a soft sigh beneath her. Her hand slipped under the pillow with care, like she was checking for a heartbeat. The watch was still there. The smooth glass face, the soft-worn strap that fit naturally into her palm; it hadn't changed. It hadn't crumbled or disappeared. She closed her hand around it, let the shape settle into her skin, then tucked it back under the pillow.

From the kitchen came the sudden clatter of metal, a pan dropped or slammed too hard, and then the sound of her mother humming. Fast. Off-key. Unsettled. Sam let out a cracked, startled cry.

Ellie's body tensed, but she didn't move. Her hands braced against the edge of the bed; her toes flexed above the carpet. She stared at the window, her eyes slowly losing focus as she forced them to not blink.

I should go....

The window stayed still, closed and quiet. The air around it felt like it was waiting, holding its breath. Ellie stayed where she was. She didn't go to Sam. Didn't call down the hallway for her mom. She watched as the light grew darker, and the moon's glow stretched across the floor. She watched the color shift from gold to gray. Her legs dangled over the edge of the bed, small feet brushing the rug. She sat, stiff-backed and silent, heart pulled small and hard.

She told herself Sam would be OK. Just for a little while. She had to be here. Just in case.

NIGHTLY VISITOR

That night came softly. Sam slept in the crib across the room from Ellie, one hand curled near his face, his breath slow and steady. The house around them was empty. Ellie's mother was gone. Too much energy to be cooped up, she'd said. She paced in circles before grabbing her jacket and slamming the door behind her. She hadn't said where she was going, nor when she'd be back. She'd skipped saying goodnight entirely. She just dropped Sam in his crib, muttering something cutting and agitated before she vanished down the hallway and out the door.

Now, the only sounds that filled the house were the sounds of age and decay, the steady shiver and knock of the pipes in the walls and under the floor, and the faint rush of wind against the house, creeping through cracks too small to see but large enough to feel. Ellie stayed still in her bed, eyes on the ceiling, listening. Waiting. Ellie felt him before she saw him.

It wasn't a sound or the cast of a shadow that caught her attention, just a weight pressing unmistakably against the room, shifting the edges of the quiet. A pause stretched across the floorboards, through the corners, and into the knot forming in Ellie's throat. Her breath slowed, caught on something she hadn't touched yet. Her skin tightened and the hairs on her arms rose, not from fright, but in the knowing.

It wasn't fear. Not exactly. It was too calm for that. Ellie felt a pull in her core that hummed beneath her ribs, familiar and hard to name.

It was recognition.

Her eyes moved to the window, already knowing right where he would be. She didn't hear a knock this time. No *tap, tap, tap,* on the glass. No whisper from the other side. But the air was full of him, like the room had breathed him in. The trees caught bits of moonlight on their bare arms. She hadn't seen him yet, but she felt him in the way the world slowed down.

She crossed the room on bare feet, careful where she stepped even though the house was empty. The carpet chilled her soles. Her fingers found the edge of the glass and pushed gently, slowly, until the window eased upward with the soft grinding sound of wood on metal.

The night air rushed in, cold and damp, brushing around her wrists as though it had fingers of its own. The air carried the scent of leaves crushed underfoot and the dark sweetness of soil. It filled the small room quickly, silently, and carried with it a tinge of something acrid. Under the earthy scents that drifted from the woods, was the faint bite of something else. It didn't linger but drifted wistfully as quickly as it was noticed.

And he was there. Already waiting.

Just beyond the window frame, standing in the patchwork of dark and moonlight, he was there. His posture was the same as the night before, still and expectant, but now it felt more certain, less of a question and more of a return. He stood in the way someone waits when they know the door will be opened for them eventually. His shape blurred slightly at the edges, his eyes the only part of him that moved. They lifted to meet Ellie's without hesitation. They held in them no warning, no alarm, only something steady, familiar and impossible to pull away from.

Ellie didn't step back.

She didn't question.

She opened the window wider, letting the cool hush of night spill over her shoulders. The glass rose with a groan, the sill firm under her fingers. She moved aside to make space, her heart thudding low in her ribs.

He didn't speak. He just stepped forward, one long leg swinging over the sill with quiet certainty, then the other. He moved like he had all the time in the world, careful and unhurried. He was someone returning to a place that had once been home. His coat whispered as he sat, folding himself gently onto the edge of her bed, the mattress dipping under his weight.

"Hello, baby girl." A smile twitched at the corners of his mouth as he spoke.

Ellie crawled back onto the bed beside him, her knees tucked beneath her, the hem of her nightgown catching under her legs. She didn't ask where he'd come from, but that question hovered between her thoughts. It drifted between them, soft as breath, but already passing. There was a stillness to him that settled into the room, like his presence rooted even the walls.

"You're cold," Ellie whispered, her voice just a thread, as she placed her tiny hand onto his.

He didn't answer. He didn't nod or shake his head. He just tilted it quizzically to one side, the movement slow and deliberate. His eyes never left her face, those same eyes that looked so tired. They were wide and waiting and terribly focused, as if blinking were reserved for later, or something optional. His hands rested in his lap.

But he was listening.

Ellie could feel it. It was the kind of attention you didn't usually get from grownups. It was the kind that made your words feel heavier, more important. She didn't know what more to say, she only knew she wanted to keep his attention. To hold it. To be seen.

She looked down at his hands. They weren't clenched. They didn't shake. They just rested there, still and waiting, like the rest of him.

"How's your mom?" he asked, voice low and warm, enveloping her like steam from a mug.

Ellie withdrew her hand and knotted her fingers together in her lap. Her words caught in her throat. He wasn't smiling, but something in his face had gone gentle, the corners of his mouth less strained, the shadows under his eyes less deep.

"She's…okay." Ellie's voice was small and careful. "Sometimes she's really tired and sleeps a lot. Or, she's not tired at all, all fast and loud and…she talks a lot and forgets stuff. She gets mad. She yells. But she always says she's sorry. Things are hard for her. But she makes noodles sometimes. I like the ones with butter."

He nodded patiently, not saying anything, just listening. His face didn't change, and his eyes stayed on her, steady, growing softer around the edges. It made her feel like her words mattered, even the ones she wasn't sure how to say.

"What about the baby?" he asked.

Ellie's eyes drifted to the crib across the room. Sam was asleep, tucked up under his little blanket with one hand half-tucked under his cheek. He looked so small.

"He's little," she said, her words growing more confident. "He cries sometimes. But not like big mad cries. Just little ones. I give him bottles, warm but not too hot. He likes it like that." She reached out like she could show him, then dropped her hand back to her lap. "And when I give him baths, he laughs a little. I think he likes the water. I think he…I think he knows more than people think he does. Babies are smart. He watches stuff."

That made the man's mouth move, a quiver at the edges. His eyes stayed soft, and he tilted his head again, this time farther and more inquisitive. His neck seemed on the verge of straining, twisted with the angle of the bend. Ellie felt her heart flutter a little faster, but she didn't move away.

"You're so good at taking care of people," he said, straightening his head back up, voice gentle, the ghost of a smile forming across his lips.

Ellie didn't answer right away. Her lips pushed together, and her fingers picked at a loose thread on her blanket. She coiled it around her finger until it cut into her skin. The words sat behind her sternum, pressing and tangled.

"I don't know," she mumbled, eyes down. "I just do stuff because someone has to. Nobody else does it, so I have to do it. And Sam needs—"

"Not everyone does it well," he interrupted. "Even when they have to." He shifted uneasily beside her, a hint of discomfort in the movement.

She shrugged, small and a little hunched. "Sometimes I forget stuff. I mess up. Like the other day I dropped his bottle. And sometimes I make him cry on accident. But I try real hard. I try and try and try…." Ellie's voice trailed off.

His eyes stayed on her. A calm weight behind them. That stillness that didn't feel mean. Just quiet. "That's more than most," he said.

They didn't talk for a while after that. The room settled into the stillness, like the air had decided to sit down and wait for them. Sam's breathing stayed soft and steady from the crib, each breath a quiet tether between him and his sister. Ellie sat with her legs tucked beneath her, back straight, her fingers resting in her lap, waiting. She was waiting to be invited back into the fold. Waiting to be held until she fell asleep. The hush made her thoughts feel bigger, louder. Was he upset? She didn't know how long they sat like that, only that it felt like time had slowed down.

"Do you ever feel scared?" he asked, his voice breaking gently through the quiet. It was careful but burned with curiosity.

Ellie didn't look up. Her eyes stayed on the blanket bunched up in her fists, her fingers digging deep into the fabric. Her throat cinched again as she nodded, just barely. "Yeah. A lot sometimes." Her voice almost disappeared with the words, then she added, "But not when you're here."

It was true. The kind of truth you didn't need to explain because your heart already knew how to carry it. The kind of truth that intertwined between your ribs and stayed warm.

That made something shift in his face. The edges eased into a hint of amusement; his eyes glinted in the moonlight. He reached out tenderly and placed his hand on top of hers. His fingers were long and cool, but not cold, and his palm was dry, the skin thin like paper worn soft from being turned too many times.

Ellie didn't pull away. Her hand stayed still beneath his, the two of them touching without squeezing, without holding, just there. His thumb brushed the back of her hand once, barely. Then he let go.

He sat back slightly, his coat creasing, and looked around the small room. At the crib. The peeling paint. The stack of books too old for Sam but too babyish for Ellie now. Then his eyes came back to her.

"I should go before your mom comes home," he said firmly.

Ellie's shoulders dropped. "Okay," she said, her voice cracking, something gripping her center at the thought.

He leaned forward again, watching her in that intrigued way, slow and steady, like nothing she could say or do was too small to matter.

"Will you do something for me?" he asked.

She nodded right away. "Yes, what?"

"Do you have something I can keep?" he asked after a pause. His voice almost folded in on itself, as though he was afraid the question might be too burdensome. "Something small. Just so I can remember you."

Ellie blinked, caught off guard by the question. Her fingers gathered a bit of the blanket in their grasp. "But…you already know me," she said, the words tentative, unsure. Her eyes searched his face for an answer, for reassurance.

"I do," he said with a nod, his tone calm and dusk-warm. "But it helps to have something real. Something that stays even when you're not with me."

She sat still, trying to think. Searching her mind. Then, with a soft grunt of realization, she shifted forward, sliding off the edge of the bed. Her toes brushed the floor as she reached for the top drawer of her dresser. It stuck about halfway, the wood stubborn and old, but she tugged it open and rummaged through its mess of crumpled papers, broken crayons and small toys. Her hand brushed against an old jelly jar that used to contain coins. He used to set the jar between them and make her his "official helper" as she'd count out the silver ones for him. "See? You're saving the day," he'd say. She'd glow and feel useful while the jar got lighter and lighter.

Finally, her hand settled on what she was looking for. Something small and plastic. A comb. It was purple, and faint sparkles clung to the plastic. A faded mermaid was molded into its spine, her tail forming the handle. The comb's teeth were uneven, a few missing. It was her favorite.

She turned it over in her palms, weighing whether it was enough. She had used it every morning since she could remember. She used it before school, before bed, before sitting quietly on the floor to comb out Sam's wispy hair. "It's not fancy," she said, her voice shy but steady as she sat back down next to him and extended her hand.

He took it from her gingerly, with both hands, like she was handing him something precious. His fingers closed around it, and he nodded again, slower this time. From inside his coat, he pulled a soft square of fabric from an inner pocket and wrapped the comb with care, tucking it away.

"Thank you, baby girl," he said. His eyes held something tender now. "It's perfect."

Ellie smiled at him, a worn-out smile, just the corner of her mouth lifting, tired but real. Her body was curled in on itself now, her arms wrapped around her knees, hugging them closely, chin tucked into the crook. Her eyes grew heavier as she watched the way he rose to his feet in one smooth motion. There was no creak of the bed frame, no shift in the shadows except where his coat settled around him.

He moved toward the window without hurry. The air stirred as he passed, not cold but changed, touched. His coat brushed against her skin and left the faintest tingle. At the window, he paused, placing one hand on the frame, fingers still. A moment of holding on.

He turned to her one last time. Just his head, just enough for the moonlight to catch the outline of his cheek and the curve of his brow. His face was unreadable there in the half-shadow. But it didn't feel empty. There was something in the look he gave her. Not sadness. Not joy. Something quieter, stretched between the two, humming with all the things they had said.

"I'll come back," he said.

SOMETHING TO REMEMBER

Just like before, after the house had gone still, after her mother's voice had burned out and the baby was asleep in his crib, Ellie's father returned to the window. She had been waiting, something in her heart open and listening for him. When the window slid open, quiet and careful, she didn't flinch.

He stepped through the window and into the room. No sound, no rush, his presence moving ahead of him like a ripple in still water. The night air followed him in, brushing against Ellie's skin. He didn't speak as he crossed the floor. No smile. No nod. He entered as if the space had always belonged to him and found Ellie waiting as if she always would be.

His jacket hung from his shoulders, damp at the hem, dripping faintly onto the floor. He stood there in the dim light, unmoving, before his eyes met Ellie's.

"Do you have another thing I can keep?" he said, his voice low. "Something small."

Ellie blinked up at him, her hands folded in her lap. The comb she had given him sat in her memory like a warm stone. That was something small and important, something already gone. She hadn't missed it, not really. She'd found an old brush in the bathroom, the handle cracked but the bristles soft enough to use on Sam's head. It wasn't the same, but it was enough.

Now he wanted more. Something small. Something hers. Something he could carry with him.

"Something to hold onto," he said, the corners of his mouth twitching into the shape of a smile.

Ellie thought hard as she stared at him in the dark. She didn't understand why he needed it, but he'd asked so gently that saying no never even crossed her mind. Only the determined thought, "What would be enough?" She got off the bed and padded across the room, careful not to wake Sam, and pried open the top drawer to her dresser again. She sifted through the jumble of old things once more: broken barrettes, crumpled drawings she hadn't finished. Nothing important.

Her hands found a scrap of paper. "Picture day today. Wear blue. You'll look pretty!" it said, scrawled in her mother's handwriting. She clutched it tight. Not this.

Then her eyes slid to her jacket, slung over the edge of the bed. The hem hung low, almost touching the floor. Her eyes honed in on the button at the very bottom. It was small, smooth, and brown. She plucked it off with her fingers, twisting until the threads gave. She stared at it before turning toward her father.

"I still got enough to keep it shut," she said, holding it out to him.

He took the button with both hands, as he had done with the comb, as if it were something fragile. He brushed its surface with his thumbs before he tucked it into that deep coat pocket where he kept the things she'd given him.

"Thank you," he said.

"It's just a button," Ellie said as she sat back down, pulling her legs beneath her on the bed, folding herself into the smallest shape she could.

"It was yours," he said. His weight sunk into the divot of the mattress, her divot. Ellie felt the pull of gravity shift, like the room was leaning into him. "That matters."

Ellie looked down again. "Where do you keep them?" she asked after a pause. "The things I give you?"

"Safe," he said. "I keep them safe. They help me remember."

"Remember what?"

His head tilted, not as far as before, but enough to make her feel that same tickle of unease down her spine.

"You," he said. "This place. The parts that still feel warm."

Ellie didn't understand, but she nodded anyway, the way you nod when you want someone to keep talking. Her fingers picked nervously at the hem of her nightgown. A loose thread had come free, and she wrapped it around her finger again and again, until it left a deep pink line across her skin.

Her eyes fell on the crib. Sam was lost deep in sleep. The fluttering sound of his breathing calmed her, even now. One of his hands rested near his cheek, his fingers twitching faintly like he was dreaming of holding something.

"You don't take things from him," she said, her voice quiet but firm. It wasn't a question, but it wasn't nothing either. It was a rule she wanted to make out loud.

He didn't answer right away. He just turned his head towards the crib, the shadows under his eyes moving with him. "No," he said at last, his voice breathy. "Only what's given."

His voice was steady. His eyes stayed on her, unblinking. They weren't watching her, they were holding her, and the longer he looked, the more the corners of the room seemed to pull inward, walls leaning just slightly, like they were listening too.

Ellie shifted on the bed. Her hands balled up in the blanket in her lap, knuckles pale and strained. Her ribs felt like they were closing in, her breath caught in a place that didn't want to move. She glanced at the door, then the crib, then back at him. She pressed her lips together, hard. Not because she didn't have words, but because something inside told her not to let them out.

"I don't like it when you go." She watched him, the way his head tilted at her words, the way his hands stayed perfectly still in his lap. He sat with the careful, motionless patience of something holding itself together.

"I don't like it when you go," she said again, this time a little louder. "You never stay long."

"I can't," he said, quiet but firm. Not apologetic.

She nodded, but only a little. She waited, chewing the inside of her cheek, eyes searching his face for something to make the answer feel okay. It didn't come. So she asked, even though she knew he might not tell her.

"Why not?"

The silence stretched, long and slow, and wrapped itself around the room. Not oppressive. Not empty. Just full of everything they didn't say.

Ellie leaned into him. Just a little. Just enough to feel like maybe they were still on the same side of whatever this was. She could hear Sam breathing steady in the crib. She could hear the faint, uneven hum of the heater ticking against the cold. But more than that, she could hear the space between them settling again. Breathing.

After that night, it became routine. He sat with her, and after a while, he would say: "Just something small. Just to remember you."

And Ellie would search. Not fast. This wasn't a game. It mattered. She needed to find the right thing. Something small, like he asked, but also something that meant a little something.

Something important enough to give, but not too important to lose.

One night she chose a sock, rolled in a ball and a little worn at the heel, with little white hearts knitted into the threads. She'd lost its match ages ago, but she'd kept this one because the hearts made her happy. It had become hers in a different way, special on its own. She smoothed it out in her hands before offering it up. He took it carefully, folding it once before tucking it away into that deep coat of his, like it was something rare. Like it mattered to him too.

Another evening, it was one of her drawings, one she'd made on the floor with her crayons pressed down hard enough to leave dents in the paper. Her crayon box had sat tipped open beside her, half the colors missing their wrappers. Thick wax lines layered over each other until the page was soft and smudged. The sky was green because she thought it looked better that way, and the grass was purple just because she felt like it. She'd drawn herself in front of a house with crooked windows and smoke curling out of a chimney. Large trees with round tops and bark the color of mustard framed the house. The sun in the corner grinned with all its teeth. She didn't remember why she gave it a face, but she liked that it was smiling.

The drawing looked like a place she wanted to visit. It made sense to her. She folded it gently, corners lined up as best she could into a square and held it out to him without a word. He took it like he always did, with both hands, like it was something important, and tucked it into his coat.

Then the ring. That little plastic one she'd found near the carts outside the grocery store. It was too big for her finger and scratched all over, but the middle had a fake jewel—a pale pink one that caught the light just enough to look real. She'd worn it on her thumb, pretending it was magic. She gave it to him because she thought maybe it really was. Or maybe giving it away would make it be.

Each time she gave him something, it felt like a promise. If he had something of hers, maybe it meant he had to come back. A secret that only she was allowed to keep.

He never stayed until morning.

The space he left behind never felt the same way twice. Sometimes it was still and quiet, like he'd never been there at all. Other times, the air held onto that tinge, that smell she couldn't name. And sometimes, she swore the blanket still carried the weight of where he'd sat, that the divot in the middle of the bed had grown just a little deeper. But no matter how many times she checked, no matter how long she stared at the spot, there was never anything left to prove it.

Except the thing he took.

Each morning, she would glance toward the place where the ring or sock or drawing had been, just to be sure it was really gone. And it always was. No trace. Like it had been swallowed by the night.

She never told her mother. Not about the visits and not about the gifts. Her mom wouldn't understand or, worse, she might make it stop. And Ellie didn't want it to stop. Even when it scared her a little. Even when it made the corners of the room feel strange, like the shadows were watching, she still wanted him to come back.

When he was there, it felt like the rest of the house didn't matter. Like the dirty dishes in the sink, the sharp words followed by the aching quiet that came after her mother slammed the front door, none of that could reach her when he sat on her bed.

When he left, it all came rushing back. The weight of the day pressed back into the corners of the room. It was like something cracked open as soon as the light returned, letting in all the noise and cold and heaviness she'd been able to ignore while he was there. The stillness left behind wasn't gentle anymore. It was hollow. Thin. A reminder.

Sam would stir in his crib, fussing, and the day would begin the way all the other days did. Her mom's voice, sharp or non-existent. School, long and blurry. Her drawings messier. Her backpack heavier. The rooms too quiet, then too loud.

School didn't feel like it used to. The days blurred together like smudged paint. Her pencil didn't always move when it was supposed to. Her drawings came out crooked, like her hands weren't sure what they were trying to say. Her backpack dug into her shoulders more.

The house seemed to breathe differently when he was gone. The walls felt closer. The hallway longer. The kitchen too bright. Every sound louder. Every silence deeper. Sometimes her muscles would lock up, right behind her ribs, like her heart didn't want to beat the same way anymore.

Dinner would come and go, sometimes barely more than toast or crackers. Her mom would fade into the couch, into her room, into whatever place she disappeared to when she didn't want to deal with the rest of them. Sam would fall asleep, warm and wiggly in his blanket.

When the sun started to sink and the edges of the world blurred again, the feeling would change. Slowly and quietly, the house would begin to soften around the edges. That was when Ellie's eyes would drift to the window. Not to just look or listen, but to wait.

Even though she didn't know where he went or how he found his way back, she believed he would come. She believed it so hard her heart beat differently in the dark. She kept the pillow beside her smoothed out. She listened for the change in the air—for the moment the room felt different, even if nothing had moved yet.

Because he always came back.

And until he didn't, until something changed, she would be there.

Waiting.

FRAYED EDGES

At first, it was just her pencil. Ellie kept turning her desk upside down looking for it, lips pressed together, eyes sweeping over the same things. The cracked box with the peeling stickers, the eraser shaped like a strawberry, the blue plastic scissors with the rounded tips, scarcely sharp enough to cut paper. Her eyes scoured the trove in her desk over and over again, and, as always, the pencil, short, dull, a bite mark near the middle, was sitting right there.

Some days, it took her a long time to start writing. Not because she didn't know the answers. She did, mostly. But because the pencil felt strange in her hand. Too light or too smooth. As if her fingers had forgotten how to hold onto it. As if her mind had to remind them one step at a time: grip, press, move.

Mrs. Rieke started pausing by her desk, her voice kind.

"Ellie?" she asked one day, compassionate and low. "Do you need a new pencil?"

Ellie shook her head. *No.*

Mrs. Rieke moved to the front of the room and picked up a dry erase marker from the tray at the bottom of the whiteboard, her voice lifting into its usual rhythm: steady, calm, the kind of voice that wanted to be kind even when it was tired. She drew lines on the white board, wrote numbers on it.

But Ellie didn't see the numbers.

She looked at them, her eyes open and pointed in the right direction, but nothing would stick in her mind. The symbols floated on the stark white surface. The lines blurred together. It was like looking at someone else's dream—shapes and marks that meant something to everybody else but stayed silent in Ellie's head. Her fingers twitched around the pencil in her hand, pressing lightly, then lifting again.

Someone giggled quietly behind her. A chair scraped as someone shifted. Mrs. Rieke's mouth was moving, her hands pointing to the board, her finger tapping a number. But to Ellie, it was all underwater. Just the shape of a sentence floating.

A boy in the front of the class raised his hand before Ellie knew there had even been a question. "Seven!" His voice rang out, confident and fast, the words snapping into place like puzzle pieces, snapping Ellie back. He laughed a little after he spoke, and someone behind him laughed too. Mrs. Rieke smiled, nodded. "That's right," she said, her marker squeaking across the board as she circled the number. She continued with the lesson, saying something that Ellie couldn't quite catch.

The classroom moved on without her.

Ellie's pencil sat limp in her hand. Her other hand rested on the corner of her desk, fingers clamped around the wood, nails digging into the edge. The blur in her eyes wouldn't go away.

The worksheet in front of her had pictures of apples and number boxes underneath, but she hadn't drawn a single line. She stared at it, waiting for something to click, waiting for the question to come back, or the instructions to sort themselves out in her head.

Ellie squinted at the board, then the page in front of her. The board. The page. The board. The page. Pencils scratched around her as she tried to focus on the neatly lined apples on the page. She counted them once. Then again. The numbers wouldn't stay in her head. They floated off, quiet and slippery. Her pencil twitched in her hand, the tip hovering just above the page.

Her legs swung under the desk, not in time with the hum of the room. Around her, classmates whispered and scribbled, their heads bent close to their work or eyes up to the board. She pressed the eraser end of her pencil to the paper, not hard enough to mark anything, just enough to feel it there.

The board stayed full of numbers. The bright, straight lines and circles drawn in marker looked like they should make sense. Little plus signs and equal signs everyone else seemed to understand. Mrs. Rieke's voice continued to float above everything, steady and light. Her voice was inviting, like she wanted everyone to follow along and was leaving a trail of breadcrumbs through the lesson. The words drifted somewhere behind Ellie's eyes, scattering before they could stick.

Ellie sat in her chair, legs dangling beneath her, the toes of her shoes brushing the linoleum floor. She didn't swing them anymore. They just hung there, heavy.

The room grew quiet, and the heads around her dropped, eyes down on the worksheets, scribbling furiously. Mrs. Rieke walked past Ellie's desk once, then again. Her footsteps made a soft swish against the floor, as if she were walking with extra care each time she passed in her carefully planned loop around the classroom. Her teacher didn't stop, but Ellie could feel the glance, quick and quiet, down at the empty worksheet and the girl staring at it. Ellie didn't move. She didn't turn her head. She pretended not to notice, even as her shoulders crept up toward her ears.

The sound of the clock was overwhelming.

Ellie turned her attention to the window. Outside, the sky was pale, like the inside of an eggshell. A line of clouds hung just above the trees, flat, quiet, and gray. Ellie stared at them. Not because she liked clouds. Not because she was dreaming. Just because they were still. Still and quiet and simple. Not like the room.

Then came the bell. Piercing. Sudden.

It was time for lunch.

The other kids were already moving, voices rising like bubbles. The line shuffled slowly forward. The smell of lunch, something salty and fried, filled the hallway outside the cafeteria doors. Ellie barely noticed. She stood behind a boy who kept bouncing on the balls of his feet and in front of a girl whose pigtails kept brushing her arm.

At the counter, the lunch lady gave her a tray. Chicken nuggets, a scoop of mushy green beans, a plastic cup of syrupy peaches. Ellie took it carefully, both hands gripping the sides like it might tip if she wasn't gentle enough.

She moved to the table near the window and sat down in the middle of the bench. Kids around her were laughing, whispering, swapping cookies for chips. One boy put one of his green beans on a spoon and flicked it across the table. A girl shrieked like it was the funniest thing in the world. Ellie peeled back the lid on the fruit cup. The peaches inside were too orange. They jiggled in the syrup. She ate one; it was cold. She chewed, then set the rest back down.

After lunch, the classes filtered outside for recess. The sun had finally pushed its way through the clouds, but the light didn't feel warm. It just made everything too bright, too sharp around the edges. Ellie's eyes hurt.

The playground was loud. It was filled with shouts and squeaking sneakers. Swings swayed in slow arcs, their hinges whining with each pass. Someone yelled from the far end of the yard. A group of four children bounced a large, red rubber ball between them. It hit the pavement with a deep, ringing thump, echoing through the playground with each bounce.

Ellie climbed up onto the big wooden castle at the far end. The wood was old and fraying. She picked at a splinter, pressing her thumb into it until it stopped stinging.

"Why are you always just sitting there?" a voice called from down below. It was a girl from Ellie's class. Her name was Courtney, or Riley, or something else. Ellie couldn't remember. She wore a red jacket that zipped all the way to her chin, and her dark braid whipped back and forth as she walked. Two more kids trailed behind her like shadows, giggling and snickering.

Courtney slapped a hand on the side of the castle, yelling louder. "Hey! I said, 'Why are you always just sitting here?' You don't play with anyone."

Ellie didn't answer. She pressed her finger against a line in the wood, tracing its pattern.

Another voice piped up from behind Courtney, higher and meaner. "She draws weird stuff. I saw it. Monsters and scribbles. She made a picture of a man with no face. And she talks to herself."

"I bet she eats worms," Courtney said, halfway up the castle's ladder now, her boots clunking against the rungs. "You a little freak, Ellie?"

Ellie's shoulders tensed, but she didn't look down at the other girl.

The laughter behind Courtney got louder. One of the kids mimicked her voice in a high, scratchy tone, "You a little freak, Ellie?" and then cackled like it was the best joke in the world.

"Are you even listening?" Courtney snapped as she climbed closer. "Or are you off in your weird little head again?"

The other kid echoed her from the ground: "Weird little head!" More laughter. A shoe scraped wood. A piece of bark crunched under someone's foot.

The bell rang out loud across the playground. Ellie slid down the slide at the top of the castle and away from the other girls, joining the others walking back inside. Her head hung low, her jaw set. Her arms stayed close to her sides, hands balled in her sleeves. The hallways smelled like pencil shavings and dish soap as steam drifted from the cafeteria dishwashers. Her shoes squeaked against the tile, too loud and too soft at once.

In the classroom, Mrs. Rieke was already speaking, her voice calm and careful, but it sounded like it was coming from underwater. Ellie slid into her seat and stared down at her desk. Her hands were cold, her fingers slow as she dug through her desk. Mrs. Rieke's lips kept moving. The whiteboard was filled with words.

She caught pieces of sentences but didn't follow: "Today we'll be using," and "Don't forget to," but the words sounded far away.

The other kids stood, gathering paper, pens, pencils, crayons, palettes of watercolors. Ellie stood too, not because she knew what to do, but because her body moved when everyone else did. Her legs took her across the room to the stacks of paper and supplies without asking her permission.

Ellie took her crayons and paper back to her desk while the other children slid stools across the floor, sitting next to each other at long tables, sharing their masterpieces. Ellie started drawing. Dark lines flooded the page. A tree, wide and too low to the ground, its trunk cracked open. Underneath, she drew a hollow, an opening too dark to see into. Around and around, she scribbled black circles, making the hollow deeper and darker. Two figures stood to the side, their bodies small, eyes too big, mouths straight and unreadable. The branches of the tree didn't reach up, but drooped low, dragging along the ground like searching hands. Reaching out from the base of the tree, she drew roots, long and curling, spilling out into the corners of the page. She colored the sky black. There was no sun. She covered the page until it disappeared under the wax.

The black crayon snapped in her fingers, startling Ellie.

She hadn't noticed Mrs. Rieke approaching her desk. The teacher came over slowly, her steps soft on the tile. She didn't speak right away. She just lowered herself beside Ellie's chair, knees cracking a little, one hand resting on the edge of the table. Her eyes flicked over the drawing—first the tree, then the hollow beneath it, then the way the sky had been scraped black.

"Ellie," she said, eyebrows raised with concern, "did you hear the directions?"

Ellie didn't answer. She hadn't heard the directions. She just stared down at the paper, the hollow under the tree filled in with layers upon layers of wax, her fist locked around the broken crayon. Mrs. Rieke watched her for a moment longer, then shifted lightly, crouching a little closer, speaking more quietly, but with an upturned, more cheerful voice.

"What's this one about Ellie," she asked.

"It's just a place," she said. She brought the broken crayon back to the page and began circling the hollow at the base of the tree again, around and around, turning the page darker and darker.

"A place you've seen?" she asked.

Ellie met her teacher's eyes. "It's just a place," Ellie said, her voice even and firm.

Mrs. Rieke stayed crouched beside the desk, one hand still resting on its edge. Her other hand hovered over the back of Ellie's chair, frozen mid-gesture.

Ellie turned back to the page in front of her and started shading with small, methodical strokes. The black crayon was almost gone between her fingers. Her movements were slow and deliberate. She didn't look up again. Mrs. Rieke watched her for a second longer, her mouth parting like she might speak. She rose slowly and moved back toward her desk, the weight of that gaze still lingering, still stretching behind her.

At the end of the day, the drawing went into Ellie's backpack. She folded it in half, and then half again, pressing the edges down flat with the side of her hand until the paper was firmly creased. She slid it carefully into the side pocket where it would be safest.

As she walked toward the door to leave, Mrs. Rieke was waiting. She placed a hand on Ellie's shoulder to stop her from scooting too quickly out the door. Mrs. Rieke crouched a little, easing down until her face was almost level with Ellie's. She held an envelope between two fingers, sealed with tape.

"I need you to give this to your mom," she said gently, her voice dipping low, careful, like the classroom was suddenly too quiet for loud things. Her eyes searched Ellie's face, not with suspicion, but with the kind of worry that tries to look like kindness. "Can you do that for me?"

Ellie's eyes flicked to the envelope then back to the teacher.

"You're not in trouble," Mrs. Rieke said, a small smile across her lips, her brow still raised.

"I'll try." Ellie reached out and took the note. She slid it into the same pocket as her drawing, fingers pressing around the paper like she needed to feel the shape of it to be sure it was real.

"Thank you," Mrs. Rieke said. She didn't sound relieved.

WRONG HANDS

When Ellie got home, the lights were off. The hallway stretched longer than it should have. The shadows reached out toward her like they'd been waiting all day. The air inside the house smelled sour, like dust and old milk. Her backpack slipped from her shoulder and thumped to the floor.

The couch was empty, blankets twisted and half-fallen to the floor. The ashtray on the table was full, ashes spilling over the sides. The TV screen was paused mid-frame. Her mother wasn't there.

But Sam was.

She heard him, screaming from down the hall, his crying sharp and raw, echoing from the bedroom. Ellie's chest tightened as she ran, as reality and her senses came flooding back to her. In the dim light of the bedroom, she found him in the crib, thrashing and red-faced, his body rigid with panic. His tiny fists punched at the air. His legs kicked at the blanket tangled around him.

"Sam," she whispered, grabbing the step ladder against the wall.

She scooped him up, her arms wrapping around his small frame, his weight pressing into her chest like something fragile and burning. He buried his face, hot and damp with tears, into her shoulder. She rocked him, standing there in the dim light, swaying on her feet.

"Shh," she whispered. "Shh, it's okay. I'm here. I'm here."

The cries softened, slowly breaking into hiccups that rattled in his chest. His eyes squeezed shut, one hand clutching at her shirt. She didn't stop rocking, not even when he'd quieted completely. She stayed there, swaying, afraid that if she stopped, the crying might start again.

When she was ready, she sat him on the floor. She peeled off his diaper and wiped him down with quick, practiced motions. His skin was clammy and pink. The wipes were cold, and he kicked a little but didn't cry harder. Afterwards, she bundled him in a towel and carried him to the bathroom. Light flickered as she flipped the switch, but Ellie didn't pause. She turned the faucet, and it sputtered out cold water. She let it run until it was warm and filled the bathtub just enough.

Sam was quiet as she lowered him into the warm water. He gave one soft hiccup, then another, but he didn't kick his legs like he usually did. His arms floated as his sides, hands limp and open. Ellie cradled his back, steadying him in the water, while the other one reached for a cloth. It was thin and fraying at the edges.

"You're okay," Ellie whispered, not sure if she meant it, but saying it anyway. She rinsed the cloth again and ran it gently over his arms, across the tiny slope of his belly. He didn't smile. He didn't cry either. He just watched her, eyes shiny and too big for his face.

After the bath, she wrapped him up in a bundle, folding the towel around his little body. He let his head fall to her shoulder, damp hair sticking to his face. Ellie dried him, dabbing at his neck and face, then hunted through the drawers for a fresh diaper and clean pajamas. She found the blue footie pajamas with the faded frogs that used to hop across the fabric in bright green. Those had once been hers. Now they were soft and pale from too many washes.

She dressed him on the floor. The zipper caught halfway up, and she had to gently tug it free before sliding it all the way to his chin. He looked up at her with wide, quiet eyes.

Ellie fed Sam with the last clean bottle. She had meant to bring home her milk carton from school that day. It sat on her lunch tray, untouched, next to the syrupy peaches she barely ate. But she'd left it behind, forgotten on the table as the noise of the cafeteria swelled and her thoughts went somewhere else entirely.

Instead, she made the bottle with the formula from the cupboard. There wasn't much left, just a powdery scrape at the bottom of the container, clinging to the sides. She used a spoon to scrape down the sides to get every last flake, stirred them into warm tap water and shook the bottle until the lumps dissolved.

Sam sat on the floor, his eyes puffy and half-shut. She slipped the bottle into his mouth and watched him latch on, slow and tired; even drinking had become too much. His hands didn't move. He just drank.

Ellie stood and crossed the kitchen, brushing her hair from her face. Her stomach pinched in a hollow, twisting knot. The loaf of bread was gone. She'd checked twice already, lifting the empty bag just to be sure. She glanced at the upper cabinets and, with a hop, climbed onto the countertops. She stretched her body tall; fingers grasped onto the shelf of the cupboard. She scanned the inside. There were empty boxes that should have been thrown away, cans without labels and a sticky bottle of syrup tipped on its side. But, tucked near the back, she saw it: a can of soup. Chicken noodle. Bent at the rim but still sealed.

She grabbed it, climbed down slowly, then stood for a moment on the linoleum, pressing the cool metal against her stomach like it could settle the ache inside. She set it on the counter and fished through the drawer for the can opener. It took her two tries to pierce the lid and longer to twist it around the rim of the can.

Ellie grabbed a bowl from the sink and rinsed it before pouring in the can of soup. Soft noodles and pale bits of carrot swam in the cloudy broth. She didn't want to wait. She sat at the table and ate it cold. Bite after bite, quiet and steady, until the bowl was empty and the ache in her stomach faded to something dull and manageable.

After they had both eaten, Ellie carried Sam into the bedroom, his head resting lightly against her collarbone. He was warm and heavy and made her shoulders ache. She lowered him gently onto the floor beside the worn playmat and sat cross-legged next to him. Sam's cheeks were patchy with the soft flush of tiredness. She pulled the plastic rings toward them, stacking them without looking, then pulling them apart again just to hear the soft clack they made. Sam swatted at the smallest one, missing it, then patting the floor instead. He made a soft noise, a sigh.

Ellie didn't talk. Her head leaned against the side of the crib as she moved the toys around, her hands working without thought. Sam's little fingers pawed at the edge of her sleeve, and she let him pull it, let him tug at her without looking away from the far wall.

Outside, the light faded slowly, one line at a time. The kind of fading that crept, that didn't announce itself. The corners of the room sank first, then the walls, until even Sam's pale pajamas seemed grayer than before. His movements slowed. He yawned without sound, eyes blinking longer between each look.

The dimness grew dense, and there was still no sound from the hallway. No keys. No voices. No crunch of gravel as her mother's car pulled up to the house. Just the low hum of things not happening. Cold pressed in from under the floor and around the window seams, leaking into the room slowly. The house felt paused again.

Sam's eyes grew heavier and his movements slower. Ellie laid him gently in his crib, wrapping him in his soft blanket with the bear. He stirred once, a broken sound escaping his throat, but then his thumb found his mouth and his body relaxed. Ellie made sure the edges of the blanket were firmly tucked under him. His breathing grew slower as sleep overtook his tiny body.

The room was dark now, the last sliver of twilight long gone from the window. Ellie's bare feet whispered across the carpet as she crossed the room. One hand steadied her on the wall, the other reaching out, fingers closing around the cool edge of the window frame. She pushed upward, slow and steady, until the pane slid open with a soft scrape like paper torn carefully in half.

He was already there.

He stood in the shadows like he'd grown from them, tall and still and sure, his shape cut clean against the night behind him. His eyes, almost glowing in the dark, found hers right away. Like they'd been watching through the glass the whole time. Like they knew she'd open the window.

Ellie didn't wave or smile. She just turned and climbed into bed, pulling the blanket high, bunching it beneath her chin, her knees folding to her chest, arms wrapped around them. The blanket felt impenetrable, grounding, protective. She let it press down on her, let it hold her in place.

She couldn't see him, but she could hear him move outside the window. A single step forward, then another, and another until he reached the window. He ducked inside in a smooth motion, hands barely brushing the wood. He didn't wobble or shift his weight. He didn't even pause. He just folded into the room like he belonged to it, like he'd never truly left.

When he sat on the edge of the bed, the mattress dipped with a hushed protest. His weight pressed into the space beside her slowly, deliberately. The air changed around him and in the room. It felt fuller, like something had stepped between the walls and filled them up without moving a single thing.

As the room filled with the presence of her father, it felt smaller, even with the window open, the night breeze drifting in. The walls folded inward the moment he entered, the shadows drawn into the shape he made sitting there beside her.

"Was it a hard day?" His voice stirred the air between them. The words were meticulous and even, like he'd sat in front of a mirror, practicing what he would say.

Ellie started to open her mouth but stopped herself. Her fingers picked at the loose threads in the blanket. She pulled one free from the fabric, winding it around and around her finger until it started to sting. The question pressed into the room's silence. She wasn't sure how to answer it. Her eyes drifted past him to the sliver of hallway beyond the cracked door where her backpack sat slouched against the wall. The note was still in there, creased in its envelope, pressed between the folded drawing and the bottom seam.

She thought of Sam. How he'd been screaming when she walked in, how hot his skin felt against her. She thought of the sound his voice made when it broke between shrieks, all his hiccups and gasps when he'd run out of cries. She thought of the way his fists had shaken, punching the air like something invisible had leaned too close.

She thought of the cupboard that had held just enough formula to mix. How she had to scrape the edges of the can to get enough. The way the powder clung to the spoon as she tried to mix it into the bottle. Then the soup that had tasted like metal and salt, eaten cold at the table.

Her teacher's voice drifted through her mind, slow and soft at the end of the school day, when she crouched down to hand Ellie the envelope. "Can you give this to your mom?" she'd asked.

Then there were the girls on the playground. The ones who laughed without hesitation, loud and sharp. Freak. Weird. The red jacket. The braid swinging like a rope. The tree line watching. All of it ran through her at once. She gave a small shrug. It was all too big to say. Too many words. Too many places to start.

"Is there anything you need to tell me?" his voice was still calm, empty.

Her fingers twisted in the edge of the blanket, the fabric pulling under her grip until it bunched in a small knot in her hands. Her eyes stayed on the wall across the room. The paint was peeling and flaking away, like a flap of skin after a sunburn.

"There's a note," she said finally, the words thin and tense. Her throat ached a little as they came out, her voice barely more than breath. "From school." She stared hard at the peeling corner.

His head tilted to the side, slow and smooth, the way a tree might lean after too many seasons of wind. His joints offered no resistance. The gesture held too long, too still, as if the air itself had nudged him sideways and left him that way. "What kind of note?" he asked, composed but commanding. He was nudging the rest of the truth into the open, piece by piece.

Ellie licked her bottom lip, then wiped her hand across her mouth like she was brushing the taste of the words away. "It wasn't a bad one," she whispered. "Not like…not like getting in trouble." Ellie peered at her father from the corner of her eye, his head unnervingly off-kilter. "She just said…" Ellie's voice caught on the edge of the sentence. She pulled in a breath, slow and shaky, and tried again. "She told me to give it to mom."

Her thumb rubbed the edge of the blanket, the fabric worn smooth under her hand. "That's all she said. Not what it was about. Just that she wanted mama to see it."

She peeked at him, quick and cautious. His face didn't move. Not even his eyes. He just watched, quiet as ever.

"She didn't tell me what it said."

His head tilted farther. "Did you give it to your mom?" he asked, finally breaking his silence.

Ellie shook her head furiously, "No."

"Why not?" his voice was measured.

"She wasn't home," Ellie responded.

"That's good." The corners of his mouth twitched. "Do you still have it?"

Ellie nodded. Slowly.

"Go get it," he said.

She didn't ask why. She slipped from the bed, her toes touching down soundlessly on the floor. The air felt colder out from under the blankets. She padded into the hallway, her shadow small against the wall as she grabbed her backpack by one strap, carrying it back into the room.

He was sitting straighter than before as she stepped back into the room. His spine in one rigid line, his shoulders squared with stillness that didn't look tired or relaxed; it looked *arranged.* His hands were folded on his knees, and his eyes were already on her. Not watching her enter. They were already there, as if they'd never left the doorway. Ellie slowed. Something about the room shifted. The air had less space in it. Her fingertips brushed the side pocket of her backpack and caught hold of the zipper.

The zipper made a short, scratchy noise as she unzipped the side pocket where the envelope and the drawing rested. Her fingers searched until they found the envelope. It was bent now, softened at the corners, still sealed at the top with the thin strip of clear tape. Her hand closed around the envelope. Behind it, the drawing rustled against the lining of the bag.

She hadn't meant to, but her grip tensed until the corners of the paper started to buckle against her palm. Her father hadn't moved.

Ellie crossed the room, the envelope pressed to her chest like a fragile thing she didn't know how to carry. Her socks barely made a sound, but the floorboard near her dresser groaned under her step, low and long, like the house was noticing her again. She winced, then took the last few steps without looking down.

"I don't know what it says," she whispered, her voice barely there. "I didn't look."

Then, with slow, delicate movements, his hand rose and his fingers curled around the paper. He turned the envelope over in his hand and tapped the edge lightly on his knee. Without a word, he tore into the seal. The tape gave way with a soft, sticky whisper.

Ellie swallowed, her arms hanging at her sides, limp and cold. He unfolded the paper slowly, deliberately, like every crease had meaning. The white of the note looked brighter in the dim room, too bright, catching what little light there was and bouncing it at strange angles.

His eyes moved across the paper. Once. Then again. But his face didn't move at all.

He let the note rest in his lap, his hand still holding it loose. "Tell me about the drawing," he said. Not demanding or even curious, just expecting. "Your teacher is concerned and wants to meet."

Ellie's voice stuck at first. She rubbed her palms on her thighs. "It's a tree," she said slowly. "Big. With roots. There's a hole underneath. You can't see inside it, but it goes down." Her fingers made a small motion in the air, like she was tracing the shape of it again. "It's in the dark. There were shapes in the dark, but I only used black crayon so you couldn't see them all.

"I added two people," she went on, her father remaining silent. "Just standing there. At the edge. They're looking in but not going. They're small. The tree's so big.... Mrs. Rieke didn't like it. I didn't follow the directions."

He nodded, slow and easy, like it all made perfect sense. "You don't have to give this to your mother," he said, folding the letter back into the envelope and placing it in the inner pocket of his jacket.

Ellie's eyes flicked up. Her voice was frayed at the edges. "She'll be mad if she finds out."

His answer was calm. Steady. "She doesn't need to know."

Ellie searched his face. "You're sure?" she asked, something unspooling in her chest, her shoulders dropping from her ears.

He nodded once. Firm. Certain. "Some things are only for us."

Ellie sat back down next to her father, comforted by the shape of him beside her, the stillness he brought. He leaned forward slightly, the fabric of his coat shifting with a soft rustle. "Was there anything else?"

Again, Ellie began to pick at the thread on the blanket. She thought of the playground, of the wooden castle, and the rough boards under hands splintering in her fingers. The girl in the red jacket calling her a freak, the way the laughter from the other kids echoed in her chest.

She opened her mouth, just a little. The words hovered in Ellie's mouth, caught behind her teeth. The shape of what she wanted to say pressed against the inside of her throat. Her lips closed again. Her fingers moved without thinking, twisting another loose thread along the edge of the blanket, winding it tighter and tighter until it tugged against the fabric. Ellie shook her head.

He didn't press. Didn't lean closer. Didn't tilt his head or ask again. He simply reached out, his hand moving in that slow, practiced way, and he tapped her knee through the blanket with two fingers. A quiet touch. It didn't hurt; it was light, barely there, but it made something shift in her chest. Made something in her thoughts settle.

"You're not a freak," he said.

Ellie's breath caught in her lungs, and she held it there. She turned to him, slowly, her eyes wide and round. She hadn't told him about the playground. About the girl in the red jacket. About the voices, the laughter, the way it made her feel hollow and too big at the same time. The way it settled in her belly like stones. But somehow, he knew.

Her voice, when it came, was small. "They don't like me."

He didn't blink. "That doesn't mean you're wrong."

"They think I'm weird."

"They don't see what I see," he replied, and his voice was warm, almost kind, but threaded with something else.

Ellie looked down at her hands again. The thread between her fingers had broken; the little knot she'd been twisting had come loose without her even noticing. It fluttered to the blanket, pale against the fabric.

He shifted slightly beside her, just enough for the bed to squeal again beneath his weight. "And you don't have to let them say those things." His voice had a glimmer of something under it, something strange.

Ellie's brow twitched. Her head tilted, just a little, like she hadn't heard him right. She squinted in the dark, trying to read his face. His eyes glinted faintly, amused.

The blanket felt heavier in her lap. Her hands slipped beneath it, folding into fists.

"I didn't do anything," she said, not to defend herself, but to name it. "They just laughed."

He didn't answer right away, but he was still smiling. Not with his mouth, with his eyes. "They won't stop," she said quietly. And in her stomach, something twisted. A flicker of heat. Not crying heat. Not hurt. Something else. The kind that rose slow and stayed. Her fingers dug in, pressing tight into her palms.

His voice dropped, softer now. "Then stop them." The words didn't hit like a suggestion; they landed like a fact.

"...How?" she asked, perplexed. Her voice was quieter than his, thin and uncertain, but it held. It didn't shake.

He smiled. It started small with the corners of his mouth lifting, twitching. The curve crept higher, pulling his cheeks in a slow drag upwards toward the corners of his eyes, until his lips parted and all of his teeth showed. They caught what little light there was and held it. The smile kept stretching across his face, too wide for his jaw. But his eyes didn't change. They stayed the same: fixed, calm, knowing.

"You'll know how," he said. "In the moment."

Ellie's breath came a little quicker as she braced at that smile. She couldn't think past the way his teeth had caught the light, or the way his eyes hadn't changed at all when the smile reached them.

Her mouth opened. Nothing came out. No sound. No breath. The words she meant to form withered before they reached the edge of her lips. The air around them pressed inward, dense and sharp in her chest, as if the walls had leaned in and taken something with them.

He didn't shift. Neither did she. The quiet stretched, saturated as wet cloth, hanging between them with weight that didn't need explaining. His eyes never left her face.

"The drawing," he said after a long stretch of nothing, almost as if he'd waited to ask until she was ready. "May I take it with me?"

Ellie blinked, surprised. "You want it?"

He nodded once. "It's yours. You made it. I'd like to keep it safe."

Her hand slipped into her lap. She thought of the tree. The dark beneath. The way the roots curled inward like fingers.

"It's in my backpack," she said softly.

He said nothing, just watched as she slid off the bed and padded barefoot across the room, her nightgown brushing her knees as she walked. She reached into the pocket.

When she turned back, she was holding the paper with both hands, folded carefully into quarters. The edges had gone a little soft, the creases worn. She stepped close again, reached out, and placed it in his waiting hands.

He took it with both hands, reverently, and unfolded the corners just enough to glance down at it. His eyes scanned it slowly, back and forth, his mouth unreadable now. Following the creases, he folded it again and tucked it inside his coat with the letter from Mrs. Rieke.

"Thank you," he said coolly.

Ellie nodded, small and tense, and climbed back onto the bed without a word. The mattress gave under her as she lowered herself, the blanket rising to meet her chin. She pulled her legs up and folded her arms close, drawing herself into a tight, guarded bundle on the sheets.

She watched him rise. One long movement, no rush. He stood straight, taller now, taller than he had been a second ago, like something in him had stretched out. The space beside her still held the ghost of his weight. The dent he'd left behind hadn't smoothed out yet. But already, it felt thinner. Like the bed was exhaling.

"Will you come back tomorrow?" she asked.

He stood there in the middle of the room, not moving, the dim light from the window throwing his shape long across the wall. His edges blurred in the moonlight, his shadow too still on the wall. Ellie waited, her breath catching on the stillness, afraid that maybe she'd asked the wrong thing.

Then he moved. Not turning. Not hesitating. Just one step, then another, quiet as fog, and the room seemed to lean out of his way. He walked toward the window again, one hand resting lightly on the sill.

"I'll come back," he said. "As long as you remember."

CORNERS OF THE ROOM

Saturday morning came, pale and gray, a fine drizzle of rain whispering down from the muted sky. Ellie woke to the sound of Sam rustling in his crib. The baby made soft little squeaks like a mouse under his blanket as he rolled around in the early morning light. She rolled over slowly, the sheets tangled around her legs and let her eyes rest on the ceiling.

The cold crept up through the floorboards and unseen gaps in the walls. The chill climbed up her legs and wrapped around her knees as her bare feet touched the floor. She eased across the room, first to her step ladder, then to Sam. He was warm against her chest, his head solid on her shoulder, his breath damp on her neck.

She changed Sam first, humming the kind of tune that loops in your head when no one's talking. His diaper was wet, and the wipes were chilly in her hands, but they smelled clean and fresh. She bundled him in layers with two pairs of socks, long-sleeves, a mitten on one hand, the other bare and pink.

Ellie carried Sam down the hall, one hand under his bottom, the other wrapped firmly across his back, pressing him close. His thumb was tucked lazily into his mouth. His body was heavier in the mornings, soft with sleep and stillness, and Ellie adjusted her arms to hold the weight of him more evenly.

The living room was dim, the weak, gray light leeching in from the blinds, stretching itself across the floor in long, tired stripes. A few toys lay scattered across the floor. Sam's little plastic keys were under the coffee table, splayed in a brightly colored heap. A glass bottle lay near the couch, and Ellie's stomach knotted.

Her mother's shoes were kicked off near the wall, one on its side like it had been dropped mid-step. Her coat was draped across the arm of the couch. Her purse slouched in a heap beside it, its zipper gaping slightly open. The bedroom door had been closed when Ellie passed it earlier. No light slipped from underneath. There were no footsteps or yawns or rustling blankets, but her mother had come home sometime in the night.

Ellie shifted Sam higher on her hip and turned her eyes away from the heap of mislaid items. She carried Sam through the living room and into the kitchen without looking back. He kicked a little as she sat him on the floor, not quite happy, not quite crying. She ran a hand through her hair and opened the cupboards slowly.

No formula. The scraping of the spoon inside the empty can from the night before echoed in her head. She climbed onto the counter on her knees, one hand gripping the edge of the cupboard door as she pulled herself up. Her socks slid a little on the surface, but she steadied herself.

She opened one cupboard, then another. Nothing soft. Nothing for babies. She regretted eating the soup last night. Sam could have at least had the broth.

Her eyes scanned the shelves for anything Sam could have. On the top shelf where her eyes could barely see, she spotted a round container. The lid was cloudy red plastic, the tan colored label pulling at the edges. She dragged it toward her and read the faded letters one at a time, sounding them out under her breath. It wasn't formula. Not the kind Sam needed. She knew that. But it was something powdery. White and soft and sweet-smelling when she popped the lid off. Like sugar. It was the stuff her mom stirred into her mug in the morning when she was awake.

Ellie dipped her fingers into the can, the powder sticking to the tips. She touched them to her tongue; the powder melted there. Sweet. Not bad. She climbed down off the counter, the container clutched between her arm and her side. It wasn't what Sam was supposed to have, but her mother hadn't brought anything else.

She stood on tiptoes at the sink. The container of powder sat on the counter, not out of her view. The water took a long time to warm. She watched it trickle out, first cold, then not-quite-cold, then just warm enough not to sting.

Sam fussed behind her, a soft whimper turning into a squawk. Ellie turned halfway to look back at him. He sat on the floor near the fridge, one sock already off, chewing on the corner of a dish towel he'd found on the floor. His face had started to go red, his eyes watering.

"I know," Ellie whispered. "I'm going fast." She quickened her pace, not wanting a screaming Sam to wake her mother.

She pulled the cleanest bottle from the rack by the sink. It was still damp. She shook the droplets of water that had collected inside out into the sink, rinsed it again just in case, then scooped in the white powder. One spoon. Then a little more. She didn't really know how much. The real formula had marks on the side, numbers and little pictures of scoops. This one didn't. She stirred it with the handle of a spoon, careful not to let the powder clump too thick. The sweet smell rose up again. Not like baby food. Not like milk either.

She capped the bottle and shook it, watching the swirl of pale water go cloudy, then creamy. She pressed the side of the bottle to her wrist. Warm, not hot.

Sam started to cry, and Ellie dropped to his side, her legs folded under her. She offered the bottle. He took it right away, both hands grabbing hold with surprising strength, his mouth latching like he'd been starving all morning. She let out a breath she hadn't realized she was holding.

"There," she said softly, brushing his hair from his forehead. "See? We're okay."

Sam drank with his eyes closed, his fists giving tiny squeezes against the plastic. Ellie sat beside him, her back against the fridge, the canister of creamer still on the counter above them. The house was quiet again, except for the gentle suck and swallow of Sam's drinking and the faint hum of the fridge under her spine.

Ellie turned from Sam and set to her task. Dishes first. She gathered them from the counter, the coffee table, and the floor where one had tipped and dried into a circle of old sauce. She stacked them in the sink with a soft clatter and reached for the sponge. It was worn nearly flat, edges fraying, the green side fraying like moss on a rock. Still, it worked well enough when she pressed hard.

She ran the water until it was warm and put the stopper into the sink, letting the dishes submerge. She plunged her hands in and scrubbed. A cup with a lipstick stain. A spoon sticky from something she hadn't eaten. One of Sam's bottles. She cleaned each one with quiet focus. Soap. Circles. Rinse.

With her hands red from scrubbing and soap, she moved next to the floor. The broom was taller than she was, but she knew how to lean into it just right, how to keep it from catching on the corners of the cabinets. It scratched across the linoleum in short, uneven strokes, dragging dust and crumbs into neat little piles. When she reached the fridge, she nudged it shut with her hip—it had a habit of not sealing all the way. The magnets on the door slid down the front faintly. She knelt to sweep the last of the crumbs into the dustpan.

Her stomach growled. Not a soft flutter, but something deep and twisting, as she pushed forward into the living room, bringing Sam and setting him with a heap of toys in his lap.

She set her mother's shoes right, one next to the other, neatly near the wall. She picked up her purse from the floor, zipped it, and placed it carefully on the chair near the window. The coat she draped near the purse. Then the blanket on the couch. She folded it in half, then again, smoothing it over the back cushions with care. The edges warped, but she tugged them flat. It smelled like sleep. Like old milk. Like something sour. She paused, her hand pressing the last corner just once before she let it fall into place.

Behind her, Sam let out a sudden laugh. Loud. Clear. It broke the quiet of the house wide open, crashing into the walls. Ellie turned at once, her heart jumping into her throat, the hairs on her neck standing straight up. He was sitting on the floor where she had left him, legs splayed out unevenly in front of him, his other sock halfway off. His hands clapped against each other in a rhythm only he understood, small palms smacking together with joyful insistence. His eyes, round and bright, were locked on a patch of empty air just above him.

Sam was giggling, soft and hiccupy, and tilting his head like he was listening to someone sing him a song. His mouth opened around another happy squeal, and he reached one chubby hand outward, fingers twitching in the air. As she watched her brother, a feeling prickled up her arms, something between a chill and a weight.

As suddenly as his laughter had pierced the quiet, Sam dropped his eyes back to his plastic keys, shaking them feverishly in front of his face before shoving them back into his mouth and gumming down. His voice dropped to a soft babble as he slapped the floor next to him while chewing, delighted, on the keys. The prickly feeling on her arms faded, and Ellie turned back to her cleaning.

By early evening, Sam had grown fussy again. His head leaned with a drowsy weight against Ellie's arm, his breath warm and uneven against her collarbone. He was tired in that squirmy, restless way that meant it wouldn't be long before he started crying again. Ellie rocked him as she moved through the house, shushing softly into the space just above his ear.

The light outside had turned golden around the edges, blurring in the place between day and night. Dust caught the light in slow, floating specks. Ellie sat Sam down on the floor again, turning to grab the red lidded can, when she heard a floorboard creak behind her. She turned as her mother stepped into the kitchen.

Her eyes were bright, shimmering with the wrong kind of sparkle, pointed and watery. Her cheeks were flush with something layered on thick, her lips smeared in bold, glossy red. The collar of her jacket was turned up like she had just thrown it on in a hurry. She moved fast, the air already too stale for her.

"Oh good, you're still up," her mother said, brushing past her toward the kitchen table, digging in her purse for something she didn't find. "I've gotta run out for a bit. Won't be long."

"Where are you going?" Ellie asked, shifting Sam on her hip.

Her mother didn't meet her eyes. "Just out. Meeting someone."

Ellie blinked. "A friend?"

A pause. Then a shrug. "Something like that."

She stood by the sink, smoothing her hair down in the reflection on the window above it, tugging her jacket straight.

"You gonna bring back groceries?" Ellie asked.

Her mother hesitated, then smiled too wide, too fast. "Yeah, yeah. I'll grab a few things. He's taking me to dinner, but after that I'll swing by the store. We might be doing something different soon anyway. He's...helpful. Got plans. Could be good for us."

Ellie nodded. Sam rubbed his face into her shirt.

Her mother walked to the door, keys already in hand. "You'll be fine for a bit, right?"

Ellie looked at her mother. Really looked. The edges of her eyes were smudged, but she was smiling, all teeth and color and perfume.

"We're fine," Ellie said.

The door shut behind her mother a moment later. "We're fine," Ellie whispered to Sam.

Ellie woke without remembering falling asleep. Her body felt heavy and her face swollen, like she had been crying, but she didn't remember doing that either. The pillow beneath her head was warm, the blanket wrapped awkwardly around her legs, one foot bare and the other still covered. Her eyes searched slowly in the dim for what had woken her, the faint light from the moon spilling across the floor. The edges of the room felt blurred, the corners pulling inward. The air had weight to it, stifling with the kind of quiet that pulled at the edges of your attention. She let her eyes move across the room, her breath soft in her nose.

Her gaze settled on Sam's crib, registering its shape before its meaning. The crib's bars cast long shadows across the carpet. And there, hunched beside it, was the shape of her father. He leaned close to the bars, his face tipped toward the baby's. Soft sounds, whispers, escaped his mouth, words Ellie couldn't understand. Sam wasn't crying. He didn't squirm or fuss.

He lay still, his hands lifted toward the man, fingers curling and uncurling in the air between them. His arms strained with the effort, but he kept reaching up and out for the figure above him. Sam's face was open, his mouth parted in a silent smile, eyes wide and shining in the dim light. The smile that spread across his face had no mischief in it, no play. It was a captivated kind of joy. It wasn't the look he gave Ellie when she made him laugh or sang to him or danced her fingers along his belly.

Ellie's body tensed as she pushed herself upright. The bed shifted beneath her, the springs giving a low groan, but she didn't stop. She watched as Sam's fingers reached again, brushing the air, just beneath the shadow of the man crouched by the crib.

Her father's head pivoted slowly, deliberately, until his gaze landed on hers across the room. His eyes were steady and full.

She swallowed, the motion slow and dry. Her fingers clutched harder at the blanket. Her eyes moved from the crib to the figure standing beside it. His hand still rested lightly against the bars, his head bowed just enough to keep Sam in view.

"What are you doing?" She found her voice, though it came out thinner than she meant it to.

He straightened fully, the coat along his shoulders catching the faintest hint of light from the hallway. His eyes lifted to meet hers. He took a step back from the crib, folding his hands in front of him. "I was waiting for you."

"Why didn't you wake me up?" she asked, her voice strained, more breath than sound.

The man across the room tilted his head in that same slow way he always did, the movement smooth and strange. A small smile played at the edges of his mouth, but it didn't quite touch his eyes. His steps were noiseless, the soles of his shoes seemingly never quite pressing down, as he crossed the room. There was no rush, no effort, as if the floor moved gently beneath him instead of the other way around.

"You needed sleep," he said. His voice didn't rise or fall. It just filled the space between them with the weight of something he'd already decided. "You've been tired."

Ellie didn't move. She wasn't sure she could. Her arms were locked at her sides, her legs drawn up beneath the blanket.

"What were you saying to him?" she asked.

He took a step closer and sat down next to her on the bed. "I wasn't saying anything important," he said softly. "Just talking."

Across the room, Sam gave a soft sigh and shifted in his crib, settling again into sleep. Ellie didn't look away. Her eyes stayed on the man next to her. On the way his face didn't move when he smiled. On the way his arm stayed lifted, open, waiting.

"I came to see you," he said again, quieter now. "Like I always do." Ellie nodded, and leaned in, settling against her father's side.

"Did you miss me?" he asked.

Ellie opened her mouth, hesitated. "Yes," she said, finally, the word nearly sticking to her tongue.

He tilted his head again, as if tasting the answer.

"I always miss you," he said. "But I wait. I don't want to come if you're not ready."

Ellie shifted under the covers. "How do you know when I am?"

His eyes shone darker than the room around them. "I just do."

Outside the window, a breeze moved past, bending the branches against the glass with a faint rustle. The shadows in the corner of the room didn't move.

"Tell me something from today," he said. "Anything."

Ellie hesitated. Then she started to talk. Just a little. About the powdered milk in the cabinet. About Sam clapping at the empty space in the living room. About sweeping the kitchen and how the sponge kept crumbling in her hands. She talked slowly, her voice steadying as she went, and he didn't interrupt once. He just listened. Eyes steady, head slightly bowed, the shadows around his shoulders unmoving.

After speaking, Ellie turned to him. Her breath had begun to steady, but something still crawled under the surface of her skin. There was the faint prickling of still lingering questions. The whispers she'd heard earlier still pressed in her mind, creeping along the walls of the room.

"What were you saying to him?" Her voice didn't shake. It came out whole.

He turned his head to meet her gaze. The shift in him was almost imperceptible—something behind his eyes deepened, two hidden pools clouding over with ink. A stillness passed across his face like a shadow overtaking the day.

"Just something to help him sleep," he said. The words hovered between them, suspended, untethered. Ellie's chest tensed with an uneasy sense that the truth had been carefully folded and slipped beneath something else.

Her father rose without a hurry. There was no groan of the mattress, no rustle from the fabric of his coat. The long line of his frame moved with quiet certainty, and when he turned toward the window, the room fell in step behind him, soundless and pulling, folding into the dark around his shoulders.

His hands didn't reach for the sill. They hovered near it but never touched, his presence shifting forward in a way that made the floor feel slanted, as if the room itself had given him a path to go. One step and half in, half out, the rest of him was lost in the black beyond the glass. Ellie sat frozen on the bed, her knees tucked against her chest, the blanket pulled high.

"You'll come back?" she called after him. Her words slipped out, frantic and unsure, and they hung there, trembling at the edges.

He paused in the frame of the window, silhouetted against the absence outside. His shape looked too tall, stretched thin and hollow, like the glass had pulled him longer than he was meant to be. He turned his head to reveal the edge of his cheek, the faint curve of a mouth that never smiled the way other mouths did.

"I'll always come back," he said.

And then he was gone, as though the night had blinked and taken him with it. The window shut behind him, soft, without a scrape or a scratch. No click of metal. No snap of wood coming together. Only the air folding closed, like water sealing after a stone has slipped through its surface.

Ellie stared at the place where he'd stood, her hand pressed to the blanket, still warm beside her. The silence returned, weighty and low, pressing against her ears until it became its own kind of noise, dense, weightless, humming.

Across the room, in his crib, Sam let out a small whimper, stirring in his sleep. There was a moment of silence before it broke. The sound that tore from Sam's throat wasn't a cry. It was a rupture—sharp, high, and raw, the kind of sound that made her suck in her ribs without meaning to. It split the quiet open like a rip in fabric. Ellie bolted upright, the blanket tangling at her knees. She stumbled across the room, legs dragging, catching herself on the side of the crib, stopping just before she collapsed into it.

"Shhh, shhh, it's okay. I've got you," she whispered, reaching through the bars with trembling hands. Her fingers found the heat of his body, kicking and flailing, and she rubbed his chest. His body jerked and spasmed, arms rigid, fists beating the air. His face scrunched, his eyes pressed together as he wailed, his breath coming frantic and shallow. His head twisted, not toward her, but past her.

His gaze stretched over her shoulder and locked on the window. His eyes were unmoving, unblinking, mouth slack and breath hitched in his throat as if something had caught his attention and refused to let go. The air was overwhelming around them, a slow press against Ellie's skin. She turned her head, unsure, her whole body tensed like she had just stepped into cold water. Her eyes fell on the window. It was empty.

She turned her eyes back to Sam, and the moment her eyes met his tiny face again, his mouth opened wide and the wail returned, raw and ripping something up from deep inside him. Ellie scrambled for the step ladder resting against the wall, her feet slipping on the carpet as she kicked it into place. She climbed up quickly, her fingers fumbling at the crib rail, and reached in to lift him. His body was warm and squirming, frantic against her chest, his little fists bunching in her shirt as he screamed into the fabric.

She stepped backward, knees stiff, trying to keep her balance while his weight shifted in her arms. Sam clung to her with every heartbeat, his face buried against her collarbone, soaking her shirt with tears and breath. She carried him across the room, her knee hitting the edge of the bed as she climbed in. She sank down without grace, one arm around his back, the blanket still twisted in the middle, where she'd been moments before. The familiar divot in the middle welcomed them both.

"It's okay," she said, though the words tasted thin. She pitched her voice low and steady, coiling herself around Sam. "We're okay."

Ellie looked once more toward the window. It was shut. Nothing loomed beyond the pane. But something lingered. Not on the other side of the glass, but inside. Around them.

Ellie gathered the blanket with one hand, pulled it over both their bodies, and wrapped herself around her brother like a shell. She pulled her knees in, forming a small hollow around his smaller one, her arms protective and stiff with worry. Sam's face pressed against her skin, his body shivering with sobs, little hiccups shaking through him.

Ellie didn't close her eyes. Not even once.

CLOVER

The weekend had passed in fits. Ellie's mother returned late Saturday night, arms laden with a few grocery bags, but neither her nor the food's presence brought any relief. Sam's cries had been relentless, echoing through the thin walls. He could not be soothed by formula or lullabies; he writhed in Ellie's arms, his cheeks blotchy and red.

By Monday morning, Sam had finally tired himself out. Ellie bundled him in a blanket and left him sleeping in the crib. She didn't eat that morning. Dark circles surrounded her eyes. Her movements were sluggish as she buttoned up her jacket and stepped outside.

The gravel crunched under her shoes, and the crunch nearly masked another sound, something frail that was almost swallowed by the wind slipping between the trees. She froze, her sneakers halfway to the cracked asphalt. It came again, clearer this time. High-pitched. Fragile. A cry threaded through the morning chill. Not the bark of a squirrel or the rustle of a bird. Not a baby either. But something young. Something small. Crying.

Ellie turned her head and scanned the yard. The sound was coming from the edge of the woods—the place just past the fence where the grass grew wild and the dirt turned soft. The trees there stood close together, hunched like they were keeping secrets.

She stepped forward, the cold twirling through her fingers. The cry came again, sharper now, more urgent. She squinted toward the tree line. Nothing moved, but the sound was still there, threading through the branches.

Her backpack was slipping off one shoulder. Her socks were too thin for the damp grass silvered with frost. Her stomach was empty. Her legs were tired. She was going to be late. Ellie walked with her shoulders hunched, eyes down. She kept walking even when the wind shifted and carried the sound after her.

The cry followed her through the hallways of the school. It followed her to her desk, to the lunch table, and onto the playground. All day, she thought about the cry coming from the edge of the woods. It stayed in her mind, behind the scraping of chairs and the too-loud ticking of the classroom clock. Even when the teacher's voice droned on about numbers and the other kids laughed and squealed, the sound echoed faintly, like a thread of noise caught behind her ribs.

She heard it again that afternoon—the same anemic, aching sound, sharper now in the colder air. It rose above the rattle of the leaves. Her sneakers slowed in the gravel as she listened closely, her eyes surveying the tree line for any movement.

Ellie dropped her bag on the porch and circled around to the back of the house, crossing the yard toward the woods, the brittle grass crunching beneath her with every step. The wind carried the cry straight toward her, clear, pulling her forward. Her breath puffed out in small clouds as she reached the fence, grabbing hold of the cold metal and pulling herself up, one shoe wedging into the diamond-shaped wire.

Her sleeve snagged on the top edge. She tugged hard. The fabric gave with a rough scrape, leaving a small tear near the cuff. The woods loomed close now, tangled and still, the bare trees pressing in overhead, their branches like arms reaching in too many directions. She stepped forward, ducking beneath a low limb. Dead leaves shifted around her shoes. The cry guided her, pulling her left, then forward, until the trees broke just enough to reveal a dip in the ground, shallow and half-sheltered by a crooked tree root and a fallen branch.

A kitten. Tiny. Gray with darker stripes, fur sticking up in wet clumps, shivering so hard its whole body seemed to vibrate. It was crouched low in a patch of soggy leaves, one paw curled beneath it, its thin sides heaving with each breath. Its eyes were sticky at the corners. It opened its mouth and a small, broken sound came out.

"Oh," Ellie whispered, breath catching in her throat.

She crouched slowly, her knees brushing the ground. Her fingers hovered above the leaves. She expected it to run, or at least flinch, but it didn't. It just looked up at her, waiting. Her hands moved forward inch by inch. The kitten didn't move. When her fingers finally touched its fur, it felt thin, damp, fragile. She slid her hands beneath its belly, lifting gently, and it let her. It nestled against her chest like it had always belonged there.

Ellie stood slowly, one hand holding the small, shaking body close, the other brushing leaves from her knee. A smear of mud clung to her palm. The woods loomed around her, tall and silent, branches overhead knitting together against the gray sky. Somewhere beyond the trees, past the fence and the brittle yard, her house waited. Dark. Still. Probably quiet if Sam was asleep. Probably not if he wasn't.

The kitten pressed its face into the crook of her arm, paws bunching against the front of her jacket. It made a sound, not quite a mew, and began to knead with tiny, rhythmic pushes, its claws too small to catch much fabric. Then the purring started. A low, steady vibration that buzzed against her ribs.

She carried it inside quietly, cradling it close to her body, keeping it warm. The house was dim. No sound from her mother's room and no sound from Sam. She tiptoed into the bathroom, flipping the light on with her elbow.

She set the kitten down in the sink, the porcelain stained at the corners, faucet handle loose. She turned the water on low. It hissed, sputtered, then warmed in her hand. She cupped a bit of it and let it drip down the kitten's back, rinsing away the clumps of dirt, small bugs drifting to the bottom of the sink. The water ran brown at first, swirling into the drain. The kitten didn't fight. Didn't squirm. It sat in the basin, watching her with wide, glassy eyes. Ellie worked gently with a washcloth, wiping its eyes clean, dabbing under its paws and along its belly. Each time she touched it, it leaned into her hand. When she wrapped it in a towel, all clean, the purring came back. Louder now. Steadier.

"You're okay now," Ellie whispered, holding it to her chest.

Ellie rummaged through a lower cabinet in the kitchen, shifting past old lids that didn't belong to anything until she found a small, shallow bowl. It wobbled slightly when she set it on the counter. She poured a little of Sam's formula in, enough to cover the bottom, then stirred it together with warm water.

Before she could even set the bowl on the kitchen floor, the kitten was at her feet. It didn't hesitate before dipping its head into the bowl and drinking, tongue flicking, eyes half-lidded with concentration.

"I'm gonna call you Clover," she said, almost shyly.

She made a bottle next, measuring the formula with practiced hands, the scoop silent against the plastic. The water ran warm, and she swirled it gently, watching the bubbles rise and settle. She carried it with her to the bedroom, the kitten tucked against her chest with one hand, the bottle held steady in the other.

Sam was stirring as she entered the room. She set the kitten on the bed, where it circled the corner once before curling into the folds of the blanket, watching with slow blinks. Ellie crossed to the crib, dragging her stepladder behind her. Climbing up, she reached in, scooping Sam under his arms, lifting him against her chest. His cheek found her shoulder, warm and damp with sleep.

"Hey," she said smiling. "I have a new friend for us."

After Sam finished his bottle, Ellie lay him on the bed beside the kitten. He sat, clumsily patting the blanket with one hand while the other reached toward Clover's tiny paws. The kitten sniffed him once, let out a low purr, and pressed its side against Sam's arm. He giggled, and Ellie smiled so wide her cheeks ached.

When the sky outside the window turned navy and the first stars pricked through the glass, Ellie lifted Sam and laid him gently in the crib. Then she gathered Clover in the towel again, folding it like a nest and placing it on the floor beside her bed, close enough for her fingers to reach in the night. The kitten settled instantly, nestling into the dip of fabric with a final purr.

Ellie climbed into bed, the mattress cool beneath her, the blanket rough under her chin. She reached down once, fingers brushing Clover's back before she closed her eyes.

Ellie woke in the night, the weight of sleep still clinging to her lashes. The room was quiet. She lay still, listening. Nothing moved. No stir from the crib. No rustle from the bed. Just the low hum of silence pressed into the walls. Sam slept with one hand tucked beneath his chin, his breath soft and steady. Clover dozed in the towel-nest on the floor, her small body folded tightly, tail giving a single twitch as she dreamed.

The blankets slipped from her shoulders as she sat up, the cool air licking at her skin. She was careful not to step on the sleeping kitten as her feet found the floor. She crossed the room and stood by the window, her heart ticking faster.

He stood back, away from the window, toward the edge of the woods. The dark wrapped around him. Ellie pushed the window open. It scraped up the frame with a faint groan, and the cold came in fast, rushing across her face, making her shiver. Her breath wove through the air between them, a pale swirl against the dark.

"Come in," she whispered, half-laughing, half-pleading. Her voice cracked with the urgency of it. "Please. I have to show you something." She waved her hand, motioning for him to come forward. He didn't move.

She leaned farther out, fingers gripping the sill. "What are you doing? Come in." Her whisper grew louder. Ellie's heart was beating hard now. "I found a kitten," she said, her voice quick and excited. "She's really little. Just a baby. I cleaned her up and fed her, and she purrs when I hold her."

She waited. The trees behind him didn't move. Neither did he.

"Please," she said. Her fingers gripped the wood with a trembling hold. "She's so little. I saved her."

His eyes narrowed, but he didn't move forward. "Why don't you want to play with me?" he asked. His voice dropped low, making the hairs on the back of Ellie's neck rise.

"I do," she said, her breath catching. "I do want to play with you. We just never…we never play."

The cold pressed harder against her cheeks. Her breath fogged between them. The blinds tapped the frame behind her, though there was no wind.

"We can," he said, his eyes fixed and shining in the dark. "You never asked." His voice dropped even lower.

Ellie began to twist her hands in on each other.

"You didn't wait at the window for me." His voice was laced with something grim.

"I still do," Ellie insisted. "I waited last night."

His face twitched, a shadow moving across his features, and for a second, she couldn't see his eyes.

"But now you've got something else," he said, his tone tilting. "Now you've got something small. Something soft. Something you can carry around and keep warm."

Ellie didn't understand the feeling in his voice, but it made her stomach twist. She took a step back from the window. Just one. But he noticed.

"You love her more than me?" he asked.

Her mouth opened. "No! No, I just...she needed help. That's all. She was alone." The words spilled out in a rush, her voice thin and trembling. "She was cold. And hungry. I didn't mean..." But the rest of it stuck in her throat, dried out and useless. She swallowed, her heart knocking hard against her ribs.

His silhouette stood fixed among the trees, swallowed at the edges by the dark. The limbs behind him seemed to lean in, angling ever so slightly. Ellie's breath hitched in her throat. The cold slipped deeper past her collar, past her sleeves. She looked down at Clover, gathered into a tight little ball, sleeping and safe. She raised her eyes back to the yard and tried to focus, but the space he'd occupied no longer held any shape. The place between the trees looked normal. The yard was empty.

Ellie pulled herself back into bed, knees to her chest, one arm draped over the edge of the bed, fingers hovering protectively above the sleeping kitten. Her eyes stayed open a while longer than usual, scanning the walls and corners. She didn't know what to make of what had happened. Her father's face. His voice. The way it had all slipped away so fast.

The warmth of the kitten's body beneath her fingertips seeped into her skin. Ellie's eyes closed.

The scream tore through the house like a crack in the sky. Ellie jolted upright, heart hammering before her eyes had even opened. The scream came again, higher this time. Sam jerked awake in his crib and began crying.

Ellie threw the blanket off and stumbled to her feet. She looked down at the small, careful nest where Clover had slept, warm and safe and sleeping. The circle of terry cloth lay hollow and empty.

"Ellie!" a shrill scream came from the next room, and Ellie ran toward it.

Her mother stood inside the bathroom, just past the threshold, hair tangled and falling in limp curls around her face, her makeup smeared and flaking under her eyes. One hand clutched her purse, still looped over her shoulder like she hadn't even taken off her coat. The other was pressed hard against her forehead, fingers digging into her temple like she could erase whatever she was seeing.

Ellie looked past her.

At first she didn't understand what she was seeing. The surface of the water was so calm, it didn't look like it had been touched at all. No bubbles. No ripples. No foam. Just the faint shimmer under the water, like glass stretched thin.

Clover floated in the center of it. Perfectly placed.

Her little body didn't drift or spin. She simply hovered there, limbs weightless, as though the water had molded itself around her. Her paws were splayed wide, toes curled as if they'd tried, at the very last second, to grasp something that wasn't there. Her head was tilted back and her ears were filled with water.

Her eyes were still open. Those bright eyes from the day before, now pale and cloudy, turned upward to the ceiling. Their shine was gone, replaced by something dull and far away. Ellie could see the light from the ceiling reflected in them, distorted and small, a smudge across the lens.

Ellie dropped to her knees with a cry that broke in her throat before it could fully form. Her palms hit the floor, and she scrambled toward the edge of the tub. Her fingers gripped the fiberglass. Her breath came in quick, shaking bursts. She didn't notice the tears flowing down her face until they landed in the water, sending small ripples out across its surface.

Ellie reached out, hand hovering just above the water, as if touching her might fix something. As if maybe, somehow, it wasn't too late.

No," she breathed. "No, no, no…" She didn't feel the cold linoleum on her knees. Didn't hear her mother pacing back a step, muttering something under her breath. The purse slipped from her mother's shoulder and hit the floor with a soft, careless thump.

"It's dead," her mother said, her voice hoarse, almost distracted.

Ellie stared at the kitten. At the small, sodden body floating in the still water. At the shape that had pressed beneath her chin the night before, tucked against her heart. The kitten that had pressed its forehead into her hand and against Sam's body. That had purred with its whole body humming like it didn't know it had been saved, only that it was safe.

Now Clover's mouth hung open. A small O of nothing. Her whiskers were stuck flat against her cheeks, waterlogged and limp. The fur across her back had puffed out from the soaking, making her look bigger than she was. She floated in the center of the tub, weightless and wrong.

"It's dead, Ellie." This time the words came sharper. She wasn't looking at the tub. One hand pressed against her temple like she was trying to hold something in, mascara trailing like faint bruises down her cheeks. Ellie stayed on her knees, watching the way the light from the window hit the surface of the water and made it shimmer around the kitten's shape.

"What is this?" her mother barked, voice cracking with disbelief and something more violent. "Why would you leave it here? Did you try to give it a bath?"

"I didn't!" Ellie's voice came out sharp and high, already breaking. "I didn't—I didn't do this—she was—she was okay. I gave her a bath yesterday in the sink! I cleaned her—she was warm—she was fine—"

Her mother raised a hand, palm out, but it wasn't gentle. It was the kind of motion that cut through words. Ellie flinched back, her breath catching.

"Enough." Her mother pressed her other hand to her forehead, knuckles white. "Just stop. Stop!"

"I didn't," Ellie said again, but her voice was slipping, the edges unraveling. Her knees ached where they met the floor, but she didn't move. The sound of Sam crying from the bedroom bled through the walls.

Her mother's head tipped back against the doorframe with a thud. Her eyes squeezed shut, mascara smearing darker. When she spoke again, her voice was low and ragged, shaking with something more than anger. "I can't, Ellie. I can't with this."

She waved one arm out toward the tub, toward the still water, toward the lifeless, bloated thing that had been warm in Ellie's arms just hours ago. Her voice rose, louder now. "Why did you do this? Why would you.... You left it in here!? What the hell is wrong with you!?"

"I didn't!" Ellie gasped. "She was sleeping next to me! She was right there, she was fine! I didn't do anything!"

Tears were pouring down her face now, hard and uncontrolled. Her mouth stayed open between sobs, gasping air between the words like she couldn't fit everything she needed to say into the same breath. "She was okay, she was purring, I fed her. She was fine, she was fine...."

"I don't have time for this," her mother snapped, stepping back from the doorway, her heels clicking unevenly on the tile. "I don't have time for this, Ellie. Things are finally turning around for me, and I can't..." She flung her arm out again. "I can't deal with...this. Whatever this is. You need to get rid of it."

Ellie blinked, her vision blurry. Her throat convulsed with another sob, and she lurched forward on her knees.

"I didn't do this," she said again, and again, quieter. "I didn't. I didn't."

Her mother didn't look at her anymore. She turned away, muttering under her breath, brushing past the wall as if she couldn't get away fast enough. "God, I can't even...."

Then she was gone. Down the hall. The sound of the front door slamming came a moment later. Ellie flinched at the noise, her shoulders curving forward and her arms folding around her middle like she could hold herself together if she just squeezed enough.

Sam was still crying in the other room.

And Clover floated in the water behind her.

Ellie lowered her head to the edge of the tub. She pressed her forehead against the cold fiberglass and let the sobs take her, rough and ugly, tearing up through her ribs like claws. Her body shook. Her voice caught. Her fingers latched onto the rim of the tub.

She knelt there a little longer, the tremble in her chest refusing to ease. Her breathing came in uneven gasps, nose running, eyes swollen. The bathroom floor pressed cold against her knees, the edge of the tub biting into her arms. She could still hear Sam crying from the other room, but he sounded far away.

Ellie lifted her head and looked down. She reached out, slow, hesitant, fingers dipping into the water. It was colder than she expected. Her fingertips brushed against the floating gray fur. Clover didn't move. Didn't twitch. Her body floated just beneath the surface, small and light and utterly still.

Ellie's whole body clenched together as she reached out again, cupping both hands around Clover's body and lifting her out of the water. The kitten felt heavier than she had the day before, like the water had settled into her bones. Ellie lay her gently on the floor.

She waded through Sam's cries to the edge of her bed and took the towel that had been Clover's bed from the floor. She moved slowly back to the bathroom, hesitating at the door when the small dark shape in the middle of the floor reached her eyes. She wrapped Clover in the towel carefully, bundling the small frame with quiet hands, tucking the edges over her face like she was putting her to sleep.

Not bothering with shoes, Ellie walked barefoot across the cold floor, out the back door, and through the brittle grass, cradling the small bundle in the towel. The air outside stung against her skin, sharp in her nose, biting at her cheeks. Her arms were tight around Clover. Her toes turned bright pink in the cold. The sky was pale, flat, just the color of emptiness.

The trees ahead stood still and silent. Ellie crossed the yard and stopped at the edge where the woods began, where the grass turned wild. She knelt and set the bundle down, the towel dampening through from Clover's body.

She started to dig. Her fingers clawed at the soil, nails breaking through its frigid crust, palms scraping against pebbles and roots. It was slow. Bitter. Painful. But she continued to pry open the earth with her hands. She made a small hollow. Her hands were red, stinging, and raw by the time she finished.

Ellie lifted Clover's delicate body, towel and all, and lowered her into the hole.

"I'm sorry," she whispered, her voice so fragile it barely made a sound. "I don't know…" Her voice trailed off. She closed her eyes and placed her hands flat over the towel one last time, water seeping through the fibers to meet her fingers.

One handful of dirt at a time, she covered Clover. She smoothed out the top when she finished, pressing the dirt flat the way she smoothed Sam's blanket over him at night. She pressed her palm deep into the mound. The earth didn't give back any warmth. In front of her, the trees creaked. A wind moved through the branches, though none of the limbs swayed.

Ellie stood there for a long time, her hands dirty and raw, her arms limp at her sides. The ache in her chest was hollow, stretching wide. She could hear Sam crying in the house behind her.

DON'T SAY HIS NAME

There was nothing left of Clover in Ellie's room. Ellie had buried everything: the kitten, the towel she wrapped her in, even the name, though it still echoed in Ellie's mind when the house was quiet. The place by Ellie's bed where Clover had slept was just a patch of floor again. Plain. Bare. There was nothing to avoid, but Ellie still stepped wide when she stepped over it.

Her father didn't come.

Not the first night. Not the second. The space beside Ellie stayed cold. She opened the window a crack, enough to feel the outside seep into the room. The blinds hung still, the trees outside didn't move, and when she looked into the dark, nothing looked back.

Each night, she burrowed deeper under the blanket, knees pressed to her chest, fingers twisted into the hem. Sam breathed softly across the room, steady and small, untouched by the silence that pressed harder into everything else. Ellie stared at the ceiling until her eyes ached. At the window. At nothing. She didn't call his name.

The nights stretched longer than they used to. Hours seemed to spool out endlessly, a slow unraveling of thread, thin through the dark. The walls that used to pull in, drawn close by the shadows, now felt wider, as if the house was slowly letting go and failing. Even the heater, which once ticked and groaned with a kind of sleepy comfort, now hummed low and distant, as if its sound came from a different room in a different house, far away from wherever Ellie was.

The window remained closed. No hand touched the sill. No boots thudded against the floor. Her father's coat never brushed the curtain, and no soft breath broke the space between her blanket and the dark. Where he had once stood stayed empty, but Ellie never stopped feeling watched. She stared at the window sometimes, half-hoping, half-dreading that something would shift.

And yet, something remained. She could feel it in the stillness, something pulled back but not gone. The air had weight, the kind that pressed at her skin. The corners of the room felt clogged, more crowded than they should have been, the shadows coiled a little more than the light could explain. When she blinked too slowly or held her breath too long, the hush of the room seemed to lean in closer.

Ellie stood in the kitchen, toes cold against the tile, arms hanging limp at her sides. Her mother moved nearby, clumsily half-awake, trying to get the coffee machine to work. Her chipped nails clicked against the countertop. Her wrist bore a smudge of makeup she hadn't wiped off fully the night before. The skin around her eyes was strained, not from sleep, but from whatever came instead of it.

"Mama?" The word came out quieter than Ellie expected, barely a thread in the kitchen air. Her mother didn't look up right away, her hand moving in slow, clumsy circles through the cup of coffee. The spoon clinked against the sides in a rhythm that didn't seem to belong to anything.

"Hm?" her mother answered, still distracted.

Ellie hesitated, her fingers twisting into the hem of her shirt. "Where's Dad?"

Her mother's hand stopped. The spoon stilled mid-stir.

Ellie swallowed. "Do you ever think about him?"

Her mother's body went still, her spine locking in place like something bracing for impact. Slowly, she turned to face Ellie, her brow furrowed, eyes narrowed in the low kitchen light.

"About who?"

"Dad."

Her mother stared at her for a second that was too quiet, too sharp. Then something passed over her face, something quick and hard and final, like a door had slammed shut behind her eyes. The spoon clattered against the counter and wobbled there as Ellie's mother slammed it down.

"Don't," she said. The words landed hard and flat. Her voice wasn't loud, but it was cutting, cold, and carved from something brittle.

Ellie blinked. "But—"

Her mother's hand came up, cutting the air between them. "No. He's gone, Ellie. He's been gone for months. He's not coming back. Ever. You understand me?"

Ellie's mouth opened, but no sound came. She looked at her mother's face, searching it for something softer.

Her jaw was clenched, her lips thinned, and her gaze had gone distant, like she wasn't even standing in the same room anymore.

"I just thought maybe—" Ellie began, her voice small.

"You thought wrong," her mother said, already turning away. "I don't want to talk about him. I don't want to remember him. And I don't want you bringing him up like that. Not now."

Ellie looked down at her feet. The floor felt colder than it had before. "But I still remember," she said quietly.

Her mother didn't turn back. "Well, don't."

She picked up the coffee cup and left the spoon behind. Then she walked out of the kitchen with bare feet and a silence that followed her like a shadow. Ellie stood there a moment longer, her heart thudding behind her ribs, soft and slow.

That afternoon, Ellie sat hunched in the narrow hallways outside of her room, the walls on either side close enough to touch with her elbows if she stretched. Her knees were pulled up to her chest, arms wrapped around them, chin resting on the soft slope where they came together. Sam rustled faintly in his crib, a shallow, tiny rhythm she'd come to know like her own heartbeat. Each faint rustle let her know he was still asleep.

From the living room, the television carried bursts of canned laughter, punctuated by clapping that always came a second too late. Her mother didn't laugh along. She let the noise run, loud enough to fill the spaces and cracks throughout the house. Ellie stayed where the walls were thin but the air was quieter. Just far enough away not to be noticed. Just close enough to hear if things shifted.

She rested her head against the wall and closed her eyes.

Her thoughts drifted to uninvited places. She thought about the last time she had seen him. The way his coat hung from his shoulders like it had grown from them. The shape of his face in the dark, familiar and wrong all at once. But it was his eyes. She hadn't stopped thinking about those eyes. Not since they had narrowed at her, sharp and shadowed, when she begged him to come inside. When she told him about Clover. His voice hadn't raised, but it was cold and crackling underneath his words.

She wanted to believe it was an accident. That she had missed something. Forgotten something. Let the kitten slip by her in the dark. That she'd forgotten to shut the bathroom door or that Clover had wiggled free from the towel nest and slipped into the tub without making a sound. Maybe the kitten had just been too small to save. Maybe it had all happened while she was sleeping a deep, dreamless sleep she didn't remember falling into. She wanted to believe that so badly her jaw ached from holding it back.

She stared down at her hands. The dirt from the woods had worn away, rinsed clean with soap and hot water, but her skin still felt raw. Her fingernails were stained dark. She kept rubbing them against the legs of her pants like she could grind the memory out of them.

Was there a part of her, broken off and hidden somewhere deep, that had gotten up in the night and walked the house without her knowing? Maybe she had carried Clover into the bathroom. Maybe her fingers had opened the tap. Maybe her hands had held her still beneath the water.

Why don't you want to play with me? That's what he'd said. Not *Who is she?* Not *Why did you bring her in?* But *Why don't you want to play with me?* The look on her father's face as he watched her from the yard when she told him about the kitten was palpable. His body was still and rigid. Ellie's skin began to hum with prickles as she thought about it.

The guilt burrowing inside her chest twisted and grew hot. Her jaw clenched until it ached, and her lips pressed into a line so tight it trembled. The anger that rose beneath her ribs wasn't loud. It didn't burst or shout. It simmered. Slow. Loaded. It filled her chest like smoke and drove her hands into hard little fists. He'd been there. Watching. Standing in the trees while she opened the window. While she smiled. While she called to him. He saw her. He heard her. And he turned away.

And then Clover was gone too.

Ellie hadn't told anyone where she buried her. She hadn't marked the spot.

Her mother hadn't asked. She hadn't even checked. By that afternoon, she was painting her lips in the bathroom mirror, already on the phone with someone who might make things easier. "Don't start," she'd said, when Ellie tried to talk. "I can't deal with this right now."

She could still hear it. Whatever "this" is.

By the time her mother came home that night, Ellie's tears had already dried into the sleeves of her shirt. Her hands were clean. Her room was quiet. And she didn't say another word. Not about Clover. Not about the woods. Not about him.

The threads along the edge of her sleeve were fraying. Ellie worked one free until it strained and broke, then went on to the next. Her fingers never stopped picking, scratching, and tugging. The corner of her blanket had gone thin from the way she folded and unfolded it. She dug her nails into her palms until they ached, until her hands shook in tiny pulses she refused to acknowledge.

She didn't tiptoe anymore. Her steps hit the floor with sound. When she passed her mother's door, she didn't glance toward it. She let her foot drag just enough to knock into the loose board, the dull thunk loud in the hallway. In the kitchen, the cabinet door bounced off the frame when she closed it. Her jaw didn't move as she ate, if she ate. Just her teeth pressing together behind closed lips.

The anger sat in her stomach and coiled around her ribs. Her father hadn't come back. The silence in her room had grown heavier with each passing night, the stillness no longer expectant, but resigned. It had made space for something twisted and hot, shifting restlessly beneath her skin.

Her mother hadn't touched her once. Not when she cried. Not when she buried Clover. Not when she sat silent through dinner, picking at cold pasta and letting Sam drool formula down his chin. Everything kept moving as if nothing had happened.

She didn't ask if Ellie was okay. She didn't ask anything at all.

And now Clover was gone. Her father was gone. And Ellie was still here, scooping toys off the floor and folding socks with holes and wiping spit-up off her shirt while her mother hummed through the bathroom door and laughed too loudly into her phone.

The laundry was piling up again. She folded shirts without looking at them, matching sleeves to sleeves, the fabric stiff with cold. She smoothed the socks and stacked them in rows. Sam dropped his bottle and began to wail. She didn't flinch. She just picked it up, wiped it once against her pant leg, and handed it back.

In the corner of the room, the shadows had returned. Not all at once, not smothering like before. But they were there. Gathering slow. Stretching long. She didn't blink them away. Didn't move. She just stared until her eyes burned and the room blurred at the edges.

The next time her mother slammed the cupboard too hard or told her to "keep it down," Ellie didn't comment. And when her father returned, if he returned, the window would stay locked.

Ellie had nothing left to say to either of them.

THE MAN IN THE TRUCK

The truck showed up on a Friday. Ellie stood at the front window with her arms crossed against her chest, each hand gripping the opposite elbow. She rested her forehead against the glass. It was cold and her breath formed a misty veil of tiny droplets on the window.

It was one of those big trucks that constantly clunked and made noise even when it was still. It rumbled, growling under its breath, long and low. The paint had once been a deep red—it may have been bright and shiny at one point, but now it was dulled by scratches, the hood bleached pale where the sun had burned through. The chrome on the bumper was smudged with brittle, dark-orange rust, and the tires were laden with mud.

Behind her, the house began to stir. Her mother was in the kitchen, humming under her breath, off-key and louder than usual. The tune wasn't one Ellie recognized, thin and aimless, the kind people hum when they want to fill the space with anything but silence. She was wiping down the counter in long, looping circles, pushing around invisible crumbs. The cloth smelled faintly of old lemon, edged with the sourness of mildew.

Her hair had been blow dried but still hung limp around her face. Heavy eyeliner framed her eyes, darkest at the corners, drawing them up and out as though that could hold them open wider. Her perfume permeated the living room, a powdery cloud with a chemical bite that clung to the air and burned a little at the back of Ellie's throat.

The truck door yawned open with a creak that cut through the sound of her mother's humming. The man who stepped out was tall, though not in a looming way. His chest and shoulders were broad, his legs thin. He wore a canvas jacket, frayed at the seams, the collar turned up. His jeans were pressed. A smile grew across his face as his eyes fell on Ellie in the window. Big and bright and full of teeth that Ellie could see were yellow.

Her mother was already at the door. She pulled it open with both hands, the screen bouncing on the hinges.

"There you are," she said, breathy and smiling, bright and eager. "I was starting to think you got lost."

The man chuckled. "Told you I'd find the place."

Ellie stood just inside the hallway, half-shadowed by the arch that led from the front room back to the bedrooms. Her mother leaned into the doorframe, her hip angled like she couldn't decide whether to flirt or lean for balance. The man stood just beyond her, holding two full grocery bags in one hand, a pizza box balanced flat on top. He was taller than he looked from the window. His smile was easy, confident.

"Come in, come in," her mother said, stepping aside. "This is Anthony."

As he crossed the threshold, his eyes landed on Ellie, unhurried and sure. "Hey there," he said, his smile creeping wider. "Who is this little lady?"

Ellie didn't move. She stood half-hidden just beyond the doorway, arms wrapped across her chest, socked feet braced against the baseboard.

"This is Ellie," her mother said quickly, voice bright but firm.

Anthony nodded, slow, like he was fitting the word into place. "Ellie," he repeated, as though tasting it. "Good to meet you. Your mother has told me lots about you."

He kept his smile but didn't push. He just turned his attention to the groceries, walking them into the kitchen like he belonged there. "Didn't know what you folks liked, so I grabbed a few things. Hope I didn't mess it up."

The pizza box gave off a low heat that cut through the cooler air of the house. Ellie could see the steam escaping when her mother flipped open the lid. The pepperoni had formed into small cups, oily in a way that made Ellie's mouth fill with spit she tried not to swallow too fast.

Her mother hovered at Anthony's side, hands moving too quickly as she opened cupboards that had been mostly empty the day before. "We haven't had time to shop," she said, brushing hair from her face that didn't need brushing. "This is great. Really, Anthony. Thank you."

Ellie lingered at the edge of the hallway, her back close to the wall. She watched as he unpacked the bags like he knew where everything should go. Boxed cereal. Eggs. A carton of milk with the cap still factory tight. Crackers in shiny foil sleeves. A frozen dinner wrapped in blue plastic—the kind she'd seen in other people's grocery carts.

"You hungry?" he asked, still facing the counter, but glancing down to meet Ellie's eyes. "I made sure to get the kind with extra cheese."

Ellie's stomach twisted again, sharper this time, as the first slice of pizza was lifted from the box. The cheese stretched and then snapped, leaving a string draped across the cardboard. She hadn't eaten since breakfast, and even that had just been dry cereal she'd fished from the bottom of a bag. Her mouth filled with a slow, simmering hunger that threatened to spill over. Her arms ached from holding back the movement toward the table.

Anthony's hands were steady as he pulled the slices apart. His shoulders stayed loose. Comfortable. Like he'd done this a hundred times before.

The hunger made her legs want to walk forward, made her imagine the taste of melted cheese, the crisp edge of crust. It made her wonder if it was warm enough to sting her tongue. Her fingers wanted to reach out, just to be sure it was real. That this food, these groceries, this quiet smile from a man she didn't know, weren't about to vanish.

Her mother turned just then, catching Ellie's hesitation. One eyebrow lifted, sharp and practiced, like it had been waiting. Ellie knew what that look meant. It was the same one she gave the check-out clerk when she forgot her EBT card, the same one she used when the neighbor asked about the noise last week.

Behave. Be polite. Don't start.

Ellie's lips parted. The word sat on the back of her teeth. It took a second push to get it out.

"Thanks."

Anthony glanced up, his smile widening at the edges. Her mother was still talking, filling the silence with fast, soft chatter about how long it had been since they'd had anything decent. The sound bounced off the cabinets and the fridge and clattered into the still air.

Ellie stood just past the threshold, one foot on the linoleum, the other still touching carpet. The line between rooms felt like a place she shouldn't cross yet. Her chest ached. The room felt overfull.

Anthony's movements were slow. Methodical. Like he was settling in. Ellie's eyes flicked to the bag on the floor. She could see the shape of a chocolate bar through the plastic. One of the ones they kept behind the counter at the store. She swallowed. Her jaw was locked.

"Go ahead and grab a plate, sweetheart," her mother said, already pulling one down from the cupboard. "Don't make him eat alone."

Anthony chuckled. "It's no trouble. I've eaten with worse company," he said, smiling in her direction like it was a joke just for the two of them.

Ellie didn't smile back, but her legs carried her into the kitchen anyway. She took the plate her mother offered and held it out toward the pizza box.

"Grab a big one," Anthony said, seating himself. "Growing girls like you gotta eat."

Her fingers hovered over the slices. She took one near the edge, not the biggest, but not the smallest either. The cheese had bubbled up and crisped on the top in spots, and the crust sagged at the tip when she lifted it. She placed it on her plate, then stepped back again.

"Sit down, El," her mother said with a lightness that didn't quite reach her eyes. She had *never* called her "El" before.

Ellie sat. Her chair gave a weary groan. Sam was asleep in the back room, and the whole house felt like it was waiting for the noise to break.

Anthony bit into his slice with a pleased sound. "Man, it's been a day," he said around the food. "Gas station sandwich for lunch. Don't let anyone tell you those things are edible."

Her mother laughed too loud, a little forced. "Poor baby."

Ellie took a bite. The heat stung her mouth, but she didn't complain. It tasted good. Better than anything she'd had in a while. Her stomach pulled with the first swallow.

Anthony glanced at her again. "You don't say much, do you?"

Ellie looked up, mid-chew. She swallowed before answering.

Her mother rolled her eyes, brushing imaginary crumbs off the counter. "She's just shy."

"I like shy," Anthony said, his eyes still on Ellie. "Shy kids are smart. Pay attention to things the rest of us miss."

Ellie looked down at her pizza. The cheese had hardened slightly at the edges, cooling in the air.

"You like school?" he asked, more casual this time.

She shrugged. "It's fine."

"You got a favorite subject?"

Her throat closed up. She didn't want to talk about school.

"She likes drawing," her mother offered. "She's always sketching in the corners of her notebooks. Half her homework comes back covered in doodles."

Anthony leaned forward slightly. "Is that right? What do you draw?"

"Stuff," Ellie said.

"Well," he said, taking another bite, "I'd like to see it sometime. Bet you've got real talent. Not that you need it, a pretty girl like you." His eyes stayed on Ellie as he chewed.

Across the table, her mother was laughing again. She had a soda in her hand and was tapping it against her lip, like she used to do when she was flirting. Anthony's leg bumped the table as he stood. He moved toward the sink and started rinsing his plate without being asked. Her mother watched him do it, her face soft.

From the back room, Sam let out a small cry, fussy and wavering at first, but growing louder into that familiar edge of frustration that meant he was ready for his own dinner.

Ellie's mother stood, brushing a crumb from her shirt and smoothing the front of her blouse. "I've got it," she said, already halfway out of the kitchen. Her voice changed as she moved down the hall. It lifted, lighter, an alien singsong tone. "It's okay, sweetheart. Mama's coming."

Anthony sat back down across from Ellie, back straight in the kitchen chair, one arm draped casually across the table, the other resting near his glass. But he wasn't drinking. His fingers hovered just above the rim, frozen mid-motion. Ellie's eyes locked on his face.

At the first sound of Sam's cry, something in Anthony's expression had changed. It was a flicker. A pause. A pinching at the corners of his mouth, a subtle drop in his brows. His smile had softened, not in kindness but in something smaller. More careful. The muscles along his jaw drew in, his breath caught and held.

"Must get tiring," he said, with a loud exhale, leaning back slightly, his fingers loosening around the glass. "All that crying."

Ellie nodded once, uncertain, her mouth dry.

He smiled again. Broader this time. Like he'd told a joke and was waiting to see if she got it.

Anthony tapped his fingers lightly against the table, the rhythm irregular. Then he leaned forward an inch, "You ever wish it was just you and your mom again?" he asked, his voice quiet.

Ellie's throat clenched. She looked down.

"I mean," Anthony added quickly, easy again, "just for a little while. Just to get a break."

Anthony leaned back farther in his chair. "Your mom tells me you help out a lot. Must be hard sometimes."

She nodded, once. Her fingers pressed into the rim of her plate.

"That's a lot for someone your age," he added, his voice lower now. "You ever get a break?"

Ellie shook her head.

He laughed, not loud. "Figured. You've got that look. Strong kid. Taking care of everybody." He reached into the grocery bag and pulled something out—the chocolate bar—the good kind with the red label and gold foil under the paper. "Here," he said, holding it across the table. "Don't tell your mom. This is just for you."

Ellie stayed still.

He tilted his head, encouraging, nudging the chocolate toward her. "Go on. You've earned it."

Ellie's fingers stayed right where they were.

He set it gently beside her plate. "It's okay. You don't have to take it now."

Anthony stood and stretched again. "You ever wanna talk, you can." He looked down at her, smile gentler now, practiced. "Doesn't have to be about anything big. Sometimes it helps just to talk."

She looked away, toward the kitchen. The chocolate bar sat next to her plate, unopened. Her fingers twitched.

"I was your age once," Anthony said, more casual now. "It's hard when people don't see how much you're doing. You get used to being the one who handles things, and nobody thinks to ask if you're okay."

Ellie met his eyes. His voice was soft and steady as he spoke, carefully measured, like he was trying to wrap each word in reassurance. His tone was gentle but deliberate, as if choosing each word to make sure she felt safe. He leaned in just a little, not too close, his eyes steady on hers.

From the hallway, her mother's voice rose, low and tired. Sam was still fussing.

"You really are a quiet one aren't you?" He reached forward and nudged Ellie's shoulder. "Come on! We're having fun! Give me a smile."

Her fingers tightened around the soft edge of her jeans, digging in through the fabric. She stared at the table, at the crumbs left behind from her half-eaten slice, at the glass of water she hadn't touched. She didn't say yes. But she didn't say no either.

"I get it," he said. "You're special, you know that?" The words came slower now, like they were meant to land gently. "I can tell."

Then he stood and moved. Just a step, but past her, behind her chair. As he passed, his hand gripped the wood. Not her. The back of the chair shifted under the weight of it, and Ellie felt the air move. And then he was gone, disappearing into the living room, his footsteps soft on the thin carpet.

Ellie stared at the chocolate bar. The shiny red wrapper caught the overhead light, the gold edge peeking out like a lure. Her hands stayed locked in her lap, fingers pressed so hard into her skin she could feel the heartbeat in her palms.

Her hand moved. Slowly. Hesitant fingers reached across the table and plucked the candy bar from where it rested. It was warm from the heat of the house, the foil already a little softened along the seam. She didn't unwrap it. She closed her fingers around the crinkling weight and slid it into her pocket.

The chair gave a soft groan as she pushed it back, the legs scraping faintly against the linoleum. She stepped carefully, her socked feet silent. The kitchen light buzzed above her, its yellow cast flattening everything into dull colors and long shadows. She crossed the kitchen with her shoulders clenched and arms close to her sides, the chocolate tucked against her hip like something stolen, even though it had been offered.

She passed the edge of the kitchen and stepped into the living room, never letting her eyes shift upward. She didn't want to see if Anthony was watching. Didn't want to meet the gaze she already felt brushing against her back. She kept her stare on the carpet ahead, then on the end of the hall where the light spilled faintly from beneath her bedroom door.

Sam was still crying.

THE SPACE BETWEEN

The sound of laughter pulled Ellie from sleep. It was low and tangled with something warmer than the house usually held. She lay still for a moment, her face half-buried in the blanket, her ears straining. The laughter came again, closer now, softer, then louder all at once, chasing itself in uneven bursts through the thin kitchen walls.

Her stomach turned, sharp and sudden. A twist beneath her ribs that didn't fade.

Voices filtered in under the laughter. First, her mother's voice, high and breathy, rising in a kind of flutter. And Anthony's voice, deeper and slower, sliding through the space with that steady ease that made Ellie's skin pull around her shoulders.

Something clinked in the kitchen. A fork or a knife against the counter. A sizzle chased after the clink, a wet crackle in oil. Underneath it all, a song played low. Soft rock, something older. The man singing sounded tired, dragging the notes behind him.

The air in the bedroom was still. The walls felt farther apart, the corners deeper. Sam's soft breathing carried across the crib bars, steady and small. Ellie sat up slowly, the blankets tangled around her legs. For a moment, she sat there, listening. The laughter rose again, too sharp now. A brittle edge beneath it.

Sam stirred in his crib.

Ellie turned toward him, drawing her legs up beneath her as she sat straighter in bed. Her legs slid free of the tangled blanket, her toes sinking into the carpet's worn nap as she shifted forward. She flexed her toes instinctively, feeling the rough weave of the fibers, a scratchy warmth that could not quite keep the chill away. The voices from the kitchen rose louder now, laughter rising and falling with a rhythm that felt unfamiliar. It wasn't her mother's usual voice. There was a pleading edge to it.

Ellie fetched her step ladder from its place near the wall. The metal felt cold under her fingers as she unfolded it with slow, practiced hands, careful not to not let it make a sound. She climbed up, steadily. She bent at the waist, her arms slipping beneath him, one hand cradling Sam's head and back, the other sliding beneath his knees as she lifted him close. For a moment, she pressed her cheek to the crown of his head and breathed in his familiar scent: baby powder, sleep-laden skin, the faint trace of milk.

Sam's head lolled against her shoulder as she climbed back down, leaving the ladder near the crib. The hallway stretched in front of her, the carpet dull and cool beneath her feet. The laughter had faded now, replaced by the low hum of voices. A faint scrape of silverware. The rhythmic clink of a spoon in a mug. Ellie kept her gaze ahead. Her shoulders tucked in. Her arms strong and sure around her brother.

Her mother sat at the table, one leg hooked under the other, her body angled toward Anthony at the stove. She had pulled her hair back in a loose knot, stray pieces falling around her face. Her cheeks looked bright and flushed, her eyeliner smudged just enough to make her look tired beneath the effort of her smile. A half-empty mug sat in her hands, fingers curled around the handle. Her laughter had faded beneath the clink of silverware and the quiet bubble of oil in the pan.

When Ellie stepped into the doorway, her mother's gaze flicked toward her, but the smile didn't break. It stretched wider for a moment, as though it had been pinned in place.

Anthony stood at the stove, one hand gripping the handle of a frying pan, the other moving a fork through a loose pile of eggs. He stirred them with lazy circles. His canvas jacket hung over the back of a chair, sleeves sagging from wear.

He glanced over his shoulder, his smile already in place before he even saw her.

"Morning, kiddo," he said, voice low and easy. "Hope you're hungry. You like scrambled?"

She shrugged.

Her mother gestured lazily toward the table, a plate already waiting. A mound of scrambled eggs steamed gently, the fork set carefully beside it. The toast was stacked in triangles, golden but a little too dark at the edges.

"He's cooking," her mother said with a quick laugh, her voice higher than before. "Can you believe it?"

Ellie swallowed. Her grip on Sam tightened slightly. His little hands twitched against her chest.

"Sam needs to eat," Ellie said softly, eyes glancing toward the cupboard, toward the place where the formula lived, then to where the bottles usually sat.

Her mother sighed, not loud, but just enough for Ellie to catch the exhale. Her eyes drifted to Anthony, then back to Ellie, and in that glance was something tired, something prickly.

"Yes, yes," her mother said, rising from her chair, smoothing her shirt like the motion could erase the edge in her voice. "Come on, give him here."

Ellie hesitated. For half a second, her arms pulled her brother closer. Sam stirred, a soft whimper rising in his throat.

"Ellie," her mother said again, the smile wavering. "Give him to me."

Reluctantly, Ellie shifted her grip and passed Sam into her mother's waiting arms. He squirmed and let out a louder fuss as the transfer pulled him from the warmth of Ellie's shoulder.

"Oh, shh, shh," her mother murmured, bouncing him roughly on her hip as she moved toward the counter. "It's okay, we'll get you fed."

Ellie watched her closely. She watched the way her mother rolled her eyes when she turned her back, the smallest shake of her head as she reached for a clean bottle. She poured water with one hand, reaching for the formula tin with the other, her movements distracted.

Behind her, Anthony leaned against the stove, the pan now off the burner. He rested the fork on the edge of a plate and folded his arms, eyes following Ellie as she hovered by the kitchen doorway.

"You've got a lot on your plate," he said before tipping his chin toward the table where the plate of eggs still waited for her. Her stomach twisted. She glanced toward her mother, who was shaking the bottle with short, impatient flicks of her wrist, with her back turned to them.

Ellie moved toward the chair, eyes on the plate. The eggs were soft, still glossy at the edges. A slice of toast sat beside them. Butter melted through the middle.

Anthony winked. "Made 'em just for you."

Anthony pushed off the stove with one slow step and crossed to the table. He pulled out the chair meant for Ellie and gave it a small nudge with his foot, just enough to make the legs scrape softly across the tile.

"Come on," he said. His voice stayed light, but beneath it, something coiled. "You've gotta eat. Can't take care of everyone else if you don't take care of yourself, right?"

Ellie's mouth opened, but nothing came.

"Look," he said, dropping his voice as if they were sharing something private. "Your mom's busy. It's just us for a minute. You don't have to be shy."

Her toes dug into the linoleum; her gaze locked on the small fold of her shirt between her fingers.

"You're a good helper," he added, watching her carefully now. "Bet your mom depends on you more than you think."

Her mother's voice cut through then, sharp and tired. "Ellie, sit down and eat. I don't want to fight this morning."

Ellie's body moved before her mind caught up, feet carrying her slowly toward the table. Anthony held the chair steady, and as she sat, his hand brushed against the back of her shoulder, a faint press. She stiffened. He stepped away, casually, like it hadn't happened.

"There you go," he said softly, returning to the counter to pour himself another cup of coffee. "See? Just trying to help."

Ellie picked up the fork with numb fingers. The eggs had gone cool around the edges; the steam thinned to nothing. Her stomach ached, but not in the sharp way it sometimes did when she was too hungry. She forced one small bite into her mouth. It tasted faintly of butter and salt. Her throat worked harder than it should have to swallow it down.

Across the kitchen, her mother sat with Sam cradled in one arm, a bottle tipped just so against his mouth. Her gaze wasn't on him though. It was somewhere behind the wall, far away. Her eyes looked rimmed and tired, dark shadows tucked beneath the eyeliner. Anthony sipped his coffee slow, his elbow propped on the table, the mug balanced lazily between his fingers. His eyes studied Ellie over the rim of the cup.

Ellie took another bite because her mother was watching now too. Watching her eat with that small, stiff smile that didn't reach her eyes. Ellie could hear her mother's voice: Be good.

Be grateful. Don't ruin this. The air felt suffused with tension, pressing against Ellie's skin.

She sat straighter and took another bite. Her mother's eyes darted to Anthony then back to Ellie. That smile held. Anthony set his cup down with a faint click and sat forward. He reached for the pot again, poured himself another splash. The smell of the coffee rose sharply between them.

"Might make pancakes tomorrow," he said, casual, like it was already decided.

The eggs sat like a weight in her stomach now. Ellie pushed the fork aside, folding her hands in her lap. Across the room, Anthony finished his coffee and rose. His chair scraped softly against the floor.

"Be right back," he said, voice light. He left the kitchen for the front room. Ellie heard the thump of the old recliner, the rustle of bags.

Her mother stood, balancing Sam on her hip as she rocked back and forth in a tired rhythm. Her free hand wiped at the edge of her mouth with her sleeve. "You could be a little friendlier," she said in a low voice, not sharp, but warning. "He's trying."

Ellie didn't answer. She kept her eyes on the plate.

Footsteps returned. Anthony came back holding something small in his hand. A bit of shiny plastic caught the light. A bracelet. Pink and cheap-looking—the kind with little plastic beads strung between heart-shaped charms.

He crouched a little to meet her eye, resting one arm on the table, too close. "Here," he said. "Picked this up on the way. Thought you might like it. Just because."

Her mother laughed softly, shifting Sam to her other hip. "Isn't that sweet?" she said, voice light as air.

Ellie's fingers wound around each other, her knuckles bone-white. She stared at the bracelet where it dangled between his fingers, the pink beads glinting in the kitchen light. Her chest felt constricted, her shoulders drawn small. She wanted to fold into herself.

"Say thank you," her mother said quietly through a clench-toothed smile.

Ellie swallowed. Her voice was paper-thin. "Thank you."

Her mother gave a small, satisfied nod. Anthony's hand lingered a moment longer in the space between them, fingers wrapped loosely around the bracelet, offering it forward. At last, he set the bracelet down gently beside her plate. His fingers brushed the edge of the table, slow and deliberate, as if placing something precious.

"Pretty hair," he said as he stood. He reached out, fingers trailing toward her head. "You've got that grown-up look already. Bet your mom's gonna have to fight the boys off in a few years." Her stomach turned hard and knotted as his fingers caught the blonde strands near her ear. The fork slipped from Ellie's fingers and landed against the plate with a metallic clink.

"She gets that from me," her mother said breezily. Anthony let his hand fall, the tips of his fingers grazing her shoulder on the way down. A slow drag across the fabric of her shirt.

"Relax, kiddo," he said, flashing her that same wide smile. "You're all tense."

As the morning wore thin and turned to afternoon, the light in the house shifted. It came harsher through the windows, cutting lines across the floor. The warmth and smell from the food had faded, and the laughter had dimmed to a steady buzz of activity.

Her mother was in the bathroom again, door half-closed, blow dryer humming through the thin walls, punctuated by short bursts of off-key humming and a click of bottles on the counter. Ellie hovered in the hallway, Sam's toy gripped in her hands—a small plastic ring of stacking blocks he had dropped by the couch.

The faint hum of the blow dryer emanating from the bathroom filled the hallway, masking the sound of the footsteps following Ellie. Quiet. Deliberate. The soft rise and fall of weight shifting across the carpet behind her. They moved at a pace to match her own, each step carefully measured and chosen.

The muscles across Ellie's shoulders went stiff as a floorboard sighed beneath a foot much larger than her own. Her skin prickled and pulled, her arms instinctively drawing closer to her sides. The air crowded against her back as Anthony slowed his pace.

"Need to grab something," Anthony said. His voice was smooth, a thread dropped behind her ear.

Ellie shifted quickly to the side, her shoulder brushing the wall as she pressed herself out of the narrow path. The hallway wasn't wide enough for two, not without touching.

He reached, one arm sliding across her line of sight, fingers extending toward the shelf in the hall closet where they kept the towels. The edge of his hand grazed her shoulder, slow, not accidental. His palm lingered there for a breath, warm through the thin fabric of her shirt. The weight of it, the choice of it, pinned her in place. His body filled the hallway, broad and sure. Close enough that she caught the scent of him, coffee, sharp and bitter, layered beneath with something sour.

Ellie's back pressed harder to the wall. The toy in her hand dug into her fingers, its plastic edges biting against her skin, too sharp now to ignore.

Anthony leaned forward slightly, his shoulder brushing past hers again, slower this time. His head turned just enough for her to see the curve of his mouth.

Not a wide grin. Smaller. Narrower. A smile meant only for this space. "You really need to relax," he murmured, voice lower now. "You're wound up."

Ellie's feet stayed rooted to the thin carpet, her knees locked until they ached. Her heart knocked hard against her ribs, fast and panicked. Her breath came in shallow pulls. The hum of the blow dryer beyond the door sounded distant now, buried beneath the rush of blood in Ellie's ears.

She could feel his presence beside her. Not touching her anymore, but close enough to stretch the space between them thin as paper. The skin along her arms prickled. The toy in her hands had stopped being a toy. It was an anchor now, sharp at the edges, her fingers locked so rigid around it her knuckles burned white.

Then Anthony's arm moved again. Higher this time. No rush, no apology. He plucked something from the shelf, a box, maybe a folded towel, Ellie couldn't tell. The sound of the item sliding forward barely registered past the drumbeat in her skull.

A breath passed. Another.

And finally, *finally*, he stepped back. Slow. Unhurried. His footsteps whispered against the carpet as he moved past her, back toward the living room. Ellie stayed frozen a beat longer. Her gaze stayed fixed on the line where the wall met the floor.

When the soft sounds of his steps faded and the air behind her felt empty again, her body unlocked all at once. A sharp, shallow gasp tore into her throat. Ellie's legs trembled as she turned toward the bedroom.

That night passed slowly, stretched thin across the hours. Ellie lay in bed, her arms curled protectively around Sam where he lay sleeping in the narrow space between them. His body was warm against hers, almost hot, little legs twitching now and then beneath the thin blanket. Occasionally, his fingers fluttered against her arm, seeking comfort even in sleep.

She hadn't told her mother anything. Not about the hallway. Not about the hand on her shoulder or the way Anthony's body had blocked her path. Not about the cold prickle that had spread down her spine when he smiled. The words tangled up in her throat, rough and jagged. They didn't fit her mouth, and she knew, with a hard, sinking certainty, that they wouldn't fit her mother's ears either. Her mother, with that bright, too-wide smile that bloomed every time Anthony walked through the door and the way her voice changed when she said his name, soft and lilting.

Sam fussed through the night, kicking free of his blankets, whimpering with a restless urgency that wouldn't settle. Ellie pulled him from his crib long before midnight, pressing his small body to her chest as she rocked him back and forth, her cheek against the top of his head. His skin was hot with sleep, his breath uneven. Every time the house murmured—a pipe shifting, a board settling, a whisper of air through the thin walls—Ellie flinched. Her arms drew closer around Sam, holding him firm. Her breath snagged in her throat.

Each noise felt purposeful, as though someone might be moving just beyond the edge of her hearing. Footsteps too soft to trace. A hand resting against the wall outside her door. Her ears strained against the quiet, her heart thudding a fast, skittering rhythm beneath her ribs.

When the heater kicked on just before dawn, the sudden hum of the vent startled her fully awake. Her whole body jerked, her heart pounding so hard she could feel it in her throat. It took a full minute for her to understand where she was, her eyes wide in the dark, scanning the room for movement. Only when Sam shifted and let out a soft sigh against her chest did her breath finally release.

For a moment, Ellie's eyes fluttered closed, and she drifted off. Not to sleep, not fully, but to that thin, fragile space between sleeping and waking where her body turned languid and her mind hovered. The room felt colder when she stirred, as if the warmth around her had diminished.

When her eyes opened again, the air stalled in her lungs. The door was cracked.

The faintest slice of hallway light touched the floor, stretched stark across the carpet. Her heart stumbled once in her chest as her gaze traveled upward. Through the gap, half-swallowed by shadow, stood a shape.

Broad.

Still.

Anthony.

Only part of him was visible, his arm, the line of his shoulder, the edge of his face in low relief against the light behind him. He stood stone still, not speaking, close enough for the air in the room to feel thinner with every breath she took.

Ellie's pulse thundered in her ears. Her whole body tensed beneath the blanket, her arm protective around Sam. She didn't move. Didn't blink. Slowly, with aching care, she let her eyelids drift closed again. Her eyelids didn't meet all the way. She could still peer through a thin slit, but they were closed enough to pretend. She willed her breath to stay even, to stay quiet.

Seconds stretched long and thin, drawn out until they felt sharp. Her mind was trapped between the hammering of her heartbeat and the need to stay utterly still. Her body thrummed with the weight of waiting.

Then came a sound so soft it might have been missed if not for the way her skin prickled with it. A faint shift of weight, the carpet fibers pressing down beneath measured steps. Slow. Careful.

One step.

Another.

Moving away.

Each one fainter than the last as though the darkness of the house were swallowing them whole. Still, Ellie didn't move. Her eyelids dragged downward, her lashes nearly trembling with the effort to keep still. Her breathing stayed locked inside her ribs, each inhale shallow, each exhale fragile.

Not until the floorboard just past the threshold of her mother's bedroom doorway groaned softly, did Ellie's mind register emptiness. The quiet that followed pressed against her skull, swollen and brimming. Her heart pounded beneath her ribs, fast and thin.

She lay there in the waning dark, her body drawn taut as a bowstring, shoulders knotted, jaw fixed. One arm cradled Sam against her chest, feeling the soft rise and fall of his breath, the other flattened against the mattress, the fabric cool and rough beneath her splayed fingers.

Ellie lay awake, gathered close around her brother's small warmth, her body locked and cold beneath the blanket. Her breath was shallow. Her limbs ached. Her eyes fixed on nothing at all as she listened for any sound of the floor giving way.

Come morning, the light pressed in harshly through the windows, thin and cold across the kitchen floor. Ellie stood barefoot on the linoleum. Sleep still hung clouded in her head, but her body stayed knotted. Her mother was already awake, bright-voiced and flushed with restless energy. Her voice murmured from somewhere far away. The smell of coffee, too strong and bitter, filled the kitchen.

"...he might stay the rest of the week," her mother said, stirring sugar into her mug with sharp clinking circles. Her words brought Ellie's attention sharply into focus.

Ellie stood by the counter, her small hands flat against the cool laminate, fingers spread wide. Her arms locked straight, her shoulders rigid as though the floor beneath her might shift if she didn't hold herself steady. The ache behind her ribs had not left her since the night before, and it grew as her mother spoke.

The spoon rattled once more against the rim of the mug before she lifted the cup. She glanced at Ellie over the edge of it, her lips pressed thin before forcing them into a smile. "You've seemed...off lately."

Nearby, Sam sat on the faded mat with his legs sprawled and his head wobbling tiredly from side to side. He fussed softly, little frustrated breaths and whimpers rising as his hands batted uselessly at the air. His face was blotched pink, eyelids fluttering with exhaustion.

"You need to stop sulking in your room so much," she said, her voice firmer now, coated with the brittle edge that came when Ellie didn't answer. "It's not healthy, Ellie. Anthony's trying to be nice. You need to try too." Ellie's heart twisted. Her mother's voice faded beneath the dull roar in her ears. The thought of Anthony in the house again, closer, for longer, turned her stomach.

Her eyes slipped past the edges of the kitchen, past the coffee cup and the crumbs on the counter, toward the window. The trees stood there, black and bare against the sky. Their long branches reached upward and outward, clawed shapes stark against the pale wash of morning. They stood like watchers.

Like they knew things she couldn't say out loud. Like they had seen what she had buried beneath them, cold earth pressed around a too-small body wrapped in an old towel.

Ellie swallowed again, her gaze still pinned to the window. The trees looked too still, their branches unmoving in the windless morning. And yet, in her mind, they shifted. She could almost see him there. Standing between the trees.

She wondered if he had been waiting for her to call him again. If he had been standing there all along, hidden between those leaning trunks. If the trees still held the shape of him, carved into the places the light couldn't reach. The thought knotted something inside her, part hope, part fear. Because if he was there, he could come back. And if he came back, maybe things would stop sliding wrong.

"Ellie," her mother said firmly, calling her attention back, her voice tighter and with no softness in it. "I'm not going to let you mess this up for me. Do you understand?"

Ellie pressed her lips together and looked down. She shifted her weight from one foot to the other, unable to stand completely still. Her mother took that silence as agreement and turned back to her coffee, humming faintly beneath her breath, the mug pressed too hard between her palms.

Later that afternoon, Ellie sat on the living room carpet with Sam. Toy blocks lay scattered around them, dull reds and blues, edges worn from too many small hands. She moved the blocks without looking, stacking them into uneven towers, then knocking them over again. Her mother's voice carried down the hallway, muted but clear enough to catch.

"She's just got to get used to you," her mother was saying. There was a soft smile in her voice. "She'll come around. You're good with her. I can tell."

Ellie's hand froze mid-reach. A red block tipped sideways between her fingers, forgotten.

Anthony's voice followed, low and easy. Too easy. "I'd like to take her out sometime. Just us. I think it'd help."

A small laugh from her mother, softer than the ones she gave Anthony when Ellie was in the room. "Maybe. She needs it. You'll see. Once she understands you're staying."

Ellie stopped breathing for a second. The words coiled around her ribs and squeezed until her chest burned. She blinked fast, the carpet pattern blurring beneath her gaze. The blocks tipped over without her noticing. Sam let out a soft whimper, batting her knee with one tiny fist, seeking her attention. The voices kept slipping down the hall, wrapping around her ears, filling the space inside her.

Sam's whimper grew louder. She blinked again and reached for him with hands that shook too much. She pulled him into her lap. His body twisted, restless, his face turning toward her chest, pushing at her with small, frustrated sounds. Ellie held him more firmly than she meant to, her arms locking around him like she could keep the words out if she just held him close enough.

"Shh," she whispered, though her voice barely worked. "Shh. It's okay. I've got you."

But her arms ached with the effort, her back stiff and sore as she kept him close, kept him wrapped against her in the place where no one else could touch him.

Later, after the sun had faded to nothing and the house had sunk into a false quiet, her mother's laughter trickled through her bedroom door, fading slowly. Ellie sat in the bedroom in the dark, her legs tucked beneath her, Sam slumped against her shoulder, finally asleep. Her arms burned with the weight of him, but she didn't let go.

She sat that way, eyes fixed on the window. Beyond the glass, the sky hung dark and low, the trees standing in their crooked line. They didn't move. But they were watching. She knew they were watching. Her throat ached. She tilted her head forward, lips parting on a breath she didn't know she was holding.

Please. Come back, she thought.

Her fingers settled around Sam's small frame, holding him like a tether.

I need you.

But the house stayed still. The trees held their place. The window stayed empty.

And Ellie kept holding on.

AN ANSWER

Ellie slid carefully from the bed, her heart pounding high and hard in her chest. Sam stirred faintly as she stood, a small sound catching in his mouth, but his eyes stayed closed. His tiny fist hovered near his cheek, soft and pink. She bent forward and pulled the blanket up to his chin and tucked it carefully around his shoulders. Her hands trembled. The floor beneath her feet was cold. The carpet gave slightly with each step as she crossed the room. The air grew thinner the closer she got to the window.

The glass met her fingers with a shock of cold that bit down to the bone. She let them rest there anyway, flattening her palm slowly against the pane. Outside, the trees stood in their line at the edge of the yard, darker than the strip of sky above them. The back porch light had been left on, its weak glow puddling on the grass.

Ellie leaned forward, her breath fogging the glass in quick, uneven bursts. She swallowed hard, the taste of fear sharp on her tongue.

"Please," she whispered. The word cracked halfway through. "Please come back."

The glass beneath her hand remained cold, the kind of deep cold that seeped through skin and bone and settled there. Outside, the trees stood in their patient line, untouched. The dark beyond them lay flat and still, a weighted shroud draped over the far edge of the yard, undisturbed by wind or light or sound.

Her pulse pounded hard against the side of her neck. Each beat felt heavier than the last, as if her heart itself were knocking, calling for something just beyond reach. Ellie pressed her fingertips harder against the glass, the faint fog of her breath blurring the view before her eyes. Her palm ached with the cold, but she didn't pull back. If there was an answer waiting, she meant to draw it through.

Then the shadows shifted. Subtle, at first. A change in the depth of the dark, no edges, no shape to mark it, but the sense of something leaning in. The line beneath the trees seemed to bow slightly, the black deepening and gathering in the spaces between trunks. Not with motion, but with weight. Presence. The airless quiet of a held breath.

The shadows drew in with the sure and steady gathering of something that had never truly left. Something that had only been waiting to be asked. And then, through the depths of it, a shape began to form.

One moment, there was only the dense weight of night; the next, something peeled away from it. The faintest rustle came first, a soft sound against the brittle grass, too deliberate to be the wind. The shape of him unfurled from the edge of the trees, as if drawn forth by the smallest thread of her voice. The air seemed thinner where he stood, the space around him pulling inward, making room.

His face wasn't clear at first. A pale impression against the deeper dark, framed by shadows that refused to settle. But his eyes were sharp. Clear. Fixed on her already, seeing straight through the glass as though it wasn't there at all.

Ellie's hands moved before her mind caught up. She unlatched the window and pushed it open, the cold biting her arms and neck in a rush. The air smelled faintly of frost. He stood just beyond the sill. His eyes held her fast in the space between them, not demanding, not soft. The kind of gaze that waits for you to remember why you called it in the first place.

"You called," he said.

Ellie nodded, her throat clogged with too many things she couldn't say yet. The cold from the window seeped into her skin, but she didn't move away. The air felt different now, denser, weightier, but in a way that made her shoulders lower just slightly, as though the tension had found somewhere else to go.

"Come in," she whispered.

He moved without a sound. One leg, then the other, folding through the narrow opening in a motion too smooth to follow. With each inch of his movement, the air turned colder, the warmth from the heater bleeding away from the walls. Sam stirred faintly in the bed, a small sigh leaving his lips, but he did not wake. His tiny fingers twitched once, then stilled.

Ellie turned to face the shape before her, her mouth open, her breath shallow and unsteady. The words tangled behind her teeth, too large to swallow, too hard to let out clean. She swallowed once and tried again. Her voice came smaller now, cracking at the edges. "Why didn't you come back?"

A pause followed. Longer than the first. The silence seemed to press between them. His mouth shifted, parted slightly, but no sound came right away. When it did, it slid through the cold in the room like a ripple beneath ice, soft, unhurried.

"You called now," he said. "So, I came."

Ellie's breath caught halfway out, stuttering in her chest. Her shoulders tensed as though her body wanted to pull itself smaller. Her voice, when it came, was uneven, scraping raw against her throat. "You were angry. That night. About...about Clover."

Again, there was a pause. Longer this time. The space seemed to pulse with it. His gaze didn't flicker. He didn't move. The shadows along the far wall seemed to gather closer, deepening along the edges of the dresser, the corners of the ceiling, dark pressed to dark.

Ellie swallowed hard, the knot in her throat growing until it felt like she might choke on the next words. "I didn't..." The sentence cracked. She forced the rest through. "I didn't put her there." The words tumbled out, too quick. "I didn't. But someone did."

The absence of an answer pressed harder than anything else might have. The space between them seemed to hum with it, as though the air itself had drawn around her ribs.

Ellie's throat ached. Her eyes burned, not with tears, but with the sharp sting of holding too many things inside too long. Her voice came out thinner, frayed at the edges. "You didn't have to be gone so long."

There was something beneath the words this time, a small edge of accusation, thin but unmistakable. A tiny, desperate blade slipped into the space between them. Her hands twisted together at her waist, fingers knotting. She could feel her own pulse racing beneath her skin.

"You called," he said once more, voice lower, softer, but weighted. "Do you want me here?"

She hesitated. Her heart slammed against her ribs in a wild, uneven rhythm. Inside her, everything tangled. She wanted to say no. She wanted to say yes. Both answers rose and collided in her chest, leaving her breathless and shaking.

Her lips parted. Her eyes stung. But before her mouth could form a word, her head moved first, a small up and down motion. A nod. An answer her body gave before her mind could close the gap and silence closed around them both.

"Mama has a man here," Ellie said at last. The words scraped raw on the way out, catching at the back of her throat. Her voice cracked on the last part, the name trembling there: "Anthony."

The figure before her didn't move at first. Then his head tilted slowly, deliberate, careful, stretching the bounds of his neck. He drew her words into himself as if weighing them on some invisible scale. "The one giving you gifts." His voice slid low and certain through the cold that pressed against her skin. It wasn't quite a question. More a confirmation of something he already knew.

"He touched me." The words hung in the air between them like something physical, a shape that neither of them could look at fully.

She drew her arms around her middle, her fingers pressing against her sides. The next words shook on the edge of her teeth. "Not bad. Not like..." Her throat closed. The rest of the sentence fell apart before it could land. She swallowed hard. "But wrong."

For a long moment, he said nothing. The space between them seemed to pull together, the dark tumbling inward until the edges of the room felt farther away. His face didn't change. His gaze didn't flicker. But something in the air shifted, as though the room itself had understood her meaning even before she'd spoken.

Ellie's breath stuttered again. Her eyes burned. The silence pressed harder than any reply would have. Her feet remained rooted where they were, her body locked as if bracing for something unseen.

At last, his voice came again, low and steady, colder than before, as though the words had settled deep before rising. "It's good you told me."

She blinked hard, tears stinging behind her eyes now, but she refused to let them fall. The knot in her throat swelled again, but this time she forced her chin up just slightly, meeting his eyes. Her voice was small but sure. "I didn't want it."

"I know," he said. His head tilted a fraction, slow and deliberate. A quiet measure being taken.

"I'll stay," he said.

His gaze swept toward the dresser. Ellie felt it the way you feel a draft pass through a room when all the windows are shut. "There is something you want me to take," he said.

Ellie hesitated. Her feet stayed rooted, the carpet pressing up through her socks, holding her in place. Her legs felt loose; her breath pressed through her nose. She forced her body forward. Two small steps. The second harder than the first. Her knees trembled beneath her nightgown, and the air felt colder as she crossed the room.

Her fingers gripped the edge of the dresser, knuckles paling beneath the skin. She stared at the second drawer, her throat clicking dryly as she swallowed. Then, slow and careful, she pulled it open. The faint groan of the wooden rails caught in her ears.

She pushed through the small, soft stacks of shirts—ones she didn't wear anymore, ones too small, too threadbare—her fingers trembling beneath the fabric. The first thing she found was the chocolate bar. The red wrapper glinted, a faint line of gold catching the window's thin light.

Next came the bracelet. She had to dig deeper for that, her hand disappearing beneath a folded sock where she had hidden it. The cold coil of plastic met her fingers, stiff and thin beneath the soft cloth. Her breath stuttered out through her nose as she freed it, her hands trembling as it left the drawer.

She lifted them both, palms shaking beneath the small weight. The chocolate crinkled under her grip, the bracelet colder than her hands. She turned back toward him, her arms locked straight to keep from shaking too badly. Her voice barely rose above the low hum of the cold air.

"Please," she said. "I don't want them."

He reached out, his long, pale fingers extending toward her, folding gently around her hands, but never touching skin. Only the objects. Only what had been given. His grasp was light but certain, like he knew exactly how much pressure to use, no more; no less.

"You will not see these again," he said.

The words fell through the cold with a weight that settled into her bones. She watched as he drew them away, the chocolate bar and bracelet vanishing between his fingers, sliding into the dark folds of his coat with no sound. The space between his hands looked empty now. But Ellie could feel the shape of what had just passed through it lingering in the air.

Ellie wrapped her arms around herself, her chest clenched and rising too fast. The cold curled in places beneath her skin where it didn't belong. Her heart still raced from the drawer, from the words she'd spoken aloud, from the weight of those things now gone. The silence that followed stretched too wide.

Her father began to hum. Soft at first. A thin vibration beneath hearing, like a sound caught between layers of air. It seemed to come from everywhere at once, beneath the floorboards, inside the walls, threaded beneath the thrum of the cold, steady and slow. Each note folding into the next with a patience that made the room feel closer.

He moved with the hum, without hurry, and sat on the edge of her bed. The mattress dipped beneath his weight in a long, careful arc, the springs sighing beneath him. He opened his arms slowly, the folds of his coat spreading like wings against the pale blanket. His eyes never left hers.

Ellie stood frozen for a moment. Her body trembled with the need to move and the fear of doing it wrong. The sound of the hum seemed to pull her forward, not with words, not with a command, but with a thread of something softer, deeper. Her bare feet pressed to the cold carpet, step by step, until she reached the bed.

She climbed onto it, careful not to disturb the space beside him, where Sam slept. Her knees folded beneath her as she crawled closer. The hum deepened. Louder now, not outside, not from the walls, but inside her head. Inside her ribs. Each note settled low in her chest, smoothing out the jagged edges still caught in her breath.

Her father's arms waited, still open, patient as stone. She hesitated, a beat, two, then leaned in. Her small frame folded against him, head settling against the firm line of his chest. The fabric of his coat smelled faintly of earth and something colder than the air, but beneath it, a steady rhythm thudded beneath her ear.

Sam shifted in his sleep. A small sigh, fingers drawing in against the blanket. Ellie reached out with one hand and drew him close, folding her arm around his tiny body so that he lay nestled against her side. His warmth pressed through the thin layers between them. His breath came soft and quick.

The hum grew stronger, filling the spaces between their bodies, slipping beneath the skin. It held no melody she could name. It was no song she'd ever known. But it rocked through her, slow and sure, weaving through the frayed edges of her fear and exhaustion until her chest began to ease.

Her eyes grew heavy. Her breath slowed. The sound beneath her ear seemed to echo with each rise and fall of her ribs. She did not remember when her arms went slack, when her cheek settled deeper against the coat, when her fingers unclenched from the fabric of Sam's shirt. She only knew that the hum stayed with her, around her, beneath her, until the dark swallowed the edges of her mind and sleep finally came.

When Ellie opened her eyes, the room was still. It was hushed in a way that made her heart beat faster. The deep, pulling hum that had wrapped around her as she drifted off was gone. The cold that had crept through her skin in the night had thinned, though the air still held a strange weight to it, like something had been pulled away too quickly and left a hollow behind.

She blinked against the pale smear of morning light bleeding through the blinds. The edges of the room were gray and soft. Her throat felt dry. She turned her head slowly, her cheek brushing against the worn blanket. Sam lay tucked close beside her, one small fist pressed beneath his chin, his tiny lips parted in a soft, slow sigh. His lashes fluttered once against his pale skin but didn't lift.

Her father was gone. The space where he had sat, where the mattress had dipped beneath his weight, was empty now. The air still seemed to hum faintly with the shape of where he had been, but the window was latched. The frost-rimmed pane reflected the dim light back at her in pale streaks.

Ellie pushed herself upright. Her limbs felt heavier than they should, as if sleep had only deepened the ache already woven through her bones. The night had left its mark. The cold of it lived beneath her skin. She let her fingers hook once into the edge of the blanket, gripping the fabric as if it might tether her to something steady. Then she slid from the bed, bare feet sinking into the worn carpet, the fibers cold beneath her skin.

The hallway light had already been switched on, casting a thin strip of sharp white across the floor. The sound of the house was loud and alive. From the kitchen came the high sizzle of butter in a pan. The air was greasy with it, sticking to her tongue. Voices floated under it, her mother's voice pitched high and fast, a brittle edge hidden behind each laugh.

Ellie moved toward the door, her hand sliding along the hallway wall. The cool paint steadied her as she crept forward, breath caught behind her teeth. Each step pressed soft into the carpet, but still she imagined every inch of the house listening.

She stopped at the edge of the living room and watched from the shadows, her body half-tucked behind the doorway. Anthony stood at the stove, spatula in hand, flipping pancakes in the pan like he had always belonged there. The sleeves of his gray shirt were pushed past his elbows, his movements loose and familiar. Nearby, her mother leaned on the counter, her mug cradled in both hands. Her cheeks were pink, her hair twisted up in a messy knot. She laughed too often and too easily.

Ellie's stomach twisted as she pressed her back harder against the wall. Her fingers clenched into fists at her sides, nails biting into her skin. She watched as Anthony spoke low and easy, his words drawing a smile that stretched wide across her mother's face.

Then Anthony shifted, head tilting in slowly. His gaze swept the kitchen once and found her in the hallway shadows. His eyes held her there, pinned, and then the smile came, thin and private, as though no one else in the room existed but her. Ellie's throat burned, her nails digging deeper. She fought to keep her feet still beneath her. Everything in her wanted to pull back, to disappear into the hallway, but her legs refused to move.

And then, beneath the scrape of the spatula and her mother's brittle laughter, beneath the sizzle and clink of kitchen sounds that no longer felt like home, she heard it. Thinner than sound. A hum. It wasn't part of the house. It wasn't part of the morning. It slipped through the seams of the walls, through the space between skin and bone, settling low beneath her ribs. She could feel it more than hear it, a vibration beneath the fragile rhythm of her own breath.

Her fingers twitched at her sides, nails pressing deeper into her palms. The hum slid around her shoulders like a second weight. It carried with it a chill she knew too well. A presence that wasn't waiting for permission. Her breath caught in her throat. Carefully, slowly, she eased it out through her nose, her gaze flicking instinctively toward the window at the end of the hall.

But she stopped herself. She didn't turn. The hum told her enough. It was there, coiled in the edges of the morning light, threading through the walls. Watching. Listening. Ellie's jaw stiffened. The room around her blurred for a moment, the harsh yellow light of the kitchen, the forced sounds of her mother's voice, Anthony's smile still crooked in the corner of her eye. They all faded behind the thin pull of the hum that wrapped around her like an answer.

A HOUSE THAT WATCHES

The sound of batter hitting the pan snapped Ellie back. A wet slap followed by the soft hiss of heat. The smell of pancakes swelled through the air; the kitchen slid back into focus one sharp line at a time. Anthony stood at the stove, one foot hooked behind the other, spatula in hand. He flipped the pancake with a practiced flick. Her mother hovered nearby, slipping her coffee, her smile stretched wide across her face.

"You're making a mess," she said lightly, a giggle following behind the words. Her voice dipped lower, play-soft. "But I suppose I can't complain if you're feeding us."

Anthony chuckled. "Spoiling my girls," he said. The spatula clicked against the pan. "You know me." Ellie's skin prickled. Her arms stayed folded across her chest.

She watched him remove the golden-brown pancake from the pan and pour another ladle of batter into the pan. The way his wrist tilted just enough to control the edges. He looked over his shoulder once, eyes glancing toward her, the smile creeping back again.

"Got a stack coming for you too, kiddo," he said.

Ellie didn't answer.

"She's shy in the mornings," her mother said, as though this explained everything. Ellie's stomach turned. Her fingers dug into the sides of her sleeves.

The pancakes sizzled, low and constant, filling the room with a syrupy, sweet smell. It wound between the buzz of the overhead light and the sharp edges of her mother's bright voice. Anthony moved to the counter, pulling down a bottle of syrup, humming under his breath now, something tuneless and off-beat. The bottle thudded softly as he set it down beside a plate with a stack of three pancakes on it.

"Let's do this right," he said as he poured a slow ribbon onto the ceramic dish, wrist tilting just so.

Her mother's voice cut in, lighter than it had been a moment before. "Oh, Ellie," she said, her tone shifting, sliding into something casual, calling her daughter's attention. "I've got to run out later. Couple errands. Won't be long."

Ellie's stomach knotted sharp and sudden. Her heart lurched up beneath her ribs, the air snagging in her throat. She swallowed hard but couldn't find her voice fast enough. Her mother's words kept going, as if they'd been rehearsed. "Anthony offered to stay and watch you two for me," she said, bright with a smile that didn't reach her eyes.

Ellie's fingers laced together, twisting until her knuckles blanched. Then her mother looked straight at her, smile thinning to something harder. "You've been holed up too much lately. You need to stop sulking in your room." The words slid out flat, not a suggestion. A command.

Ellie opened her mouth. The first word caught jagged behind her teeth. She forced her throat open around it. "Sam needs breakfast," she said, the first words she could think of to shift her mother's attention elsewhere. Her voice came out thin, rough.

For a heartbeat, the kitchen seemed to still. Anthony turned his head, that slow tilt of attention that made her skin pull across her shoulders. "We'll make sure he's got something when he wakes up," he said. His voice was light. The smile still tugged at the edge of his mouth as he flipped the next pancake with a slow, practiced motion.

Her mother barely spared a glance toward the hallway. "Of course," she said. "That's fine." But Ellie heard the shift beneath her voice, a warning tucked between the words: *Enough. No more.*

"We'll be fine," he said, words light and even. "Won't we, Ellie?"

Ellie's skin felt thin, as if the air was pressing against her ribs. She dropped her gaze to the floor. Her tongue sat clumsy, her throat locked. There wasn't a word she could force through it.

Anthony flipped another pancake. The scent of cooking butter gathered in the air, cloying now. He let the spatula rest on the edge of the pan, leaning his hip against the counter as he glanced over toward Ellie. "It'll be good," he said, his voice smooth. "We'll have fun."

"And you'll be good," her mother said, the tone edged with something hard, brittle, and impatient. "I don't want to hear about any trouble."

The words landed in Ellie's stomach. She stared harder at the floor. She swallowed; it hurt going down. Her chin dipped, one quick nod.

Her mother didn't linger after breakfast, after Sam had been fed. Once her purse was over her shoulder and her keys clinked in her hand, she leaned down and kissed the top of Sam's head without looking at Ellie. "Be good," she said quickly. "Listen to Anthony." Then she was out the door. The lock clicked with a snap that made Ellie flinch.

Anthony stood in the kitchen, watching the space where her mother had been.

"Well." His voice filled the room. "Looks like it's just us now." Anthony crossed the room in two long strides and pulled the front curtains shut. They snapped together and the light in the room dimmed, the gray morning flattened out by the dense fabric.

"Let's stay in here," he said. "Keep cozy. Just us." He grabbed the remote and turned on the TV. The volume jumped too high, garish voices shouting over cartoon music, then dipped as he pressed the volume down button repeatedly.

Ellie sat by Sam on the floor. Anthony moved past her and sat on the couch, sprawling wide, arms stretched along the back.

"You're really grown up," he said, voice dipping softer, smoother. "The way you take care of your brother." He smiled and gestured for her to come sit. "Come on. Bring your brother. We'll all hang out."

"Here," he said, reaching out. His hand brushed a strand of her hair behind her ear. The skin at her neck crawled beneath the touch. "Pretty hair," he added quietly. "Bet you hear that all the time."

He glanced toward Sam, then at a stack of toys near the wall. "Why don't we play for a bit?" he said, already reaching for one, a soft stuffed frog Ellie knew Sam didn't really like. "Here. I'll help."

She shook her head, voice too thin to rise above the cartoons. "It's okay."

But Anthony knelt beside her anyway, too close, the frog in one hand. His fingers brushed hers when he handed it over, slow, deliberate. "See?" he murmured. "No need to be shy."

Ellie's skin prickled. She shifted, scooting closer to Sam. Ellie stood up, lifting him into her arms as she rose, cradling him to her chest.

"I'm going to take him for a nap," she said, her voice clearer now, sharpened by the coil in her gut.

Anthony straightened. "Nah, leave him out here with us," he said easily, hand lifting as if to wave her off. "No sense running off. He'll be fine."

"He needs to nap," she said, firmer this time. Her feet were already moving, one step back, then another. "In the bedroom."

Anthony's smile thinned. His eyes tracked her every step, but he didn't reach for her again. He just leaned back slowly on the couch, hands loose at his sides. "All right," he said. "You know best."

Ellie didn't stop. She turned, heart pounding, and carried Sam down the hall. Her bare feet were nearly silent on the carpet. She reached her bedroom and shut the door with a soft but certain click. She leaned back against the door, arms wrapped around Sam as he squirmed sleepily against her shoulder.

She laid him on the bed, smoothing the blanket around his small body with shaking fingers. Then she crossed to the dresser. It wasn't big, but it was heavy against her small frame. Ellie braced her shoulder against it and pushed with all her weight. The wooden legs scraped faintly against the floor, a small groan beneath the carpet. Inch by inch, it slid toward the door. Her shoulder ached with the effort. Her breath came fast, a grunt escaping her lips with each push.

When it finally pressed flush against the door, Ellie stepped back, chest heaving. The knob rattled when she tested it, but the door didn't budge forward. She balled her hands into fists at her sides and stood listening. From the hallway, the TV murmured on. Voices rose and fell, canned laughter spilling out. Ellie's stomach twisted. She stayed frozen in the middle of the room, her gaze locked on the thin crack of light beneath the door.

Time crawled and the sun faded in the sky. As night loomed on the horizon, the front door opened with a bang that echoed through the thin walls. Ellie flinched, arms braced across her chest. After a moment her mother's voice carried through next, louder than before, high and frantic.

"I was only gone a couple hours! Jesus, Anthony, what's your problem?"

Anthony's voice followed, lower and clipped. The words blurred together, but Ellie caught enough. "She acts like I'm the bad guy." Another voice rose beneath it, her mother's again, angrier now, more desperate. The words slammed against each other, tangled in the hallway air.

Ellie pressed both hands over her ears and sank to the floor. The voices swelled, then retreated. Footsteps thudded unevenly down the hall. Then a new sound. The knob rattled hard against the back of the dresser.

"Ellie!" her mother's voice snapped. The door bumped against the dresser with a dull thud. "What the hell is this?"

Ellie stayed frozen.

Another hard shove. The dresser scraped an inch. A fist pounded the door. "Open this damn door right now!"

Ellie didn't move. Didn't breathe.

A grunt. A louder scrape. With a final shove, the door wedged open just enough for her mother to force her way through, the dresser groaning against her hip.

Her mother stood there, wild-eyed, her hair loose around her shoulders, face flushed. She pointed a trembling finger at Ellie.

"What is wrong with you?" she hissed. "You embarrassed him! You humiliated me! I come home and he's trying to be nice, and this is what I get?" Her voice cracked, half shout, half plea. "You don't get to treat people that way! Do you hear me?"

Ellie stared down at her knees, arms locked around herself. The room spun faintly.

Her mother's voice kept going. "You need to grow up! Stop making trouble. Stop acting like this. He's trying to help. You're going to ruin everything."

When the words finally stopped, the silence pressed heavier than the shouting had.

Her mother gave the door one more sharp shove. "Fix this." Then she was gone, footsteps storming back down the hall.

Ellie sat there on the floor, knees drawn to her chest, the dresser still wedged in front of the half-open door. The walls seemed to lean in around her. The TV still buzzed from the living room. But outside the window, the dark had deepened.

That night came sodden and slow. Ellie stayed in her room long after dinner had passed. She didn't go back out when her mother called her name once, twice, her voice strained with booze and exhaustion. Sam had finally fallen asleep in Ellie's bed; his small body resting on its side.

Ellie watched him breathe. The rise and fall of his tiny chest, steady beneath the threadbare blanket. Her own breath came shallow, every sound outside their door making her stomach clench. The muffled swell of the television. Her mother's voice, high and laughing too loud. Anthony's deeper one threading beneath it.

She drew herself around Sam when the house grew darker. Small on her side of the bed, one arm draped across her brother, the other twisted in her own hair. The pillow beneath her cheek smelled faintly of the cold night air from the last time the window had been open.

The sound of footsteps, one pair, heavier than her mother's, passed her door once, then again. The floor shifted. The hallway settled. Silence grew in the spaces between.

Her fingers unwound slowly from her hair. She rose. Her legs shook as she crossed the room. Careful. Light. She glanced once at Sam, still breathing slowly and softly, then reached for the window latch. Her fingertips brushed the cool metal. She slid the window open.

Cold night air rushed in, sharp against her skin. And, already there, was her father. He stood at the edge of the yard, closer this time. Just beyond the patch of frost-bitten grass, where the shadow of the tree line stretched its fingers toward the house. His coat hung around him like part of the dark. Ellie pressed her hands against the windowsill. The TV blared down the hall, but every sound from the living room seemed distant now, washed out beneath the drum of her own heartbeat.

"Please," she whispered, voice cracking. "Come in."

He stepped forward. One leg folded through the sill, then the other. His coat whispered as he moved. When he straightened inside the room, the air shifted, the walls leaned in.

Ellie stumbled back, her hands trembling at her sides. Her father's gaze followed her, sharp and steady.

He stood still by the window, the cold pooling softly around his frame. The weight of his gaze pressed into the room. His voice broke the hush. "You are afraid. Tell me why."

Ellie swallowed. Her fingers turned in against her palms. The words lodged at the back of her throat. "He—" she started, but it came out rough. Her voice broke, stopped. She forced it out again. "He scares me."

A tilt of her father's head, slow and stretched. His eyes narrowed slightly, a flicker passing beneath the calm surface.

Ellie's hands twisted harder. Her knuckles ached. "Mama left us alone with him. Today." The words tumbled fast, sharp-edged. "He shut the curtains…" her voice faltered, caught on the knot in her chest. She forced it out. "He kept me close. He touched my hair. Tried to stop me when I brought Sam in here for a nap." Her eyes fell on her sleeping brother in his crib.

Her voice broke on the last word. The weight of it seemed to drag her gaze downward, pulling her deeper into herself. Her shoulders shook with the effort of holding the rest of the words in, the ones she couldn't quite shape or speak aloud.

Her father said nothing. The silence stretched between them, pressing hard beneath her ribs until her breath grew shallow. The shadows in the room seemed to bend in closer. Then his voice came, sliding beneath the air, softer than the cold but more edged than the dark. "Do you want me to stop him?" The words were formed as a question but held in them a promise balanced on the edge of a knife.

Ellie's head jerked up. Her heart slammed painfully in her chest, the rhythm frantic and uneven. Her father's eyes had shifted. Gone was the calm distance of his usual gaze. Now they burned darker, steadier. Something coiled beneath that stillness, something wound and ready. The air around his shoulders seemed to pulse and flicker like heat rising off of asphalt.

Her breath came in quick, shallow bursts that scraped against her throat. The room seemed to close in around her, the walls pressing nearer, the ceiling lower. The cold had seeped through her arms and legs, but it was the weight behind her father's gaze that froze her in place. The sharpness of it caught in her chest. She wanted to say yes. She wanted to scream it. To beg him to make Anthony disappear, to take away the sick twist in her stomach and the ache in her skin. The dark in the corners seemed to lean closer now, hungry for her answer.

"Just…stay." The words shivered in the cold air. The walls held still. The shadows stilled with them.

Then her father's head dipped, slow and sure, a movement as deliberate as the hum of the dark. "I will stay." The words settled between them. The cold that had wrapped around her eased. The sharp edge behind his voice withdrew, but his gaze never left her, steady and watchful, the dark around him no longer pressing, but present.

Ellie crawled back into the bed, pulling Sam's small warmth against her chest. She drew the blanket high, wrapping it around them both like armor. Her arms locked around her brother's tiny frame, her grip trembling.

Across the room, her father stood in silence, his presence filling the space between the walls. The dark drug itself around him, folding into the pale stillness of his face. Without shifting, without stepping forward, he turned his gaze toward the door. His voice slid through the room, quiet and sure. "I will stay. And I will watch."

She drew Sam tighter against her, her arms wrapping fully around his frame. His warmth pressed into her ribs, steady and soft. His head tucked beneath her chin, his tiny breath brushing warm against her throat. Slowly, carefully, Ellie let her head drop down to the pillow, her cheek resting against the rough fabric.

WHEN HE'S NOT SUPPOSED TO BE THERE

Something wasn't right. Ellie could feel it moving just beneath her skin, a restless thread pulling, weaving. The feeling wasn't sharp, not the jagged wrong of voices raised in anger or things breaking against walls. This was a quieter wrong, the kind that settled in a room like dust.

A chill that threaded through the blanket bit faintly at the tip of her nose and wrapped its fingers around her bare toes. She huddled deeper into the thin warmth of the covers. The cold came from the room itself, not the air outside. It was the kind of cold that felt as though something was *watching*, not merely touching.

Her fingers itched with the need to be sure, to feel something solid and real beneath them. Slowly, Ellie slid her hand beneath the flat pillow. The soft cloth gave way beneath her knuckles as they found the familiar shape of her father's watch. The leather strap was worn smooth in places from her handling it, a shape her fingers now knew better than they knew her own hair.

But as her fingers closed around it this time, they stopped. The leather that should have been soft and warm from the heat of the pillow was cold—not cool—but *cold*, the kind that sank through her skin. The kind of cold that belonged to something left out too long, to something touched by hands that no longer carried warmth.

Ellie drew her hand back, the edges of her blanket scraping softly against the mattress. She stared at the pillow, the fabric innocent and undisturbed, but her heart was already knocking hard behind her ribs. She sat there in her bed, fighting the cold with the thinness of her blankets. She gathered her hand into a loose fist in her lap, skin tingling where the cold of the watch had touched it. Ellie glanced toward the window. The latch was down, the window closed against the frame. But in the weak light of the morning, something along the edge of the sill caught her eye. A smear, faint but visible, like the trace of fingers dragged through damp earth. The dirt broke in small ridges across the wood, as though someone had come, or gone, without cleaning their hands.

She swung her legs over the side of the bed; the mattress gave a muted protest beneath her weight. Her toes sank into the rough fibers of the carpet, chilled through. She sat there on the edge of the bed, arms wrapped around her knees, staring at the sill and the faint lines of dirt. For a moment, the rest of the room seemed to fall away. There was only the window.

Behind her, Sam stirred, letting out a thin sigh that sounded so very small. Ellie closed her eyes for a heartbeat, listening. The weight in her chest hadn't lifted, it had only settled lower now.

And then she heard it.

It came softly at first, barely the suggestion of a sound. Ellie thought it might have been the heater kicking on in the cold of the house, but as she sat still, barely moving, it came again. *Tap, tap, tap.* Her eyes instinctively darted toward the window, but the pane of glass stood clear and empty, the view of the backyard unobstructed. *Tap, tap, tap.* The sound feathered through the room, shifting and crawling through the walls.

Her spine went rigid as the noise threaded its way through the morning hush. It came carefully, but deliberately. Ellie didn't turn her head. She didn't even blink. She listened, holding herself completely still, the cold air around her pressing in close. The gentle tapping from behind the drywall faded after a moment; it left behind a silence that was worse than the sound itself.

The quiet that followed felt pressed close. It felt as though something on the other side of the wall was now listening back, waiting for the drumming of fingers as an answer. Ellie's eyes drifted toward the door. It was still closed, the frame faintly shadowed by the soft, gray light that touched the edges of the room. But the corners—where wall met ceiling, where floor met dresser—seemed darker, the shadows clinging like cobwebs.

Behind her, Sam whimpered again. Ellie turned and crossed to the bed. She leaned over and gently touched his cheek, smoothing his hair from his clammy face. His breathing calmed, soft and shallow, and his tiny body sank deeper into the blanket. She adjusted it around his legs, making sure it was tucked firmly, then let her hand rest lightly on his back until he settled completely. She didn't lift him. Not yet. She didn't want to move more than she had to.

Her gaze shifted back toward the window, where that faint smear still stretched across the sill. She stepped closer, slow and cautious. The streak of dirt hadn't changed, but something about it felt more certain now. Like it hadn't been left by accident. Like it had been made to be found. Her fingertips brushed along the ridges, feeling the brittle edges crumble slightly at her touch. Dry. Old. Her breath came out in a slow, uneven exhale. She wiped her hand on her pants without looking down.

She stood there for a moment, facing the window, her eyes searching the faint light for movement beyond the glass. But there was nothing there. No figure in the yard. No shadow pressed against the pane. Just the empty morning.

Ellie backed away from the window and turned toward the door. Her steps were slow, each one deliberate. She didn't glance toward the walls again, didn't try to find the place where the tapping had come from. The chill that had seeped through the blankets hadn't gone. It clung to her skin, even now. Even in the light.

The hallway was dim. The air hung stale and stagnant. Shadows bloomed in the corners where the walls met the ceiling and floor. The house shifted around her as she walked toward the bathroom. It was just the faint shift of old wood, but it made her heart skip anyway. The bathroom door stuck slightly before giving way under her hand.

Inside, she clicked on the light. It buzzed overhead, a soft hum filling the small space as the yellow glow flickered, casting uneven shadows on the far wall. Ellie stepped in all the way and closed the door behind her, pushing it shut with more care than force. She turned the lock without thinking, the sound of it clicking into place was finite in the quiet.

She turned the faucet. The pipes responded with a tired groan before giving up a splatter of water that ran cold against her cupped palms. She splashed her face, the water stinging awake the nerves in her cheeks, but it still didn't feel as cold as the air in the house had been when she'd climbed out of bed. She leaned closer to the sink, letting the water run, and lifted her eyes toward the mirror.

In the glass, over her shoulder, something moved. Not a flicker of light or a trick of her own reflection, but a shape. A silhouette. It passed across the sliver of hallway still visible through a gap in the door behind her, slow enough to be seen, tall enough to not be mistaken for her mother. Ellie spun around, her hands wet and half-lifted, heart thudding into her ribs.

There was nothing. The bathroom door was still closed, the latch steady in its place. No footsteps in the hall. No sound at all, except for her own breath, which now felt louder than it had a second ago, echoing faintly off the walls.

Slowly, Ellie turned her head and looked back at the mirror. The edges of the glass had begun to fog from the warmth of the water still running into the sink, a faint layer of condensation creeping inward. But the middle, the part where her reflection floated, was still clear. The bathroom door was now clearly closed behind her in the reflection.

Her face hovered there, pale and wide-eyed, and below it, the slow rise and fall of her breath made the glass bloom with a fresh cloud. She reached up and pressed her fingertips against it. The surface was colder than the water. Colder than anything else in the room. She pulled her hand back quickly, the tingling in her skin creeping up her fingers.

She turned away and left the bathroom without drying her hands. The cold clung to her skin as she stepped back into the hallway, water dripping from her fingertips. Each drop landed with a soft pat on the floor. She moved quickly, her breath catching in her throat as she passed through the empty stretch of hallway. The doors remained closed. She didn't look back. She didn't glance at the mirror again. The shape she had seen wasn't there anymore and it wasn't in the hallway, but the memory of it had rooted itself in the center of her chest, cold and crushing, as though it had followed her quietly out into the hall.

Ellie let Sam sleep, carefully drawing the blanket up around his small frame until only the top of his hair showed fine against the pillow. His breathing was slow and shallow. She stood for a moment, watching the rise and fall of his chest, grounding herself in the rhythm of it before she slipped out of the room. The hallway beyond was dim, lined with soft light bleeding in from the kitchen. The air felt brittle. She moved quietly, padding down the hall with her arms wrapped across her stomach. Anthony was already up.

"Ellie-bear!" His voice hit the silence hard, high and grating, too loud for this early in the morning. He stood near the counter with a white paper bag clutched in one hand, shoulders twitching with a restless energy that didn't match the hour. His jaw worked at nothing, and he kept licking at the corner of his mouth between words. "Look who's up early! I couldn't sleep, so I got us a little treat," he continued, flashing a wide, crooked smile that didn't quite reach his eyes. His gaze darted past her down the hallway before snapping back. "Where's your mom?"

"She's asleep, I think," Ellie said. She could smell something sour-sweet in the air under the artificial sugar of the donuts—sweat and something sharp.

Anthony crouched by Ellie, the bag crackling in his hand like it couldn't stay still. "You know what I always say," he said, smiling again. His jaw flexed. His fingers drummed fast on his knee. "You gotta take a break sometime." His eyes darted behind her, towards the front door. "Can you come help me with something in the truck? I need a strong kid like you."

She kept her eyes on his drumming fingers, how they moved fast, never quite landing in a rhythm. Her stomach clenched.

The air felt off around him. "I have to get ready for school," she said, the excuse coming out quickly.

His smile twitched, the corners of his mouth tugging like wires had snapped. He stood, not all at once, but in jerky movements, fingers raking through his hair as he looked down the hall again, then back at her. "Maybe later then," he muttered, his voice low like he'd already moved on to some other thought. His eyes kept flicking, like they were chasing something she couldn't see.

Ellie didn't move until he did.

Her mother was awake by the time she went to leave. She sat at the kitchen table, holding her coffee cup with both hands. She didn't say anything when Ellie walked in; she just kept staring at the wall, lost in thought. Her sunglasses were on, even though it wasn't bright inside. When she moved her head a little, the glasses slipped, just for a second. Ellie saw the dark smudge under her eye, swollen and strange.

Anthony leaned against the counter. He didn't say anything. His hands kept moving; he rubbed his fingers together, and tapped against the side of the counter. The air around him was full of something—like the sound of bees. Anthony was by the sink, tapping something out with the heel of his palm, his movements quick and sloppy. The silence sat loaded across the floor. Ellie opened the door. A rush of outside air slipped around her ankles. The click behind her as she closed the door was soft.

The school hallway stretched long in front of her. Kids talked fast, their words bouncing and tumbling through the air. Ellie stepped into the current of it, but everything sounded like it was underwater. Her sneakers squeaked, and she froze for half a second before walking again, eyes fixed on the pattern of the tiles. Her shoulder brushed a backpack. Someone laughed too loud nearby. She kept her gaze down. Something tickled the back of her neck—not a touch, but the idea of one. She turned. No one. Just kids shuffling to various doors. But her shoulders stayed tense.

She slid into her seat in Mrs. Rieke's classroom. The chair felt cold under her legs. She laid her hands flat on top of her desk and stared down at the flat surface. Mrs. Rieke was already handing out worksheets. The words on the sheet wouldn't sit still. They wobbled, like something underneath the page was breathing. She picked up her pencil. It rolled between her fingers, smooth and clumsy. Her eyes lifted towards the front of the classroom. The teacher's chair sat empty. The board had a list of words on it that she didn't want to read. But to the left of it, something moved. A shape. A stretch of shadow bending where it shouldn't.

Her head jerked up fast, eyes fixing on where the peripheral shadow had been. Nothing. Just the board. Just the chair. Just the classroom reflected back in the window across the room, wavy and warped.

She told herself not to look again. Not at the corners. Not at the board. Not at the windows. But her eyes didn't always listen. They kept tugging away from her paper, slipping toward the edge of things, toward the places where the air felt different. Where the light didn't sit right. Where the shadows pulled in. Every time she looked up, she told herself it would be the last time. And then she'd do it again.

The teacher's voice droned on. Chairs scraped against the floor. Pencils scratched across paper. Normal sounds, but none of them reached the strange, quiet part of her chest where something colder had settled.

By lunchtime, Ellie stood in the cafeteria line with her tray held close to her chest, the smell of food drifting up from the metal trays, mashed potatoes, a scoop of corn, and a chicken patty. She took what they gave her without saying anything, moving forward one step at a time. The lunch lady smiled, but Ellie didn't smile back. She slid into a seat near the end of one of the long tables. Her fork clinked against the tray as she picked at the food, tearing the breading off the chicken in small strips without eating any of it. The corn rolled in its square section, untouched. She tucked the carton of milk away out of habit.

Around her, the room swelled with noise, kids shouting, chairs scraping, trays dropping, but it all came in muffled to her ears. Ellie sat hunched over her tray, elbows tucked close, chewing on the inside of her cheek. After a while, she stopped looking at her food and turned her head to the window instead. The sky was pale and still. In the reflection, she saw her own face, and behind it, for just a second, something moving that wasn't her. A shape, slow and low, passed through the faint shine of the glass.

She blinked hard, heart thudding in her ears. When she looked again, it was gone. Only the sky. Only her own face. But her hands were shaking under the table.

In the hallway after recess, someone said her name. Soft and close, like a breath beside her ear. She spun around fast, her hair whipping across her shoulder. Her feet slipped a little on the tile, but she caught herself. No one was looking at her. The hallway buzzed with voices and footsteps and the clatter of children, but none of it matched the feeling crawling along her skin. Her neck prickled, and her arms felt numb.

She didn't remember most of the afternoon. The hours dragged, but they eventually disappeared. She stared at her desk, at the shapes on the board, at the clock. Her eyes ached like she hadn't blinked in a long time. Her lips were dry, and she pressed them together over and over again, like that might stop the strange burn growing in her throat.

By the time the last bell rang, Ellie packed her things slowly. Didn't talk. Didn't wave. She slipped her arms into her coat and buttoned it all the way up to her chin. Her backpack thumped against her back with every step. The sky outside was grayer than before. The cold reached through her coat and settled into her shoulders.

She kept her head down all the way home. She needed to see Sam. She needed to hear his voice, feel his small fingers grab her sleeve. She needed to know he was alright.

The front door stuck a little when Ellie pushed it open. She had to lean her shoulder into it until it gave way with a soft scrape. The air inside the house was still, stifled in a way that made her pause on the step just inside the door, fingers gripping the strap of her backpack. She listened for a moment, for voices, footsteps, the clatter of a dish in the sink. Nothing came.

Her shoes made soft sounds on the floor as she slipped them off and stepped into the living room. Outside, porch lights began to flicker on one by one. Sam's toys were scattered, but he wasn't there. The couch cushions were dented, one of them turned sideways like someone had sat there for a long time and then left in a hurry. The TV was off, but the remote sat too neatly on the armrest, like it had been placed, not dropped.

She moved down the hallway slowly, her fingers brushing the wall. Her mother's door was closed. She could hear a voice behind it, Anthony's. Not loud, not yelling. But sharp. Fast. Ellie's stomach turned.

She passed by without stopping, her footsteps careful. The other door was open just a little, and she pushed it gently with the tips of her fingers. Sam was in his crib, lying on his side, thumb tucked against his mouth. He was awake and staring at the wall. His eyes flicked toward her when she stepped in, and he sat up slowly, reaching one hand through the bars without making a sound.

She grabbed her step ladder and picked him up, pressed her cheek against the top of his head. He felt very warm. His small fingers clenched in her sleeve.

The voice in the other room rose, then dropped again. Something thudded against the floor, soft but certain.

Ellie didn't flinch. She sat down on the floor beside Sam's crib, holding him in her lap, legs crossed. Her eyes stayed on the doorway.

Sam coiled against her chest, his head tucked under her chin, the soft rhythm of his breathing warm against her neck. The room was dim now. The stillness inside the house grew deeper. She didn't turn on the light. The dark felt safer.

From across the hall, the voices came and went, low one minute, sharp the next. Her mother's voice floated up now and then, soft and slurred. Anthony's voice kept cutting through hers, faster, harder, the words snapping like rubber bands. Ellie couldn't make out most of what they were saying.

Sam shifted in her lap and let out a small sound that wasn't quite a cry. Ellie rubbed his back, slow circles, her hand steady even though her chest felt squeezed. He was heavy in her arms, but she didn't let go.

A glass broke. Not loud. Just a pop of sound, like something slipping from a hand that didn't mean to drop it. Then the quiet after…the kind that fills everything.

Ellie didn't move. She stared at the door. Her fingers gripped around the back of Sam's shirt, holding him close. Her throat was dry.

The hallway boards pressed and released once, but no one came.

She rocked Sam slowly, her knees aching from the stillness. The shadows in the corners of the room were growing darker now, climbing higher, stretching longer. One sat near the closet, dense and crooked, with nothing casting it directly. She tried not to look at it, but it was hard not to.

The air had that feeling again. Like something was standing just outside the door, waiting for her to notice. Sam's breath hitched. He looked up at her with wide, tired eyes, and she pressed her cheek against his forehead.

"It's okay," she whispered.

She wasn't sure who she was saying it to anymore—Sam, herself, or whatever might be listening just beyond the quiet.

In the hallway, the bathroom light flicked on. Then off. No footsteps. No door opening or closing. Just the light.

She stood slowly, lifting Sam with her, legs stiff. She didn't go toward the hallway. She didn't call out.

Instead, she went to the closet, pulled out the spare blanket, and sat with Sam tucked close in the far corner of the room, away from the door. The light from the window faded to nothing. The hum inside the walls began again, so faint it might not have been there at all.

She whispered to the dark. "Don't let him hurt us."

THE BENDING FENCE

That night, Ellie dreamed of roots. They crawled beneath the house, dark and wet, twisting through the dirt and up into the walls. They pushed up through the floorboards, slow and certain, curling like fingers around the legs of her bed. She could hear them slithering as they stretched, dragging soil behind them in clumps that scattered across her blanket. She woke with her heart pounding, her hands clenched in fists, and the feeling of damp earth still clinging under her fingernails. The room was quiet, and she reached down to press her palms against the carpet. Just floor.

The trees in the backyard seemed closer than they used to be. Ellie noticed it that morning from the kitchen window. The branches stretched higher now, longer, heavier, their tips bending toward the house, leaning in to listen. They shifted on their own, quiet and smooth, dragging their shadows across the grass. The fence had started to lean, bowing inward slightly, like it was struggling to hold the woods back. Ellie could see dark shapes moving just beyond the tree line. And the way they watched.

"You're ruining things," her mother muttered, voice low and scratchy. A sliver of sound between her lips as she stared into her coffee mug. "You always look at him like he's the problem."

Ellie didn't say anything. She kept watching the trees through the kitchen window. Her breath fogged the glass.

Her mother's head snapped up. "Did you hear me?"

Ellie gave a small nod, not turning from the window.

"I said, why can't you just be nice to Anthony?"

She still didn't answer. The words she had weren't the kind that would help. They sat in her chest like stones, hard-set and sharp at the edges. She didn't trust her voice to carry any of them without cutting something open. So, she stayed still, one arm across her middle, fingers tightening in the fabric of her shirt.

Her mother let out a sharp breath through her nose. "You think you know everything, don't you?" Her voice was louder now, rising to fill the space between them. "You act like I'm some kind of villain. Like I don't see those looks you give me. Like you're better than me."

"I didn't say anything," Ellie whispered, eyes still on the trees.

"You don't have to," her mother snapped, the mug clattering hard against the tabletop. "You sit there with your quiet face and your judging eyes, and you think you're smarter than everyone. You're not. You're a kid. You don't know what it's like to raise two babies by yourself. What it's like to not sleep. To not eat. To have someone actually stay, actually try, and all you do is look at him like he's a monster."

Ellie blinked slowly, her gaze still fixed on the branches outside. One of them had wrapped around the edge of the fence now, its shadow pressed long across the yard.

"Anthony's trying," her mother continued, her voice dropping low but still sharp enough to cut. "At least he's here. Your dad left. Or don't you remember that part?"

Ellie's shoulders tensed. She turned slightly from the window, eyes narrow, voice pinched. "You never tell me why."

Her mother didn't answer at first. She just stared into her mug like there was something at the bottom she needed to see. When she finally spoke, it came out fast. "Doesn't matter. Gone is gone."

"Yes, it does matter," Ellie said, her jaw tight.

Her mother's head snapped up. "Watch your mouth."

"It's not fair."

"You don't know anything," her mother barked, the chair scraping hard against the floor as she stood. "You think you're so smart, but you're just a little girl who doesn't understand how hard it is, how hard I try. I do everything for you. For both of you."

"I just want the truth."

Her mother laughed. "Truth? What truth, Ellie? That he left? That he didn't care enough to stay?"

Ellie's mouth opened, then closed. Her chest felt hollow, her hands cold. "He does care," her voice trailed off as she said it, not saying the full truth out loud.

Her mother was pacing now, her voice low and fast. "You don't know what it's like to be alone. You don't know what it's like to try and keep everything together with no one helping."

Ellie sat down, her legs suddenly tired. Her eyes stung, but she didn't cry. "I don't want Anthony," she said, quiet now. "He scares me."

Her mother stopped pacing. "He's not scary," she said finally, but her voice didn't sound sure. "He's trying. You have to give him a chance."

Ellie didn't answer. She just looked out the window, where the trees were still swaying even though there was no wind.

The air in the house had started to feel strange. It had gone cold. The kind of cold that sank through everything. Ellie started keeping her socks on all the time, even when she went to bed, but her toes still ached with chill. The bedroom was the worst. The air there felt still and sharp. Her breath puffed out in little clouds sometimes, even when the heater clicked on in other parts of the house.

She stopped touching the walls. Once, she leaned her hand against the hallway corner and yanked it back, gasping. It had felt like ice had replaced the drywall.

Lights blinked when she walked under them, quick flickers. The kitchen one buzzed and dimmed when she stood by the sink rinsing a spoon, the flickering glow dancing across the faucet. She tested it once, stepping away and back again. Each time, the light reacted.

She started pushing the doors closed harder at night. She made sure they clicked, even braced the step ladder against her bedroom door after it drifted open for the third time in a row. By morning, it was open again. Just a crack. Wide enough for the cold from her room to slip through.

At night, when the blankets weren't enough, Ellie would wrap around Sam and try to pretend the hum in the walls was a lullaby. It was low and steady, like something alive, something big that lived deep inside the bones of the house. It pulsed behind the drywall, behind her ribs, as if it had found her heartbeat and was trying to keep time. Only it was always just a little off. Too slow. Too loud. And always cold.

Her father's face had started to look different, like someone had drawn it from memory and missed a few pieces. The skin looked too flat. The mouth was almost right, but the smile never reached his eyes. She stared at him until her breath stopped, until her chest ached and her lungs begged for air.

"You're cold," he said. "You shouldn't be cold."

Ellie didn't answer. His eyes weren't blank, they were shiny. They passed over Sam, then landed on her, and stayed there.

She stayed too, feet pressed into the cold floor, one hand on the crib rail. She waited, her muscles pulled under tension like wire, until her father's shape began to fade, vanishing piece by piece into the corner. Into the paint. Into the wall.

Another night, she woke suddenly, her breath caught halfway in her chest, and saw him again, near the closet. He didn't speak at first. Just looked down, then up, like something had moved across the floor. Then his head turned toward her, slow and sure.

"He knows," her father said, voice flat but certain. "Babies always know first."

Ellie sat up straighter. Sam was beside her, wrapped in his blanket, asleep but frowning. She tucked the edge of the blanket around him like it might help. Her heart thudded in her ears. "Know what?" she whispered. Her father didn't answer. His face didn't change. He only stood there, quiet, until she blinked and he was gone.

The next time was just before morning. Ellie had crept down the hallway, needing something to drink, the back of her mouth dry and her tongue sticking to her teeth. The kitchen was dark except for the little flashing clock on the stove. She didn't turn on the overhead. The cold wrapped around her legs as she padded to the sink.

When she turned, he was there again. Not in the room, but just past the entryway. In the living room. Still. Waiting. Her hand clamped harder around the cup. Her feet didn't move.

"Why are you here?" she asked, her voice small and flat.

He smiled. "I never left."

When Anthony came over that night, the house held itself differently. The walls didn't move, but they felt closer. The couch looked the same, and the kitchen still smelled faintly like burnt toast, but the space between the furniture had shrunk.

Ellie sat on the edge of the bed with Sam in her lap, his warm breath against her chest, the slow rise and fall of his sleeping body grounding her. He slept so much. Ellie was grateful.

Something in the air had drawn taut. The hum she was used to, soft and low, hiding in the walls, had vanished. No tapping. No pulse. Just a stretched silence.

Through the wall, Anthony's voice spilled in too bright. "Hey, look at this. I brought something good," he said, the words riding a laugh. The rustle of paper followed, sharp and crinkling, and her mother's voice came after, small, careful. "Thanks," was all she said, but even that sounded practiced, like something said to keep something else from happening.

As they spoke, the space between their words narrowed. A pause that lasted too long. Chairs shifting on tile. Anthony's voice dropped low, the edges of his sentences scraped together. Ellie couldn't make out all the words, but the shape of them cut through the wall. Something about "always taking" about "not enough." The words blurred, dragged together like his mouth didn't quite know how to move anymore.

Anthony's voice rose loud enough to cut through the walls, fast and slurred with anger.

"You sit around like I'm the problem," he snapped. "You and that bitch of a daughter. Ungrateful, both of you."

Something hit the floor. Maybe a glass. Her mother's voice came next, louder now, but cracking around the edges.

"She's a kid, Anthony," she said, but her voice didn't sound angry. It sounded tired. Thin.

"A kid who looks at me like I'm filth," he said. "She walks around this house like she's the one in charge. I'm done with that. I'm not gonna keep coming back here just to be treated like garbage."

"Then don't," her mother snapped, quick and sharp, like she wanted to mean it. But a beat passed, and her voice changed. Softer. "No, wait. Please. Don't go. Just...just sit down, okay? Let's just talk. I didn't mean..."

Anthony wasn't listening. His footsteps stomped across the kitchen, hard enough that the floorboards gave a dry rasp. Ellie hugged Sam, trying to breathe around the pounding in her chest. He whimpered once, still half-asleep, his face tucked under her chin. The whole house felt like it was leaning sideways.

"I do everything for you," Anthony shouted from the front door. "And this is what I get? Begging and fake tears? I'm not your damn ATM."

"Anthony," her mother called, desperate now. "Please. Don't leave. Just...just come back inside."

The door slammed hard enough to rattle the walls. Then came the thud of his boots down the porch steps. One. Two. Three. Then the roar of an engine and the crackling of tires on gravel.

Ellie kept Sam close and stared at the bedroom door, waiting for it to fly open. For her mother to scream or cry or break something else.

But nothing came. No more shouting from down the hall. No shifting of the porch steps or the sound of the front door opening again. Ellie stayed on the bed, her arms gathered around Sam. She could feel the faint tick of his heartbeat, steady and soft, and tried to match her own breath to his, but every inhale caught in her throat.

Ellie's shoulders stiffened at the sound of footsteps in the hall. She held still, listening as her mother moved past the door. There was a pause, then the soft click of the bedroom across the way opening, followed by the gentle thud of it closing again. For a few moments, everything was quiet.

Her mother's crying drifted through the walls. It was faint, not big noisy sobs with dramatic gasps. This was smaller. Shaky. Like her mother was trying not to let the sounds out at all. It came in uneven breaths, sometimes stretching into silence before returning, soft and cracked around the edges. It filled the space around Ellie.

Ellie didn't move to comfort her mother. She just listened, her face turned toward the door, the soft line of light underneath it still and unchanged. Sam shifted once in her arms and let out a breathy sigh but didn't wake. Ellie drew the blanket closer around them both, her cheek pressing against the top of his head. The crying went on. She didn't try to stop it, didn't cover her ears, didn't go to the door.

When the crying finally faded, the quiet that returned made her stomach hurt. The hallway light flickered once, just a quick flash, then settled again.

She didn't sleep. She kept her eyes open long after the sounds in the house had gone still. Her neck ached from the way she was holding Sam, but she didn't shift. Her back hurt from sitting up too long, but she didn't lie down. She just waited.

Her father didn't come. Not to the corner, not to the crib, not to the space near the door where his shadow sometimes stretched. She didn't hear the low hum in the walls. She didn't feel the pull of air that always told her he was near. He had gone quiet too. It was like he had stepped out of the house the same way Anthony had.

She kept watching the crack beneath the door, but it stayed just light and dust and stillness. Sam slept on, and Ellie kept her eyes open until the first gray light of morning slipped across the floor.

The sirens didn't stop outside the house. They kept going, growing louder as they passed, bright lights bouncing off the living room walls in streaks of blue and red. Ellie had been sitting on the floor with Sam, stacking blocks into a quiet tower, but she stopped when the pitch of the sirens shifted. She stood slowly and walked to the front door where her mother was already standing, arms crossed over her chest.

Together, they watched the police cars and an ambulance rush down the road toward the bend, where the trees grew thick and the power lines ended. Ellie felt her mother's body tense beside her. One hand came up to shield her eyes from the flashing lights, even though the sun was high.

Her mother didn't say anything. She just stepped out onto the porch and started walking, slow at first, then faster. She didn't look back. Ellie followed.

She didn't call for her mother to wait. She didn't ask where they were going. She just kept to the edge of the grass, watching her mother move down the road toward where the cars had stopped, their doors flung open, radios crackling. Sam's cries started behind her in the house, muffled by walls and distance.

When they reached the end of the road, two officers were standing at the edge of the yellow tape. One of them, short and square-shouldered, looked up first. Ellie recognized him. He'd been to their house once, a long time ago—another night with yelling. She couldn't remember his name, only that he hadn't looked anyone in the eye.

"Rachel," he said, lifting a hand. "You need to stay back, alright?"

Her mother didn't stop walking. "That's Anthony's truck. That's his. What happened? What…what happened to him?"

The taller officer moved to block her path. "A neighbor saw the vehicle through the trees early this morning and called it in."

Her mother stepped to the side, trying to see past them. "Is he...was he inside?"

"Yes," the short one said, clearing his throat. "He was still in the driver's seat when we got here."

"In the woods?" she asked, blinking like she couldn't believe the question had to be asked.

"Right at the edge," the tall officer replied, gesturing toward the tire tracks in the grass. "Just past the line there. Looks like he pulled off the road.

She squinted toward the trees, her mouth parting. "Is he dead?"

The two officers exchanged a glance, and one of them spoke softly into his radio. The shorter one hesitated, then nodded once. "Yeah. He's gone."

Her mother took a step closer, her voice rising. "What happened to him?"

There was a pause. Then the tall officer spoke, careful and slow. "We think...something got to him. Maybe an animal. That's all we can say right now."

"What do you mean something got to him?" Her voice cracked. "What kind of animal?"

"We don't know yet," the other officer said quickly.

A paramedic climbed down from the back of the ambulance, talking low to someone just out of sight. Ellie only caught part of it. The word "skinned" came out low and clear.

Her mother staggered slightly, catching herself with one hand against the side of the nearest cruiser. Her knuckles were white as she braced herself. She didn't say anything. She just kept staring toward the trees.

Ellie stayed where she was, pressed behind a car, her small fingers spread against the metal. The gravel beneath her feet felt rough and steady, but everything else had gone soft and strange. The air smelled like pine and exhaust.

That night, the trees pressed closer to the house. Ellie could see them from her window. The branches leaned in, burly and long, the limbs knotted like fists. The porch light flickered once, then steadied, but its glow didn't reach far. What used to be sky between the branches had vanished, filled in by contorted limbs and bark that seemed to pulse.

She sat cross-legged on the bed, Sam nestled into her side, fast asleep with his thumb tucked into his fist. Ellie didn't move, afraid even the shift of a blanket might wake him. The silence was stretched, thin and sharp.

Ellie felt the stillness change. The air and shadows pulled inward. Her eyes moved to the doorway. Her father stood right outside her bedroom, in the narrow hall, lit by only a sliver of light through the door. He stood there, his body taking up the whole frame. His head was tilted to one side, the way a person might lean in to hear better. He was smiling.

"I didn't let him hurt you," he said.

Ellie didn't speak. Her arms gripped Sam.

"He wanted to, but I didn't let him."

He didn't move toward her. He stayed in the doorway, but his presence filled the space between them. The walls seemed to bend around him. He looked taller than he had earlier in the week. His hands hung by his sides, stiff.

Ellie's voice came small, uncertain. "Did you…did you hurt him?"

He smiled wider. "You're safe now."

A QUIET FALLING APART

Ellie stood in the middle of the living room with one shoe dangling from her fingers, the other nowhere. She knelt and peered under the couch, lifting the blanket that always ended up crumpled there. Nothing. She pushed open the hall closet, the door groaning on its hinges. Still nothing. She checked behind the TV stand, under the armchair, and even behind the curtain by the front window where shadows pooled in the afternoons. No shoe. She stood again, turning slow, trying to remember if she'd worn them to school. Or was that yesterday? Or the day before that? It all slid together now. Mornings didn't start so much as happen, sometimes with cereal, sometimes with silence, and sometimes just with the feeling that the dark had backed away enough to let the house move again.

At school, Ellie sat at her desk while the other kids filled in their worksheets with their pencils and quiet hums of thought. She stared down at hers, but the numbers didn't make sense. They floated on the page. Her pencil slipped from her fingers and bounced once before rolling under her chair. She watched it settle near the leg of the desk in front of her. Around her, the classroom buzzed with soft noises, paper crinkling, chairs scooting, someone whispering a joke, but it all felt far away. She folded her hands on top of her worksheet and waited for the noise to make sense.

Her papers started coming back with more red on them. Lines and circles and little question marks left by Mrs. Rieke's pen. Her letters leaned to the side now, like they were trying to slide off the page, and her words didn't always finish. Sometimes she stopped in the middle of a sentence and never came back to it. She forgot where to put periods.

She didn't always write, anyway. Not when she could draw instead. She filled the edges of her papers with pictures, twisting staircases that disappeared into the ground, narrow hallways lined with doors that didn't open. When she drew people, she only drew herself and Sam with full faces. Their eyes were big, but they looked like them. Her mother's face was always turned away or blurred with the side of her hand. Her father's eyes were round and dark, colored in thick with crayons.

It must've been Thursday, or maybe one of the days that felt like Thursday, when Mrs. Rieke asked her to stay in from recess. The other kids were already pushing toward the door, laughing loudly, coats half on, sneakers squeaking against the floor as they raced to the playground. Ellie stayed where she was. Her hands stayed folded, fingers laced, knuckles white.

The scrape of a chair came next, soft and slow. Mrs. Rieke pulled one from a nearby desk and turned it sideways beside Ellie's. Her knees bent awkwardly in the little seat. She tried a smile, warm but careful.

"Ellie," she said, low enough that it didn't bounce off the walls. "Can I ask you something?"

Ellie didn't move. She kept her eyes on the corner of her desk where someone, a long time ago, had scratched a star into the wood. It only had four points. Not five. Not a real star. She traced it lightly with her finger.

"I've noticed your drawings," Mrs. Rieke said after a beat. "They're…I just wanted to ask if everything's okay at home."

The carved star felt deeper today. Or maybe her finger just pressed harder. She didn't speak. Maybe if she waited long enough, the question would get tired and leave.

After a while, Ellie shrugged a little, more with her shoulders than her voice. "Things are fine."

Mrs. Rieke's eyes softened as she continued to watch her.

Ellie added, "Sam sleeps more now."

"I see," Mrs. Rieke said gently. "And your mom?"

Ellie blinked slowly. Her finger stopped tracing. "She's quiet too."

"Has she said anything that made you feel upset or scared?"

Ellie shook her head. "She just stays in her room."

"And you?" Mrs. Rieke asked. "Have you been okay?"

Ellie's mouth tugged a little, not quite a frown. "I forget stuff sometimes."

"Like what?"

"Shoes. Where I put my backpack. What day it is." She looked up then, just a flick of her eyes. "But it's not bad."

Mrs. Rieke gave a small nod, but her face didn't relax. "And your drawings? The stairs and the…hallways?"

"They're just pictures," Ellie said quickly. "I like drawing."

"I know," her teacher said, a small smile pulling at the corners of her lips. "I like them. I just wondered why they feel different now."

Ellie didn't answer. It was quiet again. The kind of quiet that soaked into the fibers of the room.

After a long moment, Ellie's voice came, soft but clear. "My dad's back."

Mrs. Rieke sat up a little. "Your dad?"

Ellie nodded once. "He comes to my room. But only I can see him."

Mrs. Rieke's brow furrowed. Her face stayed mostly still, but her smile fell away. She blinked, slow. Her hand moved slightly, maybe toward Ellie's, but it stopped before it got there.

"And...what does he say, when he comes?"

Ellie looked up. Just for a second. Her eyes weren't watery. They didn't shake. They looked steady, but far away.

"He hums to me sometimes," she said. Her voice didn't rise or fall. "I don't know all the songs, but he does."

Mrs. Rieke stayed very still. She didn't smile anymore.

"He tells me not to be scared." Ellie picked at the edge of her desk, her fingernail working loose a little splinter.

"He takes things sometimes. Not bad things. Just little things. To remember me." Her voice got quieter, almost a whisper. "My drawings. A button from my coat."

Ellie's eyes narrowed as she looked at Mrs. Rieke. "*He* likes my drawings."

Mrs. Rieke opened her mouth like she might say something, but nothing came right away. Her eyes were wide, watching Ellie.

Ellie looked down at her lap. "He says it's so he won't forget. That way, even when he's not there, he still has pieces of me."

The wind pushed against the windows then, a long groaning sound like something dragging its fingers across the glass.

Ellie rubbed the carved star again. "But I don't think he forgets," she said. "I don't think he ever did."

Mrs. Rieke didn't speak right away. She seemed to be choosing her next words with care, letting the quiet stretch just long enough that Ellie almost thought the conversation was over.

"Does he ever tell you to do things?" the teacher asked gently.

Ellie shrugged again, a little one. Her shoulders moved, but the rest of her stayed still.

"He says things," she murmured. "Things that are true."

Mrs. Rieke tilted her head. "Like what?"

Ellie's eyes stayed low. Her fingers found the corner of the desk again, rubbing at the star.

"He says I don't have to let people be mean to me," she said. "Not anymore."

Somewhere down the hall, someone was still laughing. Sneakers still squeaking. The wind tapped once against the window, not hard. Just enough to remind them the outside was still there.

Mrs. Rieke's hand hovered over Ellie's shoulder, then pulled back. "Would you like to join the others? You can still catch some of recess."

Ellie shook her head, slow and quiet.

Mrs. Rieke's eyes found the gap where a button should be on Ellie's coat. "Do you want me to sew a new button here?" she asked, rubbing the fabric between her fingers.

Ellie didn't look at her teacher again, and Mrs. Rieke didn't press. They just sat there in the stillness, the sun dragging long shapes across the tile as the clock above the board ticked forward without hurry.

The last bell rang, and the other kids surged toward the door, voices climbing over each other. Zippers zipped. Chairs scraped back. Someone dropped a pencil. Ellie stayed in her seat, blinking like she'd just woken up. Her legs ached, even though she hadn't run during recess. Her back felt tired. When she finally stood, her limbs were stiff.

She didn't stop as Mrs. Rieke's eyes followed her out of the door.

Outside, the wind picked up around her coat. The trees along the sidewalk creaked, their limbs stretching long and crooked across the sky. The walk home felt longer than usual. The street kept slipping beneath her feet, never quite the same shape from one step to the next. By the time she reached the front door, her socks were damp inside her shoes. Her fingers had gone red from the cold.

The house looked the same, but the light in the windows had a gray tint to it. She let herself in quietly—not because she was sneaking, but because everything in her felt quiet. Her backpack slipped from her shoulder and landed with a soft thump near the door. No one called out hello. No footsteps came to meet her. There was just the hush of the house.

She went to the kitchen and opened the fridge. The light buzzed faintly as it flickered on. She stood there for a long time, staring at the shelves. There was milk near the back maybe. Or juice. She couldn't remember what she was supposed to get. A snack for Sam? Dinner? Her hand hovered near a container of something but didn't close around it. She leaned her head against the door and let the cold spill over her.

From down the hall, a sound reached her, soft and papery and dry. Ellie shut the fridge and stepped quietly across the kitchen, down the narrow hallway, each board under her feet groaning.

She pushed open the bedroom door with slow fingers.

Sam was lying in his crib. One arm was tucked up near his face, but it didn't move. His other hand rested open on the blanket, empty. His eyes were half-lidded, staring at the wall above the crib, not blinking.

"Sam?" Ellie whispered.

He didn't turn his head.

She came closer and reached between the slats to touch his cheek. It was very warm. This was stale warmth, a burning under his skin. He didn't lean into her touch. He just accepted it. His breath came in slow, dry little pulls. The rise and fall of his chest looked practiced and methodical.

He blinked, once, and that was all.

Ellie stayed beside the crib, her fingers resting against his arm. He didn't grab them like he used to. Didn't fuss or coo or smile. He just lay there, quiet and still.

The house made a low noise behind her. A groan in the wall. The press of cold air threading around her knees. Ellie didn't look away from Sam.

Ellie's stomach started to ache. It finally remembered it was empty. She hadn't eaten since lunch. Maybe not even then. She couldn't remember anymore. Sam still hadn't moved, but Ellie knew he'd need something too. Even if he didn't cry. Even if he didn't reach for her. She gently brushed her hand over his blanket once.

The hallway stretched in front of her. She padded softly across the floor, arms folded across her chest. Her mother's bedroom door was cracked just enough to show the edge of the dresser. Inside, something rustled. A drawer opened. A zipper maybe. A shuffle of clothing. Not voices. Just her mother, moving around like a ghost rearranging her own grave.

Ellie had almost reached the kitchen when the phone rang. It sounded far away at first, muffled behind the bedroom door, maybe under a pile of clothes or blankets, but loud enough to snap the stillness in half. She stopped in the middle of the hallway, feet flat on the rough carpet, listening.

The bedroom door opened a few seconds later. Her mother's footsteps came quick and sharp across the floor. Ellie stood there, one hand resting against the wall.

She didn't hear all of it. Just her mother's voice, first low, then louder. Edges sharpening with every word. There were no pauses. No *uh-huhs*. Just her mother talking fast and hard, beating back against the words coming from the other side of the call.

Ellie knew the call ended when her mother went silent. When the barrage into the phone stopped. For a second, there was nothing. No footsteps. No movement. Just silence that made Ellie's ears ring.

The quiet stretched. It filled the hallway, close and insistent, seeping into the corners and pressing against her chest. Ellie held her breath. Her fingers tightened against the wall. The air felt strange. The walls and shadows all leaned in to listen.

Ellie's mother stood in the hallway. One hand clutched the phone, and her back was stiff, shoulders high and tense. The shape of her body had gone rigid, like she was bracing for something. Ellie watched from a few steps back, unsure if she should speak or stay silent.

"What did you say?" Her mother's voice cracked, wild and high. Her body jerked sideways as the phone fell and clattered against the floor. Her other hand reached for the wall. She needed something to hold onto too. "What did you tell them?"

Ellie shrank as her mother stormed down the hallway, her robe dragging across the floor. Ellie pressed her back to the opposite wall and slid down until she was sitting on the floor, legs pulled up, arms around her knees. Her mother's breath hitched, caught, and restarted, louder than before.

Down the hall, the bedroom door swung on its hinges, still open from before. Ellie could just see the edge of Sam's crib in the dim light, and the top of his head. She wondered if the sound hurt his ears the way it hurt hers.

"You...you talked to your teacher?" Her mother's voice cracked again on the word *teacher*. "You told her something about your dad?"

Ellie's mouth opened, but no sound came out.

"You can't just say things like that!" her mother screamed, both hands flying to her head, fingers digging into her hair. "What the hell is wrong with you?"

Her mother's hand hit the wall with a loud, flat slap, the sound bouncing down the hallway. "You think this is funny? You think people won't ask questions? You think they won't come here and take you, take Sam, away?"

Ellie's eyes went wide as she tried to make herself even smaller.

"You're gonna ruin everything! Do you want people thinking we're crazy? Is that what you want?"

"I just said—"

"I don't care what you just said!" her mother snapped, voice jagged, spit at the corner of her mouth. "Do you even understand what you're saying? Do you?"

Her mother stared at her, chest heaving, eyes red and wide. "Sometimes I wonder if you're doing it on purpose. You sit there with that look on your face."

Ellie said nothing. The hallway felt smaller than it had a moment ago.

"You're just like him," her mother said suddenly, her voice low now, and shaking. "You know that? You look just like that worthless piece of shit."

Ellie stayed on the floor, arms tucked in close. Her mother towered over her, chest rising fast as she tried to catch her breath. Her hand clenched at her side, still shaking from where it had hit the wall.

"You think I want to go down there tomorrow?" her mother snapped. "You think I have time to sit in a school office and explain why my daughter's making up stories?"

"It's not made up…" Ellie's voice went unnoticed.

"You know what that teacher's going to think of me now? Of us? You have no idea what it's like trying to make everything work while you're pulling things apart."

Her mother started pacing, three steps down the hall, back again. She couldn't stop even if she wanted to. "I have to meet with her, Ellie. I have to go in and smile and nod and pretend everything's fine while they look at me like I'm the one who's lost it!"

She slammed her fist into the wall again, cracking the thin drywall. Ellie flinched.

"You could've just kept your mouth shut," her mother hissed. "But no. You had to make it about you. Again."

She disappeared into her bedroom. The door slammed with a thud that echoed in the vents.

The hallway stretched quiet and narrow, and her mother's door firmly closed. Ellie didn't want to pass it.

Ellie went back into her room and sat down hard beside the crib. The air in the room had weight. The vent above the dresser let out a soft sigh, enough to remind her it was still there. She stared across the room at the far corner near the closet. It wavered.

The shape of the room gave way. The lines of the walls didn't hold the way they were supposed to. That clean edge where ceiling met wall softened and sagged. The dark in the corner pulled back like a curtain.

It folded and gave way in pieces, allowing something to climb out from behind it. First a shoulder, then an arm. He didn't blink into the room. He poured into it. The light near him didn't flicker, but it lost something. Lost warmth. Lost shape. It faded, a little at a time.

The quiet around her settled across her shoulders and down her spine like a blanket lowering itself over her. Even the hum in the walls had gone still. No tapping. No wind.

The flash of teeth that opened across her father's face was bright in the dark. It slipped ahead of the rest of him, slow and wide, his lips pulled too far back like when someone hooks their fingers into their cheeks and stretches. The teeth that filled the space were packed closely.

Ellie's hand found the edge of the crib. She didn't look at Sam. She could hear him breathing, soft and shallow.

"I used to sing to you."

The words hit like they were trying to form a memory. Like they were trying to be something she'd heard before and forgot until now.

"You were small. You'd fall asleep in my arms, and I'd keep singing even after you would leave for school."

He didn't blink. The smile never dropped.

"You don't remember," he said, head leaning a little closer, just enough that his eyes found hers in the dark. "But you liked it."

Ellie sat still, the crib firm against her spine. Her knees were pulled up close, but she wasn't hiding.

"You're strong," he said. "You'll have to be."

There was no goodbye. He didn't vanish like smoke or like a shadow when the light returns. He simply thinned. Bit by bit, his shape lost its edges, folded itself back into the place where the room didn't hold right, where the lines bent and didn't meet clean. The dark stretched a little longer as he went, reluctant to let go. And when he was gone, the air didn't shift back.

He said he used to sing. She remembered the nights. Crying in her crib, feet cold through her pajamas, waiting for someone who didn't come. She remembered the sound of the door slamming at the end of the hall. The voices never softened.

He never sang.

UNDER THE PILLOW

Ellie sat on a bench outside the office, backpack hugged to her chest. Each time the front door opened, it let in wind that smelled like chalk and the parking lot. She pushed gently on her front tooth with her tongue. It moved. Then she pulled back on it from the front. It moved again. Back and forth as she pushed and pulled with her tongue.

Inside the office, the secretary spoke softly into a phone. The clock on the wall ticked away. Ellie watched the minute hand crawl forward and tried not to count how many times the front doors opened and didn't bring her mother with them.

When Mrs. Rieke finally came out, she knelt beside the bench and gave Ellie a smile that didn't reach her eyes. "She said she was on her way," the teacher said, voice light. "We'll just wait a little longer."

So they waited.

Eventually, the teacher brought Ellie back to the classroom, turned on the overhead lights that buzzed faintly, and gave her a book to look at. Ellie didn't open it. She watched the window instead, the gray outside emboldened as the shadows stretched long across the blacktop.

The classroom door swung open, and her mother stepped in with her hood half-up and sunglasses still on. Her hair was pulled back, messy. One sleeve of her hoodie was wet near the cuff. She didn't greet the teacher. Didn't glance Ellie's way. She just dropped into the plastic chair across the desk and let her bag thump against the floor.

Ellie hovered at her desk until her teacher gave her that soft smile again. "Why don't you wait in the hall for a bit?" Mrs. Rieke said gently. "We'll just talk for a few minutes, okay?"

Ellie nodded, stood, stepped out into the hallway, and slid down the wall until she was sitting, knees pulled to her chest. The classroom door didn't close all the way.

She heard her mother sigh first. Then her voice, flat and tired. "So…what? She's not doing well?"

There was a pause. The teacher said something Ellie couldn't quite hear. Calm. Careful. Something about being worried. About how Ellie seemed different lately.

"Yeah, well." Her mother's voice scratched out again, low. "Her dad took off. Left the damn car parked by the woods like some kind of goodbye note."

Another pause. "Was he with someone?" the teacher asked quietly.

"Probably," her mother said. "Wouldn't have been the first time. Honestly, I don't know. I don't care anymore. I got the car back. That's all I needed."

There was another stretch of quiet before her mother added, "He's not coming back. He's gone. That's it."

Ellie pressed her cheek to her knee and stared at the floor tiles.

"Ellie's been quiet," the teacher said. "More than usual. Is she…does she talk to you at home?"

Her mother let out a dry laugh. "She never talks. She just stares at me like I did something wrong. Like she's waiting for me to mess up."

"I don't think that's what she's doing," the teacher said gently.

"She looks at me like I'm the reason everything's falling apart," her mom snapped. "Like I wanted this."

There was a pause, and then Mrs. Rieke's voice came again, softer. "I know this has been hard on you too."

"She doesn't get that," her mom said. "She acts like she's the only one who's hurting. But she's not. I'm tired. I'm so tired I can barely stand up some days."

"Kids don't always know how to show what they're feeling," her teacher said.

"She knows," her mother whispered. "She knows more than she lets on."

Ellie pushed her tongue gently against her tooth, felt it shift. Not ready to come out yet, but it wouldn't be long.

"She needs help," her mother said with a long sigh. "And I don't know what to give her anymore."

"Listen, Rachel, I'm a mandated reporter; my job is to keep Ellie safe…" Mrs. Rieke's voice trailed off as Ellie's attention shifted.

Ellie's legs had gone numb from sitting so long. The tiles under her felt warm where she had been sitting, but the rest of the air around her was cold. The voices in the classroom kept drifting out, muffled words, sharp breaths.

Ellie stood up slowly, brushing the back of her legs with her hands. She didn't look back at the door. Her shoes were quiet on the tiles as she walked down the empty hallway, past the rows of artwork taped to the walls, past the nurse's office with its light off and door cracked open. The front office was empty now too. Everyone had gone home.

The door at the end of the hallway gave a soft sigh when she leaned into it. The air outside hit her face, sharp and cool. She crossed the blacktop, her eyes on the big wooden castle that sat at the far edge of the playground. She walked, one foot after the other, until her fingers brushed the splintered edge of the lower ramp.

It smelled like damp wood. She climbed up, the boards protesting under her weight, and settled in the upper part where she could see the fence line but not the road. The school building looked smaller from here. Far away.

Ellie sat cross-legged, hands in her lap, and let her tongue press against the aching place in her mouth. Her loose tooth wiggled again, soft and sore. Ellie could see her mother through the classroom window, still deep in conversation.

She didn't hear them coming until they were already close, feet clomping across the mulch, voices bouncing up through the tower.

"There she is," one of them said, laughing. "Told you she was hiding."

"I bet she lives up there now," one of the other girls said, giggling. "Like a little troll."

"Hey, Ellie," Courtney called. "You live here now or something?"

Ellie stayed still.

"Ellie," Courtney called again. "What are you even doing?"

More laughter. Ellie heard one of them whisper, "She's always watching stuff that isn't there."

"Maybe she's talking to ghosts," Courtney said. "Or maybe her dead dad."

"Gross," said the one with the pink clips in her hair. "She probably sleeps in here and eats bugs."

Courtney pulled herself up into the tower, her braid swinging like a rope behind her. Her shoes thunked hard on the wooden planks as she stood. The other two girls stayed below, peering up, their shadows sliding through the slats in the floor.

Courtney stepped closer. "I saw you," she said, grinning. "From my window." Courtney pointed at a yellow house across the street. "You just walked outside like a zombie. Do you even know how weird you are?"

Ellie kept her eyes on her knees.

"What're you doing? Sitting up here like it's your clubhouse?" Courtney crouched low, leaning in like she was telling a secret. "Is your ghost dad up here with you?"

The other girls giggled from below.

"I bet he hides under the floor," one of them said. "He's probably listening right now."

"She probably talks to him at night," Courtney said. "I bet he tells her to do creepy stuff."

Ellie's hands clenched in her lap. Her fingers tightened slowly, her nails digging into the soft skin of her palm.

"She doesn't talk," said the girl in the purple jacket. "My cousin said she can't. That she's crazy."

Courtney wrinkled her nose. "Her mom's crazy too. I saw her once in the gas station, wearing slippers and yelling at everyone."

"Why do you always look like that?" Courtney asked. "Like you're gonna cry or bite someone."

Ellie stood.

Courtney's grin widened, like she'd been waiting for it.

"Aw, are you mad now?" she said, stepping closer.

The wind shifted. Ellie's hair tickled the side of her face. For a second, the trees behind the fence leaned in. And in the space behind her thoughts, something quiet stirred.

You don't have to let people hurt you.

Courtney squinted at her. "What, are you gonna cry now? Are you gonna tell on me?"

Ellie stepped forward and shoved with all of her strength.

Courtney's eyes went wide. Her feet scrambled for the edge, but she missed it. Her arms swung out, grabbing at air, and then she dropped.

The thud was loud as the back of her head cracked against a rock below.

The girls below screamed. One of them ran, yelling for help. Courtney was splayed on the mulch, not moving.

Ellie stood near the edge of the platform and stared down at Courtney's small, folded shape on the mulch below, the rise and fall of her breath barely visible. A low sound started coming from Courtney. A dark patch was growing beneath her head. Blood. It seeped slowly, pooling in uneven rivulets before soaking into the dirt.

Footsteps pounded from the direction of the school doors. Mrs. Rieke was the first to appear, sprinting awkwardly in flats that kicked up bits of gravel. Ellie's mother came right behind her, her hoodie flapping open, her keys still clutched in one hand. Both women skidded to a stop beside the playground.

"Oh my God," Mrs. Rieke said, dropping to her knees beside Courtney. "Courtney? Courtney, can you hear me?" She fumbled in her pocket for her phone and pressed it to her ear with shaking fingers. "Yes. Yes, I need an ambulance. Green Acres Elementary School playground. A child fell from the play structure. She's conscious, but…please hurry."

Courtney let out another groan, sharper this time.

Ellie's mom stood behind Mrs. Rieke, breathing hard, her eyes darting between Courtney and Ellie. "What happened?" she asked, but the words came out flat.

Ellie didn't look at her. She stayed at the edge of the tower; her toes dug into her shoes.

"I don't have to let people hurt me," she said. "I don't have to let them say mean things."

Her mother blinked, like she wasn't sure she'd heard right.

Mrs. Rieke turned her head, her mouth parting, but whatever she was going to say was lost as she returned her attention to Courtney, whose breathing had gone thin and fast. The blood around her head continued to spread, glistening wet in the fading light.

Ellie's mother exhaled slowly and stepped back, her face unreadable. "Get down," she said, her voice quiet now. "Come on. Now."

Ellie took one last look at the spot where Courtney had landed, then backed away from the edge and climbed down the tower ladder.

Mrs. Rieke was still talking to the dispatcher, her voice clipped and shaking. "She's moving her fingers now. There's head trauma. We need someone here fast."

Ellie walked past her mother and didn't look up. She stepped into the grass, into the gravel, onto the sidewalk. Her mother followed a step behind.

"She's suspended," Mrs. Rieke called after them. "Rachel, she can't come back tomorrow. I'll talk to the principal, but for now...just take her home."

Her mother didn't answer. She didn't turn. She walked beside Ellie down the path toward the parking lot, the keys still clutched in her hand, her jaw clenched.

The ambulance siren started somewhere in the distance.

Ellie continued to roll the loose tooth back and forth with her tongue, the ache dull now. When they reached the car, she opened the passenger door herself and climbed in, quiet.

"I didn't want to push her," Ellie said, once the seatbelt clicked into place.

Her mother paused, hand on the door.

"She said mean things about you," Ellie said.

Then her mother laughed, but it wasn't an amused laugh. It was cruel and tired and too loud in the small car. She slammed the door and twisted the key in the ignition. Gravel kicked under the tires as they pulled away from the school.

"You don't get to do that," her mother snapped, her voice cracking through the silence like a slap. "You don't get to use me as your excuse."

Ellie shrank down in the seat, clutching the buckle across her chest.

"Are you kidding me?" Her voice kept rising, bouncing off the windows, hot and fast. "You pushed her! She hit her head! What the hell were you thinking?"

Ellie didn't answer. The words sat in her throat. She looked out the window, counting the trees as they flicked past.

"Oh, but she said mean things," her mother mocked, her tone twisted and sharp. "Poor you. You don't even talk to anyone, and then the second you do, it's to shove a kid off a tower?"

Ellie shook her head, eyes stinging.

"You think the whole world's out to get you. You think you have the right to hurt people?" Her mother's knuckles were white on the steering wheel.

Ellie opened her mouth, but her mother wasn't done.

"I've got enough going on, Ellie. I am trying. Do you get that? I am trying to keep food on the table and lights on in that damn house, and now I've got to deal with this? You getting kicked out of school for acting like a little freak?"

Ellie pressed her forehead to the window, her breath fogging the glass.

When they pulled into the driveway, the car jerked to a stop. Her mother yanked up the emergency brake and turned to her, eyes wide and furious.

"Go to your room. I don't want to look at you right now."

Ellie unbuckled the seatbelt with stiff fingers and got out. She walked up the porch stairs and opened the front door. Inside, the house felt cold again. Still.

She went straight down the hallway, past the darkened living room. The light above her blinked once, then steadied. She closed her bedroom door and sat on the floor, jacket still on, her backpack still sitting in the classroom back at school.

Ellie sat on the floor with her back pressed to the side of her bed. The door swung open. Her mother stepped into the room and didn't even look at her. She walked straight to the crib, lifted Sam with one arm, and turned to go. Her voice came out flat, brittle with exhaustion. "Just stay in here tonight, Ellie. I don't want to hear anything from you." The door clicked shut behind her.

Ellie stayed where she was, the blanket gripped in her hands. She listened to the sound of her mother's footsteps fading down the hall, the soft creak of the floorboards swallowed quickly by the stillness that followed. Somewhere deeper in the house, Sam gave a little fuss, just a whimper, and then quieted.

She stayed hunched in place, waiting. Her ears strained for the sound of the cupboard doors opening, the rattle of dishes, the beep of the microwave, the scrape of a chair pulling out from the table. She imagined the sounds in order, one after the other.

Time stretched thin. Her stomach pinched, slow and hollow, and the ache crawled up into her chest. The room had grown colder, and she drew her knees closer, tucking her hands beneath them to keep them warm. Her tongue found the loose tooth again, working the edge, but the pressure only made her jaw throb.

Outside the window, the last of the daylight faded into a dull gray. Shadows pooled under the furniture, soft and wide. She didn't turn on the lamp. The house stayed quiet. And dinner never came.

Her father stood in the doorway, his body outlined in what little light was left. His frame filled the space, like the door had shaped itself around him. His eyes were bright and sharp, his arms slack at his sides, his shoulders set.

Ellie didn't move. The fear wasn't new. It hadn't rushed in. It had been there already, sitting with her like it always did, a part of the room. Her hands balled into small fists against her legs, nails pressing half-moons into her skin. Her tongue found the loose tooth again, but this time she didn't press on it. She let it sit there, aching gently, something small and sharp she could still control as he stepped into the room.

The air grew close, slow in her lungs. The light didn't touch him the way it touched everything else. It caught on his shoulders and faded, dimmed. Ellie's gaze didn't leave his face. She watched it closely.

He walked farther into the room, the space around him darkening, the shadows moving with him. His feet made no sound on the carpet, and when he stopped, it was beside her, near enough that she could see the lines in his face more clearly, the way they pulled at the corners.

"You pushed the girl," he said.

"She said mean things," Ellie murmured. "About you. About Mom. About me...." Ellie's voice trailed off as her eyes began to sting again. "I didn't want to," she added after a pause, quieter than before. "But she wouldn't stop."

He crouched beside her then, enough that he was no longer towering over her. His face was close; his eyes held hers.

"She would have kept hurting you," he said. "Words can do that. Even when they're small. Especially when they're small."

Ellie blinked slowly. "I didn't mean to hurt her that bad."

"I know," he said. "But sometimes people don't stop unless you make them." His voice was calm.

"She cried," Ellie said. "And there was blood. I saw it on the ground. I heard her hit her head."

He didn't blink. "I told you, people like her don't stop… unless you make them."

"She said nobody liked me."

His eyes narrowed slightly, not angry, but focused.

"She said you were hiding under the floor," Ellie said. "She said you were dead."

A slow smile pulled across his face. "She's wrong," he said.

Ellie looked up at him. Her tooth ached, sharper this time. "Will I get in trouble?" she asked.

He stood again, and the cold in the room rose with him.

"You did what you had to do," he said. "People forget that sometimes."

Ellie took a deep breath. "Mom said you don't care about us," she said quickly.

"She says a lot of things."

Ellie sat up a little straighter, the blanket slipping from her shoulders.

"Can you stay?" Her voice came out quiet, rough around the edges.

"For a while," he said. His voice had settled into something flat again. "I think you have something for me."

Ellie's fingers twitched where they rested in her lap. She didn't understand. Her eyes searched his face for clues, as the light bent strangely around him. She felt a chill move across her skin.

His smile stretched slow and wide, revealing teeth that looked bright white in the dark. His cheeks didn't lift. His eyes didn't crinkle. The smile didn't belong to the rest of his face. It hung there and Ellie's stomach turned.

Her hand moved to her mouth, her fingers pressing into the soft place behind her lip. The tooth sat there, loose and sore. She pressed on it, just a little. The pain bloomed fast and mean. She drew her hand back and looked at the tip of her finger and found blood.

She tried again. This time, she pinched it. The roots held. She pulled harder. Her tooth tore free with a wet pop, quick and sharp, and the pain bloomed through her gum like a spark catching dry grass. Her eyes watered. A metallic taste filled her mouth. She cupped her other hand beneath her chin just in case.

The tooth sat in her palm, small and pale, the root pink and raw at the tip. Her gums throbbed where the blood welled, warm and sticky against her tongue.

"I was gonna put it under my pillow," she said, her hand covering her bleeding mouth. She closed her fingers slightly around the tooth, like she might hide it away again. "The tooth fairy...she's supposed to come if I do that."

His hand lifted, slow and steady, palm open. "There is no tooth fairy."

WHAT IT KNOWS

Yesterday sat in Ellie's chest. The playground. The tower. Courtney's face crumpling in surprise before she disappeared over the edge. The sound when her head hit the rock. The blood that soaked the ground beneath. The other girls had screamed, but Ellie hadn't moved. Not until the adults came running, shouting her name like it belonged to someone else. She remembered Mrs. Rieke's voice crackling into the phone.

She couldn't go back to school. Not now. Not for a while. Maybe not ever. She should have felt relief. No more girls whispering. No more hallways that buzzed. No more worksheets with letters and numbers that wouldn't hold still. But all Ellie could feel was cold.

Ellie padded into the hallway, leaving Sam to sleep, her steps light, careful, the chill biting through even the carpet. She paused outside her mother's door, ear tuned to any movement on the other side. The latch hadn't moved since last night.

The house didn't feel like the same place she'd gone to sleep in. The hallway felt like it had grown overnight, the corners looked deeper, the edges softer and darker.

She walked into the kitchen without flipping the light on. The blinds were half open, and the daylight had already made its way in, pale and cold. The air inside still felt stale. The heater clicked in the walls, but it didn't seem to be doing anything. The floor cracked softly under her weight.

Her father didn't turn when she stepped into the room. He didn't say her name. Didn't nod. Didn't move. He stood there with his back to her, shoulders squared toward the counter, arms resting quiet at his sides. The light from the window stretched into the kitchen but stopped when it reached him.

He wasn't supposed to be here like this. He had been shadows in corners before, reflections that lingered too long, but this was full daylight. He stood in the kitchen, still and whole in the pale morning light, standing at the counter like he'd been there all along.

Her breath caught, shallow in her throat. The cold in the kitchen felt heavier, deeper; it stung her skin and settled beneath it. It crept along her arms under the fabric of her shirt and hung around her knees. Her feet ached where they touched the linoleum.

He hadn't turned. He hadn't moved. But he filled the space anyway. The heater gave a soft, metallic pop, then settled. The hum from the refrigerator crawled out, low and brief, then disappeared. The room stilled. The corners seemed to lean inward just slightly. The ceiling felt lower. Like the whole house was being pulled toward him.

Ellie's fingernails pressed into the seams of her palms. A muscle jumped in her cheek, then went still again. The light stayed flat and weak against the floor, too dull to cast anything that resembled shadow.

"You asked me to stay," he said without facing her.

The words dropped into the space between them with no echo, no breath to carry them, no shift in his posture to mark them as his. His voice didn't sound angry or gentle. It didn't even sound human anymore. It simply existed.

Ellie watched as he crossed to the kitchen table and scraped the chair legs against the floor before easing himself into the seat, his hands folding on the tabletop. He gestured to the chair across from him. The bottoms of her pajama pants brushed her ankles. Something in the way he sat so still and practiced made her skin crawl. She crossed the room in short steps; her sleeves bunched in her fists. Her hot breath showed faint in the light. His didn't.

"You were so little," he said, his voice soft, low enough to sound like memory. "On mornings like this, before there was school, you'd be out in the backyard. Singing, digging, wearing those old pajamas with the ducks on them. I used to sit and watch you play."

Ellie stared at a crack in the tabletop. Her fingers dug into the cuff of her sleeve. The chill in the air had crept into her wrists, and her legs felt small dangling beneath the chair.

"No you didn't," she said after a beat. Her voice didn't lift. It barely made it out. "You stayed on the couch. You always said you were tired."

"I remember watching you," he said again, steady, quiet. "Every morning."

"No," she said, a little sharper now. "You didn't. I used to ask you to come outside. You'd say maybe later."

His hands sat still on the table. The fingers were long and smooth. His smile didn't waver.

"I never missed a morning," he said. "You just don't remember it right."

Ellie's eyes stayed down. "I remember," she said.

A pause stretched between them. The kitchen ticked in tiny sounds, the refrigerator humming, the heater knocking once, the blinds rustling from a draft no window should've let in.

His voice came again, just above the sound of her heartbeat. “That’s not how it happened.”

A lump rose in Ellie’s throat.

“You always needed someone to watch you,” he said. “And I did.”

Ellie looked up and met his eyes.

“I was there,” he said. “Even if you didn’t see me.”

He smiled again, the edges of it too long.

The room held still around them. The light from the window stopped short of his shoulders, dimming there like it wasn’t allowed to go any farther. Ellie’s hands burrowed deeper into her sleeves.

“Why are you saying that?” she asked.

His smile didn’t change. “Because it’s true.”

Ellie’s lips stayed pressed together, and her hands gripped the edge of her chair, fingers clenched tight beneath the hem of her pajama top. The cuffs had stretched, and the faded ducks printed on the fabric seemed to tilt forward as she hunched. The light from the window had faded behind the blinds, soft and gray. It reached the table but didn’t touch his arms. His shadow didn’t stretch. It sat beneath him unwilling to move.

Her gaze drifted to the window, where the trees had pressed closer to the house, their branches crawling forward across the yard. Only thin lines of light slipped through the gaps in the branches. Across from her, he was still watching. Not blinking. Not breathing. His eyes held the shape of her face inside them, tiny and fixed.

“You used to be smaller,” he said. “You used to need me more.”

He stood slowly, the legs of the chair dragging across the floor in a way that made her teeth clench. The light around him didn’t shift. His shape moved without pulling anything with it.

He walked past the table and into the living room, his footsteps making no sound at all.

Ellie stayed in her seat, her hands gripping the edges, her back straight.

He reached the living room and didn't stop. The dim shape of him passed beyond the threshold, where the corners had softened into dark, and as he moved, he faded. His shoulders thinned, his legs vanished first, and then there was only the curve of a head in shadow and the whisper of something no longer present. And then there was nothing.

The chair across from her stayed empty. Ellie's hands stayed gripped around her seat's edges, fingers numb at the knuckles. The cold had settled into her arms. By the time she stood, the light outside had faded to that strange, sour color it got in the middle of the day when the sun never quite broke through the clouds. She wandered through the house slowly, eyes slipping from door frames to corners to the hollow stretch of the hallway. The boards beneath her feet didn't creak anymore. They sighed.

The house felt different as she walked back into her room, her feet soundless against the carpet in the hallway. The door to her mother's bedroom stayed closed, the hollow quiet on the other side pressing outward as she moved past. The cold that had settled into the house dug into her ankles.

Sam was still in his crib, bundled into his blanket, tiny hands resting on his chest. His eyes stared up at nothing, wide and unblinking. She watched him for a long moment, expecting some sound or small gesture, but he only breathed. When she reached into the crib, his body was lighter than she remembered. The blanket smelled faintly of milk and sleep. She held him close as she crossed the threshold, feeling the softness of his cheek against her collarbone and the slow, steady rhythm of his chest. She kept him tucked against her.

By the time she reached the living room, the light had shifted again, become thinner. She laid him gently onto the floor, hands moving slowly as she pulled the blanket from the couch and arranged it around him. His eyes were glassy and round, fixed on some point above him that held his full attention. No hands reached up when she settled beside him. No smile broke across his face. Only the slow flex of his fingers and the rise and fall of his breath. The light from the window barely touched him. She touched his cheek with the back of her hand. It was hot.

"Hey," she whispered, bending close until her cheek brushed his. "You okay?"

Sam's face was warm against her skin, the heat pressing through the softness of his hair and into her. Every breath came quick and shallow, his chest rising and falling in uneven little pulls. His gaze didn't follow her voice. It stayed fixed on the same blank corner above him, his mouth slightly parted, hands fisted weakly against the folds of his blanket.

Ellie shifted onto the floor, drawing in next to him so she could feel the heat coming off his body. She rested one palm lightly over his belly and felt it move under her touch with each short breath. Behind her, a floorboard whined with strain as the house leaned in on itself.

Her mother's door hadn't opened all morning.

In the kitchen, she moved by habit, hands reaching for the formula tin, the bottle, the sink, the microwave as she warmed the bottle. The overhead light buzzed faintly but gave off little light, its yellow glow making the countertops look tired. Sam whimpered once, soft and dry, as she offered him the bottle, his hands trembling. Sam's mouth only opened a little and then he turned away.

Ellie sat on the kitchen floor with Sam in her lap, the bottle untouched beside her. The light above buzzed faintly, casting long shadows across the floor. She tried everything, rocking, singing softly, wetting a cloth and laying it across his forehead. She even whispered nonsense into his ear, words she made up just to hear something other than the quiet that wrapped itself around the walls. Sam didn't fuss. He just blinked slow, his breath rattling in shallow bursts, eyes glassy and distant.

She pressed the nipple of the bottle to his lips again. He turned his head weakly. The formula sloshed inside, still warm from the microwave, but he didn't want it. Her hand dropped, the bottle rolling to the side and thudding softly against a cabinet.

Her arms ached from holding him, but she didn't let go. She sat there until the buzzing overhead turned into a low drone in her ears, until the light seemed like syrup, draping everything in yellow.

She carried Sam back down the hall because she didn't know what else to do. He was so hot now. She wrapped her body around his, her arm settling across his middle, the other cradling the back of his head. His curls were damp with sweat, the shape of his skull sharp beneath her fingers.

Outside, the sun disappeared without warning. The shadows didn't stretch or drift. They took over, covering the windows, pressing against the glass like skin pulled thin. From the far side of the wall came the sound again, thin, dry, a scraping that started slow and dragged long. A single branch, maybe. Or many. Her eyes stayed on Sam. Her hand stayed on his chest. The scratching at the window went on. And on. And on.

HIS VOICE, NOT HIS HANDS

Ellie sat with Sam in her lap, his face pressed to her shirt, his breath hot against her collarbone. The bottle lay on its side beside them, the milk line unmoved. Dust drifted through the room, catching in the corner of her eye. The house felt worn through, edges dulled, corners stretched.

Ellie stroked Sam's back once, then again, slow and even. He didn't stir. The only sign that he was still with her was the faint flutter of breath at her throat.

Ellie watched the hallway from the edge of the bed, her eyes following the shape of the doorframes, the seams in the walls. The house didn't shift anymore. The vents clicked now and then, a tired mechanical sound, but nothing moved past the bedroom. Nothing creaked or sighed or rattled in the kitchen. No faucet dripped. No toilet flushed. Her mother's door never opened.

She imagined dust settling over her mother's body, the shape of her still beneath the blanket, pressed deep into the mattress. Ellie had stood in that hallway more than once, toes pointed toward the door, hand halfway to the knob, and each time, she had turned back before touching it. It felt sealed.

Ellie eased the bedroom door shut behind her. Sam's breathing stayed soft on the other side, a steady rhythm beneath the fever heat. She drifted through the hallway, arms wrapped around her middle. The house held onto the cold. She walked without making a sound, toes gripping against the carpet.

In the living room, the coffee table had shifted a little off its usual square. One of the picture frames tilted the wrong way, its corner resting against the lamp instead of sitting flat. She paused near the wall and stared at it. She didn't remember bumping it. She didn't remember her mother hitting the wall. But the frame had moved.

Ellie stretched her hands up, rising to her tip toes, setting it straight. The glass was cold under her fingers. Dust swirled where she disturbed it, rising into the faint strip of light filtering between the curtains.

She moved through the cleaning motions: straightening a blanket tossed over the arm of the couch, picking up a single sock from the floor and dropping it into the laundry bin, wiping her palm along the table edge to clear it of dust. The movements helped keep her stomach from twisting.

At the back window in the kitchen, she paused. Her eyes flicked toward the fence, half expecting to see something pressed against it. The trees were still behind the fence, but their branches were stretched higher. Not close enough to touch the house. But they leaned, reaching.

At the front door, her hand found the knob almost by habit. It turned without resistance, smooth and quiet, but the door itself barely moved. A narrow sliver opened, just enough to let in a stripe of pale light across the floor. The bottom edge caught against something hidden. There was no scrape, no sound, just a firm, unmoving stop.

Ellie pressed harder. Her shoulder met the wood, and her heels anchored into the rug, but the door refused to give. The gap stayed thin. The air that slipped through was warmer than the house behind her. It moved slowly across her cheek. She leaned closer, squinting through the crack. Her mother's car sat in the gravel driveway, the hood veiled with fallen leaves, its windows clouded from the inside.

She pressed her fingertips to the edge of the doorframe and looked past the car to the road. Nothing moved out there. No neighbors coming or going. No dogs barking. The mail hadn't come.

She stepped back. The door remained ajar by that same inch. She waited to hear her mother's voice, sharp and annoyed. But the hallway behind her gave nothing. Only the hush of a house that was starting to forget how to sound lived in.

Her hand stayed on the knob a moment longer. Not pulling. Just resting. Like maybe, if she waited, the door would open on its own. Let her out. Let them go.

The light faded slow and sour as the afternoon thinned. Ellie moved through the house more carefully now, her steps softer on the carpet. She passed the living room window but didn't look out.

The hallway narrowed behind her as she reached the bedroom door. When she pushed it open, the air that met her felt colder than the rest of the house. The cold settled in layers, starting on the skin and sinking down through the bones. She paused just past the threshold, her fingers clenching on the doorknob. The curtains hadn't been drawn, but the dim light coming in didn't seem to reach the bed. It stopped halfway across the floor and flattened against it. Ellie's eyes adjusted slowly.

Her father sat on the edge of the bed, Sam in his arms. His arms bent at the elbows, but they weren't relaxed. The way he held Sam looked right at first. But when Ellie looked closer, she saw the strain in it. One hand pressed against the back of Sam's neck, the other wedged under his legs, fingers gripping the fabric of his onesie with too much force. Sam's body sagged in the middle, limp as a doll.

He didn't cry. His eyes were wide, round, too glossy. They stared up at the man holding him.

"I was just keeping him warm," her father said. His mouth moved. Just his mouth. The rest of his face stayed slack. No crease in his forehead, no pull in his cheeks. Just the shape of his lips shifting as the words came. His smile stretched across his face, slow and easy. "You were gone a long time."

Ellie stepped in, her arms wrapping around her stomach.

"He's hot," she said. "He needs medicine or…or his bottle."

She didn't blink either, not while she watched his fingers tightening around Sam's leg.

"I can take him," she added. Her voice sounded steadier than she felt. "I know how."

He tilted his head slowly, stretching his neck to the side, his eyes widening slightly.

"You're a good sister," he said. "But you don't need to worry. I've got him."

Ellie took another step forward, eyes still locked on Sam.

"I think I should hold him now," she said again. "You can stay. I just…I need him."

"You don't have to be scared," he said, his lips curling around his teeth. "Not anymore. Not of anything."

"I'm not scared," she said. "But he's mine."

That made something in his face shift. A small pull at the corner of his mouth.

"Is he?" he asked, voice just above a whisper.

Ellie didn't answer. She stepped closer, holding out her arms. Her father's hand moved, brushing through Sam's hair like a motion that was meant to soothe.

"He's fine now," he said. "I've got him."

Ellie's eyes tracked the line of his shoulders, the way the fabric at his collar hung too loose. She looked at the skin near his jaw. It sagged, just slightly, over the edge of his cheekbone. And still, he didn't blink.

"I should take him," she said again. "Please."

His head straightened. The smile stayed in place.

"You don't need to," he said.

The lights in the room buzzed once overhead and held. Her hand stayed at her side. Her feet didn't move. And Sam, still staring, didn't blink either.

Ellie held her arms out, steady but not forceful. Her palms were open, fingers spread, the way her mother had once shown her when Sam was brand new. She remembered that. Not the words, just the shape of her mother's hands under his tiny body.

Now Sam looked heavier somehow, his skin too red, his breathing shallow. His arms twitched.

"I think he's tired," she said, softer now. "I can help."

Her father's fingers flexed against Sam's side, like he wasn't ready to let go. The bed let out a strained whisper beneath him. His eyes stayed on her, clear and flat.

"I've always helped," Ellie added. "You said I was a good sister."

Something about that seemed to please him. His smile stretched again, longer.

He nodded once.

"You don't have to be scared," he said again, and this time it sounded almost kind.

His arms unfolded slowly, almost reluctantly, the way someone might hand over something that still felt like theirs. Sam came away without protest, his body soft against Ellie's chest. The heat of him soaked into her immediately, deep and alarming. She shifted him higher, pressing her cheek to his damp hair.

Ellie lowered herself slowly to the floor, one leg bent, the other folded beneath her. Sam's weight settled against her chest. His forehead pressed to her collarbone, damp and hot. She kept a hand cradled behind his head, the other across his back. Her father didn't move from the edge of the bed. His knees stayed bent, hands folded over each other, fingers pressing lightly together.

"You used to sit out in the backyard," he said. "Right where the grass thinned near the fence. You'd pull all the clovers out of the dirt and make piles and whisper to them like they could hear you." Ellie winced at the word Clover, the bundle buried under the cold earth flashing in her mind.

Ellie kept her arms around Sam, her eyes on the carpet instead of him. Her fingers stroked lightly over the soft back of his onesie. "You never came outside," she said, keeping her voice low and steady. "You stayed on the couch. I remember asking."

"That's not how I remember it."

"You weren't there," Ellie whispered.

He turned his head, not blinking. "I was. Every time."

"I would've seen you."

He leaned forward a little, elbows to his knees, chin resting in one hand. "You're not supposed to remember it like that."

Ellie pulled Sam closer, feeling the weight of his fevered body tucked against her chest. Her breath caught, but she didn't look away. "I do."

He watched her, the edges of his smile still hanging there, waiting to be believed.

They stayed there like that, the three of them. Sam between them, the dark drawing its line across the room inch by inch. The window glass had started to frost. Outside, something tapped once, then stilled.

The smile lingered a moment longer, then fell. He sat back slowly, the mattress barely dipping under his weight. One hand dropped to the blanket, fingers brushing the corner. He didn't look at Ellie when he spoke again.

"You've done a good job," he said at last, voice low and smooth, his fingers tracing the blanket. "Keeping him warm. Keeping him safe."

Her fingers moved along the curve of Sam's back, slow and careful. The heat rolling off him hadn't faded.

"He's tired," her father said. "A body that small shouldn't have to hold so much."

Her stomach twisted. She looked down at Sam, his lashes resting soft against his cheeks, his skin damp near the hairline. Her thumb brushed his temple.

"You must be tired too."

She nodded before thinking. "A little."

The creature's gaze softened, his voice slipping into something closer to a lullaby. "You've carried him long enough."

Ellie blinked. Her arms ached. Her back had started to tense when she leaned.

"Let me help you," he said.

She shifted Sam again, almost lifting him.

"I think..." she started, her throat catching halfway. "I think I should get Mom. She'll know what to do."

The air pressed harder against the walls.

"You don't need her," he whispered. "You don't need anyone else."

Ellie looked up, and his face was closer now. Still. His eyes lingered on her.

"You're safe here," he said. "With me. You always were."

Her jaw moved, but no sound came. Sam stirred, his small hands flexing once in his sleep before drawing in again.

"I just want to lie down," she said, voice thin as paper.

His smile stayed. "Of course."

He rose from the edge of the bed without effort or sound, the mattress barely shifting as he pushed up. The space he left behind held his shadow for a breath longer than it should have, then smoothed back out. He stood at the bedside, watching, his figure pale and long in the fading light.

Ellie stood, slow and careful so she wouldn't jostle Sam too much. The sheets were cool against her knees as she crawled in, turning her body sideways to make room for him against her chest. She eased down onto the mattress inch by inch, cradling his weight as she went, until her head sank into the pillow and her arm wrapped protectively around him. The warmth of his fevered skin bled into her. The blanket came last, drawn up to her chin with a soft drag, closing them in together. Her arm wrapped around the curve of Sam's belly, and she felt the heat of him pulse steady against her.

The mattress dipped behind her again, but only slightly, just enough to know her father had come back. He didn't press close. Just settled into the space at her back, folded into the shape she'd left behind. The air around them cooled.

He wrapped himself around them both. The room grew quieter. Her eyes drifted closed, lashes brushing her cheek. Sam's chest moved beneath her palm, soft and rhythmic.

"You don't have to worry anymore," her father said, his breath touching the back of her neck. The words folded, warm and coaxing, barely more than a vibration behind her ear. "I can help you."

Ellie's lips parted. She meant to answer. She meant to tell him no or maybe ask what he meant. But the weight of sleep settled into her limbs, and her voice slipped before she could catch it.

"Okay," she breathed.

OPEN DOOR

Ellie jerked awake with a sound caught in her throat, her hand flinging out across the mattress before her eyes even opened. The sheets were cool under her palm. Her fingers searched blindly, digging through folds of blanket, sweeping across the bed where Sam should have been. The space beside her was flat. She sat up fast, heart thudding against her ribs, hair clinging to the back of her neck with sweat.

"Sam?" Her voice cracked on the name.

She pushed the blankets off in one motion and scrambled to the edge of the bed, knees slipping against the sheets. Her eyes darted to the shadows in the corners, to the carpet on the floor, to the soft dent where he'd slept. Empty. She dangled her head over the edge of the bed, peering underneath, as if he'd simply rolled off and rolled under.

The bedroom door stood wide.

She slid off the mattress quickly, the frame creaking behind her. Her heel struck the floor hard, a sharp jolt rising up through her ankle and into her calf. She crossed the room in a blur of bare feet and cold air, one hand dragging across the wall to catch herself. Her breath hitched partway up her chest.

The hallway met her; the shadows there were deep, pooling near the corners, smeared up the walls. The overhead fixture flicked once and gave up, leaving only the half-open front door at the end of the hall to glow. It stood there, perfectly still, cracked open wide enough to see the pale light bleeding in from outside.

Ellie's toes bunched against the carpet. The space beyond the door held a strange stillness. The yard looked flat and colorless in the early light, its edges soft where the grass met gravel. The sky felt stalled above, hazed over with low clouds.

Her heart pushed harder behind her ribs, steady but clumsy. The quiet outside pressed into the hallway, slipping past the threshold and settling across her skin. She felt it in her throat first, then her chest, that prickling awareness that something had shifted when she wasn't looking. She took a step, then another, the carpet brushing her soles in short, dry lines. Her fingers grazed the wall as she passed.

Ellie stepped into the yard barefoot, the small stones biting up into the soles of her feet. The cold came sharp up her legs, numbing her skin in patches.

"Sam?" Her voice came out hoarse. She swallowed and tried again. "Sam!"

She crossed the porch and dropped to her knees in the damp grass, peering beneath the steps, behind the shrubs where the morning frost still clung in the shade. She crawled further under the porch skirting, ducking her head to look deeper into the dark gap beneath it, heart hammering. The ground there was bare and still.

She stood again, wiping her palms on her pajama pants without looking down. The driveway stretched to one side, the gravel wet with dew and marked only by old tire lines. She ran to the edge of it, scanning both directions down the street, her breath slipping out in clouds. No figures on the sidewalk. No passing cars. Just the quiet sprawl of yards and closed windows and drawn curtains.

Ellie took a few more steps along the front walk, "Sam! Sam, where are you?" Her voice cracked at the end. No curtains twitched. No doors opened. Only the wind, moving soft along the edge of the street, stirred the grass at her feet.

She turned in a slow circle, eyes darting from bush to bush, yard to yard, her breath speeding up with every heartbeat. The street lay blank and wide, her footprints the only marks in the frost.

"Sam!" she called, louder this time.

She ran to the edge of the yard, the thin line of gravel bleeding into the tall weeds near the back fence. Her breath came in sharp bursts now, mouth open, eyes scanning for any shape, any small movement. She checked behind the trash bins. She circled twice, three times, her hands stinging from where they caught on rough wood and thorned vines.

Ellie turned back toward the house, bare feet slipping against the cold edge of the porch step as she stumbled up. The open front door yawned ahead of her, the light from outside pooling in the hall beyond. She pushed through it fast, breath catching in her chest, and turned down the hallway. Her mother's door was still closed.

Ellie shoved it open, the handle slamming against the wall as she crossed the threshold. The room smelled flat and stale: old air, unwashed fabric, something sour and lingering that clung to the walls. Her mother lay folded on her side beneath a tangled heap of blankets, face turned away, hair matted against her cheek.

"Mama," Ellie gasped, already at the edge of the bed, her hands reaching. "Mama, wake up...he took him, I can't find him...please get up...."

She grabbed her mother's shoulder and shook it hard, her small fingers digging in through the fabric of her shirt. The body beneath the blanket gave a sluggish twitch, a groan slipping out.

"Mmmn't now," her mother mumbled, the words muffled, barely there. "Just…lemme sleep, baby."

"No…Mama…he's gone," Ellie cried. "Sam. I can't find him. He's gone."

She yanked the blanket back hard, the covers sliding down to reveal her mother's arm, pale and slack, her wrist bent at an awkward angle, her fingers drew inward toward her palm. Her mother squinted up at her, eyes glassy.

"What're you yelling for?" she slurred, her voice slow and dragging. "What time is it?"

Ellie's heart was thudding. "He's gone. He took Sam. I looked…I looked everywhere."

Her mother blinked once, slow. "He's…he's in his crib. Just check his crib, Ellie. You're just…just tired. Go lay back down."

"He's not in the crib, Mama!" Ellie said, louder now. "He's gone. Please! Please come help me…."

But her mother only groaned and turned her face toward the wall, one arm dragging the blanket back up to her shoulder.

Ellie moved across the hallway, one hand brushing the wall to steady herself. Her fingers felt stiff, the cold from outside still clinging to her skin. She turned into her bedroom without turning on the light. The shadows were long now, bending over the corners of the furniture. The bed still held the impression where she had laid, where Sam had been.

She crossed to the dresser and crouched, pulling the bottom drawer open with a dull scrape. Her jeans were crumpled in the back corner. She yanked them out, the denim stiff and cold, and sat on the edge of the bed to shove her legs through. The fabric tugged against her knees and clung to her calves. Her coat was balled near the corner of the bed frame. She grabbed it and forced her arms through the sleeves.

She left her room fast. The hallway seemed to stretch longer in front of her, her shoulders tensed as she ran forward. At the front door, she crouched again and grabbed her sneakers. She stepped into them without untying the laces, heels crunching down into place. Outside, the wind moved thin across the porch. The neighbors weren't far. She would run. She'd tell them. Someone would answer. She'd go knock and tell them. *He took Sam, please, please help me.*

Her fingers closed around the doorknob, the metal cold under her grip. It turned easy, but the door didn't move. A harder twist strained her wrist. Still nothing. She braced and yanked, feet sliding on the floor, but the latch held fast.

She bolted to the back door, yanking the handle. The glass refused to slide. Her palms slammed against it, echoing once through the quiet. Breath fogged the pane. Outside, the yard sat unchanged. The trees bent forward slightly, one branch crooked over the fence. The wind wasn't blowing. Nothing moved out there.

Ellie tried the front windows next, fingers scrambling for latches. Each one stayed sealed. She hurried down the hall to her room. Condensation blurred the glass, but when she turned the latch it gave with a scrape, but the window held, stubborn as stone. Her palms slipped against the cold surface, leaving damp streaks on the glass that faded almost at once.

She hurried down the hall, brushing the door frame with one shoulder as she turned into the room. The window was rimmed with condensation, its surface clouded and cool beneath her fingertips. Moisture clung in thin lines along the edge of the glass, blurring the shape of the fence beyond.

Her fingers found the latch. It sat familiar in her grip, smooth from use. She turned it slowly, expecting resistance, but it gave with a low scrape, metal shifting against metal as the lock pulled free. The breath she didn't know she was holding slipped out. She pressed both hands to the glass and pushed. The window held.

Her thoughts drifted to the bathroom. She thought of Clover. The kitten in the tub, water-slick and limp. The same pull gripped her now as she reached for the bathroom door. The knob was icy under her palm. It turned. She flicked on the light and stepped in slowly, one foot then the other. The overhead light buzzed faintly, catching the edges of the mirror and bouncing pale against the ceiling. The tub sat bone-dry now, the surface smooth and dull.

The walls pulled close as she slipped from the bathroom and moved back toward her room. Each board beneath her feet groaned in quiet protest. Her hand brushed the edge of the doorway as she entered. The corners were darker now, edges blurred by the dull stretch of afternoon light bleeding through the curtains. Her bed waited where she'd left it, the blanket still tangled and half-fallen to the floor.

She stepped over it, knees aching as she sank into the mattress. Her legs folded stiffly, the muscles in her back drawing taut with the motion. The blanket came with her, dragged up with absent fingers, and she pulled it over her chest before smoothing the fabric flat again and again, until the shape of it settled.

"I didn't mean it." The words vanished into the stillness.

Her eyes drifted to the doorway, half-expecting to see him standing there. But the frame was empty. No long shadow waiting. No smile that stretched across his face. The room was still.

The blanket around her legs felt heavier, pressing down, rooting her to the bed. Knees drawn up and arms empty, she stared into the far corner where the shadows stacked, quiet and close. The stillness wasn't waiting. It had already settled, sure of itself.

His voice came back to her, soft and careful, but wrong. It had never been his laugh, his touch, his smile. She had always known. It wasn't him.

The ache in her arms deepened. The space where Sam should have been was still empty, growing colder. Her breath stuck halfway in her chest.

He hadn't come back, because he couldn't.

The light flickered once, hard and final, then went dark. The heater gave a hollow tick. The refrigerator's hum cut mid-breath. Outside, the sky pressed in, colorless and flat, the dark sliding deeper against the glass. Air shifted around her ankles.

Her breath shuddered out. She loosened her grip on the blanket and let it fall across her legs. Her feet touched the floor. Her shoes were still on. The room was drained of sound.

Beyond the window, the last strip of sun slipped behind the treetops. Shadows climbed the walls, stretched across the floor, into the hallway, into the bedroom. Before the light could even fully slip away, the dark had already taken its place.

THE PATH SHE FOLLOWS

"Mama," Ellie said, soft at first. Then again, louder. "Mama!"

No response. She moved closer, each step making the floor groan a little under her weight. She reached the edge of the bed and touched her mother's shoulder, giving it a small shake. The warmth of her body was still there, but no tension.

"Mama, you need to get up. Please." She shook harder this time. "He took Sam."

Still nothing. No flicker of an eyelid. No sigh of waking. Her mother's skin felt strangely hot where it met the air, and Ellie let go, her hand falling to her side.

"Please," she whispered. "Just wake up."

She stood there for another moment, watching her mother breathe, waiting for something to change. A shift. A groan. A word. But the figure in the bed didn't stir. It didn't turn. It didn't reach. Whatever sleep her mother had sunk into was deep and unyielding. Ellie backed out of the room without another word, pulling the door closed behind her, the latch catching in the quiet with a soft click. She stood there for a moment, coat still clinging to her shoulders, her breath catching at the top of her throat. Back in her room, the air was cold but familiar. She stepped across the floor slowly, her shoes dragging against the carpet. She sat on the edge of her bed, her fingers twisted together in her lap. Her eyes fixed on the window.

Her thoughts ran in a slow circle, a path worn down in her mind. Anthony had been found in the woods; she remembered the way the officer's mouth had twisted when he said it. Just at the edge of the tree line. Her father's car too, abandoned and cold, no one inside, no one waiting to be found. And now Sam. Gone without a sound.

Her hands were clenched in her lap. The thought of that place in the woods pulled at her like gravity. She had never gone in very far. Just to the edge. Just past where the fence ended. Only as far as she'd needed to go to find Clover. But now she could see the line clearly in her mind, the place where the grass gave up and the trees took over.

That was where Sam had to be.

The words settled first in her chest. She repeated the thought inside her head, letting it echo. That's where he had to be. The woods. It's where everything seemed to be.

No one else was coming. No knock at the door. No crackling voices on the radio. No grown-ups with flashlights and clipboards. The neighbors were just windows now, lit or dark, with no faces behind the glass. The world had pulled back, peeled itself away from the edge of their yard, and left them alone. Her mother wouldn't come. That door stayed shut now, as much a wall as anything else in the house.

Ellie sat very still on the bed, her coat buttoned all the way up to her chin. She only looked at her shoes. At the floor. At the place where Sam had last been. Her arms still felt the weight of him even though he was gone. Her palms remembered the fever of his skin.

Ellie exhaled slowly, then moved to the window and looked out again. The trees were waiting. Still and certain in the dark. Their limbs hung low and sagging. The space between the porch and the first row of trunks looked longer than it had in the light. She watched the patch of ground that divided them, her fingers pressed flat to the sill. Something tugged behind her ribs. Ellie pressed her forehead to the cool window glass, breath fogging a small circle in front of her mouth.

She had to go.

The words circled again, soft but sure.

Her eyes swept the room. The door wouldn't open. The front wouldn't budge. The back had sealed itself. Every window she touched had fought her hands. She stared down at her shoes and thought of the path waiting on the other side of the fence.

How was she supposed to get out? She turned back to the window. The latch sat open.

As the thought settled, the room seemed to shift. A low hiss whispered through the sill, steady and quiet. She leaned closer and the air whispered against her face. Her hands found the underside of the frame. She pressed upward, slow and careful. This time, the window moved. It lifted an inch. Then more.

Ellie turned to the other side of the room, grabbed the step ladder with both hands, and dragged it across the floor. It bumped once against the crib. She climbed up, knees stiff beneath her, and pushed the window higher until it hung open wide enough to let her through. The night air fully met her face, cool and damp, full of the scent of dirt and bark. She climbed through. One knee, then the other.

Ellie lowered herself slowly onto the porch, her shoes hitting the wooden slats with a soft, hollow sound. The house stayed quiet behind her, the window yawning open. The air outside pressed cold against her cheeks.

She moved across the back porch, her eyes scanning the space between where she stood and where the grass began. The light from the window barely reached that far. Something small caught her eye, barely visible in the dark. A single button sat right at the edge of the porch, right where the step dipped low. Dark, plastic, scratched at the edges. She bent down and picked it up.

Her fingers brushed her coat front, moving along the seam where the fabric crossed her chest. She felt the empty space, the missing thread still dangling loose from the hole. She turned the button over in her palm, then wrapped her fingers around it and stood. The trees waited. Still. Watching.

Ellie's eyes lifted toward the fence line. Dangling from a low branch, just above the chain link panels, where the fence leaned back from the weight of time, hung one of her socks. It was tied in a loose knot around the branch, the cuff limp, swinging slightly through the air.

She stepped to the fence, her fingers coiling through the cold wire. The metal chilled her skin instantly. She wedged one shoe into the open diamond of the fence, then the next. She climbed fast. Near the top, her coat caught. The seam at her hip jerked and held. She pulled harder, twisting her body sideways. The fabric ripped. The fence gave way behind her with a final clatter; the sound swallowed fast by the trees. Ellie dropped into a crouch on the other side, her hands pressing into the cold earth to keep her balance. The ground felt loose. It was damp, soaking through the knees of her jeans as she landed.

With each step, her shoes sank into the ground, moss and leaves giving under her heels. Above, the branches drew closer, their limbs folding toward each other, arching into long, narrow curves.

As she walked, her eyes adjusted to the dark. There was no moon, but the dim shape of things became clearer with each cautious step. The air had changed the moment she passed the fence. It pressed against her skin, clinging in her clothes and in her chest. Her breath came out ragged, loud enough that it made her pause, listening again, checking the trees for movement. But they didn't sway, they just leaned forward.

The ground sloped gently in places, but Ellie's attention was pulled to the shapes. A comb near the base of a tree, half-buried in damp leaves, its broken plastic teeth dulled with dirt. The mermaid was still visible in the handle, her glitter dulled but present. Ellie tucked it into her pocket.

She walked slower, eyes darting from trunk to root to shadow. There, pressed against a wide patch of bark, something else. One of her drawings, rippled now, its lines blurred with moisture. The sun had a crooked smile. She didn't remember giving this one to her father. She didn't remember anyone saving it.

Farther on, another thing. A barrette. One from a set of three, shaped like flowers. It sat wedged in a split in the bark; its faded yellow petals tilting sideways. Her footsteps sank deeper now. The soil clung to the soles of her shoes. hunched not from cold but from how close the trees had grown. The path continued, narrowing.

Ellie stepped over a root that arched like a question across the narrow path. The full moon loomed overhead. Her fingers brushed the rough bark of a tree to steady herself. The trunk felt damp and colder than the air. The trail continued to curve, gentle and long, leading her deeper.

Another shape caught her eye up ahead. It hung from a low branch, swaying slightly though nothing else moved. A bracelet. Plastic beads, threaded unevenly. She remembered making it when she was smaller. The string had snapped, and she had cried over it. Now it swung quietly in the hush between the trees. She passed beneath it, her shoulders brushing a branch that left something wet along her collar.

Each step tugged her farther from the edge of the world she knew. The sky was replaced with the weave of branches above. They had knitted themselves into a ceiling, moonlight fighting through the gaps, and beneath it, the forest breathed slow.

Ahead, the path began to dip. The trail of lost things narrowed too. Fewer now. A button here. A clip of hair once tucked into a baby book there.

The trees finally broke open. The clearing wasn't wide, just enough space for one massive tree to spread its limbs outward, the ends gnarled and low. Its trunk was split in two at the base, like something had forced it apart from the inside. Moss clung to the lower half, and the bark puckered where rain had once carved slow lines into its face. Beneath it, sunk into where the roots folded back from the earth, was a hollow.

Ellie froze at the edge of the clearing. Her legs didn't want to move anymore. The shape of the hollow was exactly as she remembered from the picture she'd drawn in school, the one that had scared Mrs. Rieke. A black space cradled in the crook of a tree, wide enough for something to crawl into or out of.

Bones littered the dirt, some snapped clean through, others still smeared with something that hadn't dried. Scraps of flesh clung to one caught on the edge of a root. A plastic hair clip sat among them, teeth cracked. Just beyond it, the corner of a T-shirt poked from the soil, pink, faded, child-sized.

Ellie's stomach folded inward. Her mouth filled with something sour, but she swallowed it down, pressing her sleeve to her nose. The cold here had turned dense, full of things that had once breathed but didn't anymore. Her fingers tightened around the hem of her coat as she forced herself to take one step forward. Then another.

Ellie tried to step carefully over the bones, but they crunched beneath her feet. Tiny rib cages scattered like dried leaves and spines strung like broken necklaces. Others sat scattered and pale, picked clean by time or something worse. The air no longer smelled only of wet earth but also of rot. A scent that made the back of her tongue taste like pennies. She stopped when she reached the base of the tree. It stretched open, wide and ready, a wound in the wood.

Something shifted inside. The sound reached her before the shape did, low and quiet. A tune broken at the edges, familiar only in pieces. She stepped closer, her body rigid. The hollow exhaled. And there, inside it, hunched within the curve of the trunk, was her father. Or what still looked like him.

He crouched in the shadows, knees wide, arms cradling Sam with the loose delicacy of someone holding something already broken. Sam didn't cry. Didn't squirm. His head lolled softly to the side, one hand rested near his chest.

Behind him, tacked and wedged into the rough bark of the hollow, were her drawings. Dozens. Maybe more. Some she knew she'd made. Others she wasn't sure. The paper had gone soft, edges warping in the damp, color bleeding down the grain. Shapes of trees. A figure at the window. Sam's crib. Skies and suns and flowers. All stuck there like they were propping the tree up. The tune stopped, a breath held. The figure looked up and smiled.

The figure that turned toward her was still wearing her father's skin, but the flesh had started to pull, to stretch, to lose its grip on the thing beneath. It sagged under the eyes, loose and wet, the jaw shifting oddly beneath slackened cheeks. At the corners of the mouth, the skin had split open in fine, weeping cracks. A seam had begun to part along the left cheek, where something larger and darker bled through. When he smiled, the smile didn't lift. It tore. Slowly, with the sound of something peeling.

His hands shifted under Sam. The flesh had ruptured across the knuckles, the tips of the fingers pushed long and sharp, bones piercing through like claws, the skin bunching around them. They wrapped around Sam. The grip was possessive.

The rot had taken his shoulders too. Where the coat had once draped, it now slouched, the fabric torn open to show soft, blackened folds underneath. Ellie could taste the rot.

Sam's chest moved. A slow, rhythmic rise and fall, shallow but there. His mouth hung open, and his hands twitched in sleep. His hair was damp, pressed to his skin. His weight sagged against the creature's crooked arms.

Ellie's breath caught in her chest. Everything in her leaned forward, mind, body, bone, drawn to the shape of her brother alive and close and almost touchable. The thing in the tree tilted its head, the loose skin folding at the neck, wearing the ruin of her father's face like a costume it no longer needed to fit.

The creature shifted its weight slightly within the hollow, the bones of its hands adjusting beneath Sam's blanket with a whisper of cracking joints. Its face turned fully toward Ellie now, and though its smile never changed, the voice that followed was soft.

"I was sleeping," it said. "Deep. For quite a long time."

The eyes watched her without blinking.

"I didn't know you. Not yet. Not until the crying started."

The creature went on. "You cried in the dark. Under blankets. Into your pillow. You cried so quietly, they didn't hear. But I did. That kind of sadness…it doesn't go unnoticed."

Ellie's hands squeezed shut at her sides, fingers stiff in the cold.

"You were the first voice in a long time that reached this deep. It wasn't a scream. It wasn't a prayer. It was grief. It tasted sweet on the wind."

Sam exhaled, soft and uneven. Ellie took one step forward.

"I didn't take him to hurt you," the creature said. "I took him so you would follow."

Its head shifted again, that loose remnant of her father's face dragging behind the movement. One eye drooped slightly. The other locked on Ellie without blinking.

"You said yes," it continued. "You gave him to me."

Ellie's breath caught. Her lips parted, but her voice didn't work.

"You whispered it," it said, softer now. "You were so tired. So alone."

Its head tilted, the ruined face drooping as the creature studied her. "They made you sad," it said, voice low, almost gentle. "She forgot you. He left you. And still you cried for them. Every night, you cried." The jaw shifted too far as it spoke, the tear in its cheek widening with the movement. "But he left first, didn't he?"

Ellie's fingers twitched at her sides. Her arms wrapped closer around herself. "Daddy…" she said, the words brittle. "What… what did you do to him?"

The creature leaned forward. The thing inside the face, the shape that squatted behind that sloughing skin, stirred again. It lowered its gaze to the child in its arms, then looked back at her. "You had such love for this face," it said. "Even when he didn't deserve it. Even when he turned his back on you, even when he left." Its fingers moved lightly over Sam's back, its exposed bone glinting in the dark. "I thought it would make you happy."

"You're not him."

"No," it agreed. "But you never would have wanted to look at the other face. The one under this, you would have run away." It leaned closer to the edge of the hollow, its bulk filling the frame of the opening. "And the other skin I took was wrong. The other man scared you. His smile. His hands. You never wanted him near. Even when this face began to fail, I could not wear his. He would have only driven you away."

Its hand rose to the decaying flesh across its skull. "This one kept you close to me."

Its head bent again, the sagging face twisting unnaturally as it glanced at Sam. "And this one," it said slowly, "this one I cannot wear. Not yet." A pause stretched. "Still too small."

"No," Ellie's voice cracked as it left her, sharp in the hush between them. "Give him to me."

The creature didn't flinch. Its long fingers adjusted slightly beneath Sam's weight, gripping tighter. The exposed bone where the skin had peeled back gleamed damp and pale in the shadows of the hollow.

"He's not yours," Ellie said again, louder now, her feet shifting closer across the soft, wet ground. "You don't get to keep him."

The creature tilted its too-loose face. One ruined eye narrowed, the other gazed at her, glassy and round.

"I kept him safe," it murmured. "I held him close. I rocked him. I was gentle."

"Give him to me," Ellie said, again. Her voice was stronger this time. She took another step forward.

The creature's hands didn't move.

"You tricked me. That's not the same." Her arms lifted slightly, ready to receive her little brother. "So now I want him back."

Sam shifted faintly, a tiny sound escaping his throat, his lashes fluttering once against his cheek. Ellie's breath caught. She reached forward for him.

"Please," she whispered.

The creature stood, its limbs bent at sharp, unnatural angles, the bones that jutted through its fingers. The skin across its face had sagged farther. A fresh split opened along the edge of its jaw. Ellie stepped closer. Her hands remained raised, ready to take Sam. "You said you didn't want to hurt me. Then give him to me."

The creature tilted its head, and this time the gesture came with a sound, a quiet crack, like something splintering deep inside.

"I can give him back," the creature said again, voice steady, almost soft.

Ellie blinked. Her arms trembled. "Then give him to me."

The creature's gaze didn't leave hers. Its smile had slackened, one side of its mouth tugging low where the cheek had torn.

"But things taken have to be traded," it said. The sound came out brittle, catching in the folds of skin where its throat should have been. The arms holding Sam shifted again, a stuttering movement. Sam's head tilted, his mouth slack, breath fogging faintly beneath his nose.

Ellie's shoes sank under her weight half an inch deeper into the unsettled earth. Her fingers pulled in toward her palms.

The creature's arms trembled beneath the small weight. The flesh of its elbow cracked slightly as it bent, and the voice that came out was quieter now.

"He can go. He will grow." Its head turned from Sam back to Ellie. "He will forget." The smile that came didn't reach anything but the corners of its mouth. "But you won't."

The silence pressed in around them, thick with rot and roots.

"You were crying," the creature murmured, gaze drifting toward her chest like it could hear her heart. "At night. In the dark. You wished someone would stay." Its chin dipped with the loose roll of skin sliding across a shape underneath. "So I did."

Its eyes shifted again to Sam. The skin around its fingers looked hollow now, like the bones had grown too long inside. "I kept him warm," it said. "I was gentle."

Ellie's arms twitched.

Her gaze stayed on Sam. He hadn't woken. Hadn't stirred. But he was breathing. He was still here.

"He can go home," the creature said, arms shifting once more, ready. "But you *are* home." Its shoulders hunched again, spine bowing like a branch under snow. "You already know that."

Her feet stayed planted in the soft, damp earth, the edges of the hollow yawning just inches behind her. She could now hear Sam's breath, shallow and soft, each exhale cutting through the silence like thread. The creature held him with arms that shook now, its joints bowing under the baby's weight. Its head tilted, her father's borrowed face sagging in uneven folds, the edges buckling as the mask continued to collapse.

"You've already come this far," it said, voice wet at the edges. "Just a little more."

Ellie nodded. She took one step forward, then another. The ground dipped beneath her feet, soft and giving. The curve of the hollow surrounded her now, the air denser inside, fouled with the smell of damp rot. She kept her eyes on Sam, not the walls, not the roots twisted like ribs around the inside of the tree. Just his little face half-shadowed in the crook of that thing's arm.

The creature leaned toward her, its arms unfolding to present Sam like an offering, but it didn't let go. Its face lowered with him, close to her own. The skin twitched where it hung loose, strings of something dark and wet trailing from the cracked corners of its mouth. It brought its face inches from hers. The eye that still worked held her steady, wide and waiting.

Ellie reached forward slowly, like she was ready. Her hand moved to Sam's side, her fingers brushing him lightly. Her other hand stayed in her coat pocket, hidden.

The creature exhaled. "You've come home," it whispered.

Her fingers gripped the small plastic comb, and in one breathless movement, she drew it up and stabbed it straight into the creature's eye.

It staggered back, Sam sliding in its grip as it clawed at its face. The comb stuck out from the ruined socket, shaking with the force of its shudder. Its knees buckled, and its arms went loose. Sam dropped and hit the ground.

Ellie lunged forward, her arms wrapping around her brother. He was still warm. Still breathing. Her fingers locked at his back as she turned and ran. The creature shrieked, loud and long, behind her, clutching at its face.

She bolted through the mouth of the hollow, her breath slicing cold through her throat. The forest bent around her, the path closing in strange arcs. She held Sam close, each step pounding through the softness of the ground.

And somewhere behind her, the creature called her name.

THE LAST CHOICE

The path ahead was wrong. It no longer matched the way she'd come. Where there should have been space, the ground funneled inward, narrowing into crooked turns that wound deeper instead of out. The trees hunched close, their trunks angled unnaturally, leaning into the trail. Roots rose from the soil like twisted fingers. The forest was folding in on itself, reshaping to hold her fast.

Something moved in the distance behind her. Not the crash of something breaking through the brush—the quiet parting of leaves, branches whispering apart, footsteps landing with the patience of a predator that never missed.

"You don't have to be afraid," it said. It smiled through the words—she could hear it. The shape of its teeth sat inside the vowels.

Ellie drew Sam closer, her jaw locking hard. The air scorched her nose as she breathed. His small fingers caught weakly in the fabric of her coat, and the touch sent a jolt through her chest. She hitched him higher against her, arms braced firm beneath his weight.

The trail ahead narrowed more with every stride. The way she'd come was gone, swallowed in front of her. The branches above arched and knotted, weaving into each other until the sky disappeared entirely. There was nothing but a low ceiling of limbs bowed heavy under their own weight. The trees hunched in close, leaning into the trail. Roots lifted from the soil like twisted fingers. The forest was folding in, reshaping itself to keep her close.

Behind her, leaves parted again. The sound didn't rush. It didn't panic. Each step landed with deliberate rhythm, the cadence of something patient.

"You don't have to be afraid," it called again.

The voice poured through the trees like oil.

Ellie pulled Sam closer. His arm shifted, limp and trailing. She could feel the heat of him now. Her chest burned, her breath scraping up dry. One of her feet caught a rise in the dirt and she stumbled, falling to one knee, nearly toppling. A branch cracked somewhere behind her.

She forced herself upright again. Clutching Sam close, her arms quivering beneath his weight, Ellie pushed forward. Her steps dragged but never broke. The path looped in on itself once more, the trees pressing close, the air sharpening colder. The way out had to be ahead. It had to be.

The cold bit into her face, raw and sharp. She could feel her pulse thundering in her teeth. Her breath burst ragged in front of her and disappeared into the dark. Sam became heavier with every step. Her arms screamed from holding him.

The forest continued to close around her, the branches weaving above like ribs, the path ahead narrowing to a seam. Brambles clawed at her sleeves. Leaves tangled in her hair. Each footfall landed in mud and her steps began to slant, slipping sideways. She pushed forward anyway, teeth clenched, vision smeared with sweat and cold. Behind her came the rhythm of something moving with care, not speed. Leaves shivered and settled. Bark groaned low. Just one step, then another, deliberate and constant.

"You're going the wrong way."

The voice rolled through the trees like smoke. It slid into her ears and stayed there, winding around her thoughts.

"You're tired. You don't know where you're going. You'll only get more lost."

Ellie didn't answer. Her legs burned. Her lungs rattled. Sam's cheek stuck to her collar where the sweat clung.

"You don't have to carry him anymore. Let me help you. That's all I've ever wanted, Ellie."

Her foot landed in a shallow pit of mud, and she went down to one knee again, the shock of it shooting through her legs. She gasped, shifting Sam and bracing with one palm to keep him from touching the ground.

"I stayed when no one else did."

She swallowed hard. Her mouth tasted like dirt and blood.

"I listened when you cried. I waited when no one else did. And now you run from me?"

Ahead, something changed in the trees. A thinning. The lines between trunks grew wider. Pale light gathered at the edges.

"I stayed."

The trees thinned all at once and Ellie broke through a last curtain of low-hanging branches and stumbled into the clearing. The world opened in front of her, and there, just beyond the churned edge of earth where the woods ended, stood the fence.

It cut across the far end of the yard. Bent in places, flecked with rust. Her chest rose sharp. Her eyes stung. Her shoes hit the packed dirt harder now, her knees nearly giving with each step. The fence loomed closer. She reached it in only a few strides. Close enough to press her hands against the cold links. The metal clanged under her touch, shaking faintly. The porch light across the yard hadn't come on. The house stood dim and waiting.

She hit the fence running. The fingers of one hand hooked through the mesh to hold her up, the other cradled Sam against her. The metal was slick beneath her fingers. She tried to climb, footing the lower mesh and hoisting herself up. Her center tipped back. The rubber soles of her shoes skidded.

Ellie's breath hitched. She adjusted Sam again, hoisting him higher, but her arms screamed. Her sleeves were soaked to the elbow. Sam was burning in her grasp, skin damp, breath shallow. Her back hunched under his weight. The fence rose higher than she remembered, slick from frost. Her foot slipped as she tried to find a grip in the links. No traction. No leverage.

She slid back to the ground with a gasp, knees buckling. She tried again, higher this time, wedging her toe into the link, dragging herself up. Sam shifted in her grip and her elbow slipped. They dropped again, harder.

"No, no..." she gasped, already lunging back up, one hand on the fence, the other struggling to keep Sam close. He moaned, low in his throat. Behind her, the brush whispered. The sound of a branch folding beneath something tall.

She shoved the toe of her shoe into the lowest diamond of wire and lifted again. One foot. Then the other. But her arms were shaking. Sam's weight dragged her down. Her grip broke again. She hit the ground, bracing Sam against her body.

The ground pressed cold through her knees as Ellie crouched at the base of the fence, Sam tucked against her. Her arms trembled, but her grip didn't loosen. His breath came soft and fast against her collar. His skin burned through her coat. The metal fence rose high above them, lit by nothing but the pale smear of moonlight.

"It's okay," she whispered, her mouth close to his ear. "You're going to be okay."

Ellie pressed her lips to his forehead once, then pulled back. She looked up at the fence again; it stood tall. She shifted Sam in her arms, found his weight with both hands, and lifted him above her head. Her arms shook. Her shoes slipped. Her spine locked into place as she reached higher.

"Hold on," she breathed. "Just for a second. Hold on."

Her muscles screamed with the effort, her legs trembling as she pushed upward. The fence pressed into her front, its cold links biting through her coat. She lifted him higher, higher still, balancing him on her palms as the cruel unfinished wire bit into the backs of her hands. Her arms shook, nearly buckling. Then, with one last lurch, she shoved him over the top. The shape of him vanished from her hands.

Sam landed with a soft, final thud. Grass muffled the sound, but Ellie still flinched. Her breath caught in her throat. A cry pierced the dark, thin and high and alive. It cut through the stillness like a thread drawn sharp and sudden. Ellie sagged forward, the air rushing from her lungs in a shuddering gasp. Her knees folded under her, her forehead dropping against the fence with her hands pressed flat against the cold metal.

Ellie felt the air change behind her. It crowded the edges, pressed inward. The weight of it settled against her back. Her breath caught, and her spine pulled straight. The leaves seemed to hush, the damp earth going still beneath her shoes. The pull of it dragged at her as the shadows pulled toward the thing at her back. Exhausted, she turned.

The creature's limbs gathered close to its sides, jointed and twitching. The face it wore, the one that had once belonged to her father, had failed. The skin sagged at the neck, puckering at the edges. One eye drooped. The other was nothing more than a destroyed, oozing orb. Its ruined head turned unerringly in her direction, as if scenting her fear. What fixed itself on her now wasn't a man. Wasn't a father. It was something old and listening. Something that had waited for her in the trees, in the quiet places of the house, in the folds of her sadness.

Her hand slid from the fence. Her fingers fell open. Behind her, Sam cried again, sharp and wet, his breath ragged with fear, his voice catching on the edge of the wind. The sound tore something open in her chest.

The creature stepped forward, its limbs uncoiling, dragging pieces of itself through the dirt. Long, thin digits spasmed and stretched and spasmed again, their tips splintered and scraping furrows into the ground. Its body shifted with the motion, folding in strange places, the seams of its skin pulling open to show what writhed beneath. Where the mask of her father's face had once clung, only strips remained now, flaps of flesh that twitched at the edges, clinging to cheekbone, lip, brow. Each step it took came without sound, but the air changed with them, bending around the thing like the woods themselves had bowed to make room.

Ellie rose and stepped forward. The fence was behind her, the sound of Sam's crying thinning into distance. She didn't let herself look back. One step, then another, arms listless at her sides. Her coat clung to her shoulders. The cold bit through the seams. But she walked forward. Because something in her had already decided. She couldn't let it follow. Couldn't let it try again. Couldn't let it touch Sam ever again. The woods seemed to exhale as she moved, the space between trees parting just enough to let her pass.

The creature folded itself around her gently, as though it meant to keep her warm. Its limbs wrapped slow, draping, sliding into place with a strange patience. The weight of it settled across her shoulders first, then along her spine and down her arms. It moved with care, its surface shifting with each breath, slick where the skin had gone thin and stretched, coarse in places where bone had pushed through. It smelled of rot and damp earth, of something pulled too long from the dark. The pressure of it wrapped her completely, the way blankets might if you were being buried in them.

Its mouth never moved. The teeth remained bared in a frozen grin, but the sound came anyway. A voice that didn't belong to lungs or lips.

"Goodnight, baby girl."

The words didn't pass through the air. They threaded between her ribs and sank beneath her skin, following the line of her spine. It filled her up without force, seeped in soft. The voice didn't hurt, but it replaced something. Pushed something else out to make room.

The creature's heart beat slowly and deliberately through her body. It came from somewhere below the clearing. Not inside the creature, but underneath them both. A pulse that reached up through the dirt, into her feet, her legs, her chest. One beat. Then another. It echoed in the bones of the trees. It hummed in the roots.

The last thing she heard was Sam's cry, thin and trembling through the trees. It carried over the fence, just enough to reach her ears, one sharp breath. It caught in her chest and she tried to hold onto it, to keep it separate from everything else tightening around her. But the sound began to fade.

The heartbeat rose, steady and low. It pulsed through the dirt and into her feet, filled her bones, pushed against her ribs from the inside. She could feel it in her jaw, in her teeth, in the space behind her eyes. It drowned everything else. Sam's cry disappeared into it. Swallowed whole.

And the forest moved in. The trees gathered around her and the creature. Their limbs stretched. Bent. Folded. The branches drew together one by one, closing her in, until even the heartbeat in her bones went silent.

WHAT THEY FIND

Out here, at the edge of town, houses didn't cluster together. They stood apart, each one stitched to the next by gravel drives and wire fences, with wide open lots and sagging sheds between them. And beyond all that, behind every backyard, the woods waited, dark and tall and hunched, pressing in against the property lines.

The crying had been going on for hours—a faint, broken sound that rose and fell in the dark, like something tugged up by instinct, then dragged under again by exhaustion. It was the kind of sound that could almost be mistaken for some wild thing in the distance, tangled in a snare. But as the hours passed and the darkness began to lift, the sound sharpened.

She stood at her kitchen window, one hand braced on the counter, the other cupped around a mug. The floor tiles were freezing under her bare feet. The cry floated up through the glass, thin and ghostlike. It reached into the walls, into her ribs.

When Mrs. Emmons finally heard it, it had become raw and thin, paper-edged and frayed. The voice behind it was stretched to its last thread. There was nothing in it that asked to be picked up or comforted. It didn't even sound like it expected help.

The mug hit the counter with a flat, hollow clunk, splashing a few cold drops of leftover coffee up over the edge. She yanked her coat off the back of a chair, arms disappearing into the sleeves as she moved fast, her breath catching in her chest. The coat hung open as she stepped out the back door and down the porch stairs in her slippers.

Her yard dipped at the back, sloping toward the trees. The grass was brittle underfoot, cracking with every step. Her slippers were soaked through in seconds, but she kept going, moving along the narrow path between the garden beds. The yard gave way to a scatter of dead leaves, and past that, the woods crouched low, waiting in the half-light.

She almost stepped past him. Her foot was already lifting to take the next step when something caught the edge of her vision, too pale to be part of the leaves or the frost-glazed ground. She stopped short, her breath catching, eyes narrowing against the shifting morning light. There, slumped at the bottom of the fence, was something small. A soft sprawl of limbs and cloth, the faintest trace of color, off-white, gray-blue, and stained dark in places. It wasn't moving. Fabric clung to tiny limbs, slack and sagging, the kind of soaked-through stillness that said he'd been there for hours.

Mrs. Emmons's coat hung open, and the wind sliced through the fabric and up her back. The trees in front of her gave a slow lament as their limbs shifted against each other. The shape in the dirt twitched, one hand fluttering weakly against the ground. His head rolled to the side and from somewhere deep inside his chest came a sound.

She was on her knees before she could think about it. The baby was drawn in on himself, his small frame twisted like someone had dropped him there and he hadn't moved since. His legs were drawn up as far as his little body would allow, arms locked around his midsection, one elbow caught beneath him at a wrong angle. His face was blotchy, the skin around his eyes so swollen she couldn't tell if they were open or shut. His lips were cracked.

His clothes clung to him, stiff with cold and soaked through in patches. He was trembling, small, stuttering spasms that rolled through his chest and arms in waves. She pulled off her coat and wrapped it around him with clumsy, desperate care. The fabric swallowed him completely, and she tucked the sleeves underneath his feet, pressing the coat closed with her arms. He let his head tip forward, his body folding into her touch.

"It's okay," she whispered, her voice catching in her throat. "Shhh. I've got you."

The walk back to the house felt impossibly far. Her slippers slipped on the frozen ground. Her door stood open ahead. She pushed it wider with the side of her body and stepped inside, the warmth of the kitchen blooming around them.

She fumbled to find her phone with the baby still pressed to her chest, her chin resting lightly on the crown of his head. The screen blurred once before her thumb found the numbers. 911.

The voice on the other end of the line asked questions, clear, practiced, clipped, but Mrs. Emmons could barely answer. She gave her address. She said "baby." She said "the woods." Her voice shook too much to say much more. The dispatcher told her to stay on the line, but she set the phone down gently on the counter, already rocking back and forth with the child in her arms. His skin was still cold beneath her collarbone.

A low wail, distant at first, came from far off down the road, but rose fast. The familiar echo of sirens, splitting the quiet wide open. Mrs. Emmons stepped to the window, careful not to jostle the child in her arms. The blinds were still half-drawn, but she could see them coming, flashes of red and blue flickering through the trees.

Mrs. Emmons didn't wait for the knock. She opened the front door before anyone reached it, the baby still cradled to her chest, his face hidden beneath the oversized fold of her coat. The wind caught the door and slammed it hard against the outside wall.

"He was at the fence," she said, her voice raw and flat, stripped down to the simplest truth. "I think...I think he was out there all night."

The officer on the porch stepped forward. He was square-shouldered, short, his jaw dark with early stubble. He slowed, just slightly, his boots dragging half a step on the porch boards. His eyes dropped to the bundle in her arms.

A medic came up fast behind him, efficient and silent, hands already gloved, a bag swinging at her side. She didn't wait for permission. She crouched low, voice even and calm as she reached for the coat. Mrs. Emmons shifted just enough to let her in.

The medic's voice came low: "Still responsive. Breathing's shallow. Let's go."

She scooped him up with both arms and turned without looking back. As she stepped off the porch toward the waiting ambulance, the officer finally spoke.

"Wait..." the officer said, quiet at first. His gaze followed the child. Something shifted behind his eyes. "That's..." His mouth opened, then closed again.

He stepped forward, out from under the porch light, into the dawn.

"That's Rachel's kid," he said, his voice tired. "Sam."

He stood there for a moment, still. The lines around his mouth deepened. "I've been to that house," he said. The words came slow. His eyes drifted toward the woods, then came back. "She has a daughter too. Was there a little girl?"

Mrs. Emmons shook her head. “No one else.”

The officer gave a small nod, his expression hardening. He turned without another word and stepped off the porch, his boots sinking slightly into the grass as he crossed back toward the road. The cold hadn’t broken. It still hung over the yards and rooftops, pressed into the ground, clinging to windows. Each step he took was quick and deliberate, his body moving forward, but his thoughts were already ahead of him.

The house stood quiet across the way, its paint dulled and peeling, the porch sagging under its own weight. The screen door hung askew, the frame warped, and the front window was clouded with grime. A wind moved through the yard, tugging at the loose pieces, making the screen tap softly against the siding. The place looked hollow.

He climbed the steps carefully, his boots testing the strength of each board, the wood sagging with a tired rasp beneath his weight. He raised his hand and knocked, firm and steady. The sound echoed in the space behind the door and was swallowed by it. He waited, listening, watching for the flicker of movement behind the glass, but saw nothing.

He knocked again, louder this time, his knuckles hitting the frame with a thudding, hollow rhythm. “Rachel? It’s the sheriff’s office.”

His words rang out into the stillness, stretching into the corners of the porch, into the narrow spaces between the walls. He stepped back, looked toward the windows, but the curtains didn’t stir. No footsteps, no voice, no rustle from inside. Just the wind at his back and the brittle sound of the screen shifting against the siding.

He raised his voice again.

“Rachel, it’s the police. I’m coming in.”

He waited one more second, eyes fixed on the door like he expected it to open on its own. When it didn't, he reached for the handle. The door gave way under his hand, slow and soft, swinging inward with the reluctant dragging sigh of swollen wood.

The air that met him was stagnant and stale. It rolled out past the frame and the smell was immediate: old cigarettes, mildew, the sour trace of food left out and forgotten.

He stepped over the threshold, leaving the door open behind him. The living room was dim, the curtains drawn uneven, letting in just enough of the morning to trace the outlines of worn furniture and scattered toys. A blanket draped over the arm of the couch. A glass resting on the floor beside it. A single shoe tipped on its side near the door.

He moved forward slowly, his boots soft against the floorboards. The air in the house felt stifling.

"Rachel?" he called out.

He followed the narrow hallway, his steps sinking into the carpet.

At the end of the hall, the bedroom door stood ajar. He pushed it open with his knuckles. The hinges let out a long, weary sigh, slow and drawn-out. The room was dim, curtains drawn. Rachel lay curled on the bed, facing the wall. One leg twisted up beneath her, a bare foot hanging off the edge of the mattress. Her hair was half stuck to her cheek. An empty bottle lay on its side beside the bed.

He stepped closer, careful, watching the slow, shallow rise of her back. Still breathing.

He crouched beside the bed, placed one gloved hand on her shoulder, and shook her, firm.

"Rachel."

She didn't move. Her body gave a slight sway under his grip but offered nothing back. He shook her harder, hand clenching through the fabric of her shirt.

"Rachel. Wake up."

Still nothing.

She breathed, slow and shallow, but her face didn't change. Her eyes stayed closed, lips slack, head pressed into the pillow. The smell coming off her now was stronger and sour. Sweat, old liquor, something else beneath it.

He stood halfway and came back down harder, voice raised now, sharp.

"Rachel! Hey! Wake up! Come on!"

A groan slipped from her throat, low and dragging. Her head rolled slightly toward him. One eye cracked open, unfocused, her mouth working against the air. She squinted up at him, confused. He grabbed her shoulder with both hands and gave her a full jolt, enough to rattle her in the bed.

"Get up, Rachel! Get up!"

Rachel winced at the sound of his voice, her face twisting in irritation. Her hand flailed weakly across the bed, trying to push him away, but it was slow and clumsy. She blinked again, longer this time, and her brow knit slightly as her eyes began to focus. The slack in her mouth pulled tight.

"Jesus," she muttered. Her voice was dry, cracked at the edges. She dragged the back of her hand across her mouth. "What the hell…what time is it?"

He didn't answer. He crouched lower again, right into her field of vision.

"Where are your kids, Rachel?"

Rachel pulled her arm over her face. Her lips moved, barely forming the words. "They're…they're in the bedroom," she mumbled. "They're sleeping."

He shook his head hard, voice rising again, fierce now.

"No, they're not," he snapped. His voice rose, all patience gone. "We just found your son outside. Barely breathing. Where the fuck is your daughter, Rachel!?"

Rachel jerked her arm off her face, eyes wide now, confused but starting to sharpen.

"No…no, he's not," she said, shaking her head. "Sam's here. I put him down last night…he's in the crib." She pushed herself up onto one elbow, her breath catching in her throat. "He was crying, but I…he's here."

"We found him outside, Rachel. Out by the fence. He's in an ambulance right now."

Her mouth opened, then closed again. She blinked at him, lips parting, unable to find any words.

"No. That's not…" she started, but the words trailed off.

"Get up," he snapped. "Get your ass up! Now!"

She swung her legs over the side of the mattress, unsteady. Her feet hit the floor; one hand gripped the edge of the nightstand, her knuckles white.

He didn't wait for her to argue again.

"We found Sam, Rachel. Outside. Alone in the cold." His voice didn't rise this time…it dropped lower. "You tell me where your daughter is. Right now."

That landed.

Rachel's eyes snapped toward the hallway. She pushed past him, stumbling toward the doorframe, dragging herself forward like instinct had finally caught up to her. She moved fast now, barefoot and weaving, almost tripping over her own feet as she reached the bedroom across the hall. She threw the door open so hard it slammed against the wall.

"Ellie?" she shouted. "Ellie!? Sam!?"

Nothing.

She stood frozen in the doorway, one hand gripping the frame, her other arm wrapped across her stomach. Her breath came shallow and quick, chest hitching as she scanned the room, waiting for the child she swore was there to suddenly appear from under the bed or behind the door. Her eyes moved frantically across the mattress, the small pile of blankets kicked toward the foot of the bed, the pair of child-sized socks crumpled near the dresser.

She turned, quickly, and looked back over her shoulder. Her eyes were glassy, unfocused, the shock starting to bleed through. "She's not…" Her voice cracked in the middle, barely more than breath. "She was here. She was here. Last night. She went to bed right there."

The officer stepped into the hallway behind her, his boots loud on the worn wood.

"Go outside," he said, voice low but firm. "Now. Go sit on the porch."

Rachel didn't move. He took another step closer, close enough that his voice hit her more squarely when he spoke again.

"Rachel…" His voice trembled, breaking. "Go outside. Sit on the porch."

She blinked, slowly, and her mouth parted as if she wanted to argue, but no words came. She turned and started down the hallway, each step slow and dragging. Her hand trailed along the wall for balance, her shoulders hunched inward, her robe bunched beneath her elbows.

He waited until the door clicked shut behind her, then lifted his radio.

"I need backup guys," he said. His voice was flatter now, pinched at the edges. "We've got a second child unaccounted for. Start a search team. We…we may need dogs."

He stepped into Sam and Ellie's room.

There were no signs of struggle. No blood. No broken glass or footprints. The window shut. He backed out slowly, closing the door behind him as he left. The hallway stretched long in front of him, the light growing brighter by the minute through the windows.

By midmorning, more patrol cars had pulled up along the road, their tires skidding to a stop, doors swinging open in practiced rhythm. Radios crackled, boots struck the pavement. A second unit stepped onto the porch and was waved inside, heads already bent together, voices hushed but purposeful.

Room by room, drawer by drawer, they searched the house. Nothing was left untouched. The kitchen cupboards were bare, a crusted jar of something green in the back of the fridge. Empty liquor bottles rolled against the baseboards. In a rusted tin in Rachel's bedroom, one officer found two glass pipes nestled among a scattering of white crystals. Another tin, beneath the couch, held a needle and a folded piece of foil.

Outside, the woods began to fill with movement. Officers combed the tree line, working in pairs. Orange markers were planted in the ground. The area where Sam had been found was cordoned with tape. More units moved deeper into the trees, heads low, boots breaking slowly through the crust of dead leaves. Dogs were brought in. Volunteers too: quiet-faced neighbors in gloves and knit hats, forming lines and waiting for instructions. Some had known of the family. Most hadn't.

Word spread. By afternoon, the lot beside the Emmons house held three cruisers and a line of cars parked half in the ditch. Someone had already printed flyers on their home computer, Ellie's name in bold across the top, the picture below taken on school picture day that year. The paper lifted at the corners before they'd even finished taping them to the telephone poles.

People talked. They stood at the edge of the yards, arms crossed, voices low. One man said he'd seen Rachel shouting in the driveway three nights ago. Another swore he'd heard a scream. A teenager from down the road said Ellie was always alone, walking home from school.

Mrs. Rieke told the officers everything. That it started with drawings—the hollow tree, the figures with warped faces. She told them Ellie said her father had come back. How he came into her room at night. How he hummed to her. How he took things, buttons, drawings, small things, so he could remember her. How he told her not to be scared, and she didn't have to let people be mean to her anymore.

Mrs. Rieke's voice shook when she said it out loud. She didn't look at the officer's notepad while she spoke. She just kept her eyes on the trees behind the house.

She said she'd reported it. Called the school counselor. Called Rachel in for a meeting. Sat across from her in the front office while Rachel insisted it was all just stories. Nightmares.

And then, Ellie got suspended for pushing a little girl off the big toy on the playground.

"Ellie wasn't violent," Mrs. Rieke said, her voice catching at the edges. "She was tired."

Questions were asked. Rachel didn't have answers as the officer led her to the back of the police cruiser. She stared out the window, her face pale in the flash of blue and red spinning across the dash. Her hair was pulled back in a rough knot. Her slippers were damp.

At the station, they gave her water. Asked if she needed anything. She shook her head once, barely. She didn't touch the paper cup. When the detective sat down across from her and opened his notebook, she flinched slightly.

They asked when she'd last seen Ellie.

"Last night," she said.

They asked what Ellie had been wearing.

"I don't know," she said. "Whatever was clean."

They asked if she remembered putting Sam to bed.

She didn't answer that one at all.

When pressed, she shrugged or looked down at her hands.

They asked about the woods. Whether Ellie ever went out there.

Rachel blinked slowly. "No," she said. "Never."

They asked about Ellie's father.

Rachel's jaw stiffened at that. She looked past them at the wall, at the clock above the door.

"Gone. He took off," she said.

They asked when.

"Six months ago," she muttered. "Right after Sam was born."

They asked about Ellie's drawings. The stories she'd told at school. They asked about the meeting with the teacher, about what she remembered from that conversation. Rachel rubbed at her temple with one hand and said Ellie made things up sometimes.

"She had a big imagination," she said. "That's all it was."

They let the silence hang, long and pressing. Eventually, they asked her again: "When did you last see your daughter?"

Rachel leaned back in her chair, eyes half-closed. No matter how they came at it, direct, sideways, soft or firm, she gave them nothing new. She stayed quiet until they walked her back outside. The morning had grown sharper, the air brittle with sunlight, the wind pulling harder now against the corners of the buildings.

They opened the cruiser door again. Rachel slid in without a word. Hands still folded. Face turned toward the glass. She didn't ask where they were going. She didn't ask if they'd found anything. She didn't even ask if Sam was all right. She stared at her own reflection in the window. Thin and washed out. Her eyes sinking below the surface.

The cruiser pulled to a stop in front of the house that evening. The sun was out, but it had started to fade. Light skimmed over the porch, and the trees at the edge of the yard didn't move. The cop she'd spoken with earlier, the short one with square-shoulders, opened the door to let her out. He didn't look at her when he stepped back. He just stood with his hands at his sides, waiting.

She climbed out slowly, one hand bracing the frame, her feet hesitant on the gravel like the ground might shift under her weight. Her robe had come loose again. Her eyes drifted toward the side yard, to the place near the trees where the tape still fluttered in the breeze.

He cleared his throat behind her. "You'll be contacted by Child Protection Services," he said. His voice was clipped, flat. "Probably today."

Rachel nodded faintly, her eyes not leaving the woods.

"They've placed Sam in emergency foster care," he added. "He'll be somewhere safe."

That made her blink. Her jaw twitched.

He stepped forward then, closer, his shadow long against the porch.

"You need to stay the fuck away from him," he said, low and deliberate. "Do you hear me? Unless the state tells you otherwise, and God willing they won't, you don't go near him. Not the hospital. Not the foster home. Nowhere."

Rachel's eyes shifted to him, slow and unfocused. There was something dull behind them. She nodded once, barely. It could've meant anything.

He watched her for a long second more. Then he turned and walked back to the cruiser without another word. The engine rumbled to life with a low, mechanical growl, the tires crunching deep into the gravel as he backed out onto the road. She didn't watch him leave. She stood where he'd left her, in the shallow dip between the frostbitten grass and the porch.

Rachel climbed the porch steps one at a time, slow and unsteady. The wood groaned softly under her weight, and for a second, she paused at the top step, one hand on the railing, her eyes blank and unfocused. The front door hung cracked wide enough for cold to slip through the house and settle in the seams of the floor. The draft slipped around her ankles, up through the folds of her robe. She stepped through the threshold without touching the door.

She crossed the room, her slippers making no sound on the floor, and walked straight through to the back door. Her fingers found the latch by memory. She turned it slowly, letting the hinges whine open. The light outside was thinner now, stretched low across the grass, cutting long, gray lines through the yard.

She lit a cigarette with trembling hands, her thumb missing the lighter wheel twice before it caught. The smoke drifted up into her face. She sank into the porch chair slowly, bones stiff, robe dragging across the weather-worn slats as she settled in. Her slippers were still damp from the walk, the chill of them seeping up through her soles. She didn't react to the cold.

Officers swept the forest in slow, overlapping lines. Boots left shallow prints in the dead leaves, bright tape marked paths through the brush. Dogs passed through, tongues lolling, noses low to the ground. Volunteers from town moved in quiet groups, calling Ellie's name. Flashlights cut through the undergrowth in wide arcs. People with clipboards knocked on doors, asked if anyone had seen anything. If anyone had heard anything strange.

Each night, the lines got thinner. The sweeps grew shorter. Flashlights moved slower. The dogs were called off. The questions slowed. Voices grew quieter as the trees soaked up the light and the cold settled deeper into the ground. Most volunteers stopped showing up after the second or third day. They went home, closed their doors, and told themselves someone else would find her.

But Mrs. Rieke stayed. She searched late, long after the others had gone home. She brought her dog, a flashlight, and an old red scarf she wore high over her chin, knotted under her coat. Each night, she walked into the woods, the beam of her light swinging low and steady across the brush.

The flyers, once bright, began to peel from telephone poles and wooden fences, their edges fluttering in the wind. Rain washed out the ink in some of them. Others were torn by passing hands or tugged loose by the wind.

Seasons nudged forward. The trees went bare. Then green again. No new footprints appeared by the fence. No new drawings were found in the grass. The case file stayed open. Long after the search parties had stopped walking the gridlines, after the tape had come down and the last flyer had fluttered loose from its staple, Rachel sat on the porch in the dark. The sky above her was cloudless. The moonlight cast pale shapes across the lawn, and the air was still.

A small sound, soft, drifting, slipped from between the trees with the lightness of breath. It floated across the yard like mist, so faint it might have been imagined, so clear it couldn't have been.

"Goodnight, Mama."

ACKNOWLEDGMENTS

Writing a book is never a solitary act, and I am deeply grateful to those who have helped shape *The Hollow One* into what it is today.

First and foremost, I owe immense thanks to my editors, Holly Royle, Rachel Moulton and DJ Schuette, for their keen insight, patience, and unwavering belief in this story. Your sharp eyes, thoughtful guidance, and encouragement have elevated every page, and I could not have asked for better partners in this process.

To my most avid readers (you know who you are), thank you for your enthusiasm, for staying with me through drafts and rewrites, and for reminding me why stories matter.

To my family and friends, who offered love, patience, and encouragement—even when my head and heart were buried in Ellie's world—thank you for keeping me grounded.

And finally, to you, the reader: Thank you for choosing to step into this story. The world of The Hollow One comes alive because of your willingness to walk its paths, face its shadows, and hold onto its light.

ABOUT THE AUTHOR

Author photo by Jim Louvau

Corinne Westbrook is a writer and journalist whose work explores the darker edges of art, music, and storytelling. She has written for outlets including Metal Injection and Knotfest, covering album reviews, features, annual "Top Albums" lists, and cultural commentary rooted in the strange and unconventional.

Raised in rural Oregon, Corinne discovered her love of writing early. Her first poem was published when she was ten years old. A lifelong horror devotee, she grew up staying up late with friends to watch Tales from the Crypt, drawn to stories that blur the line between the real and the unreal.

She believes the most haunting stories often have roots in reality. While The Hollow One is a work of fiction, it is shaped by emotional truths and experiences pulled from real life. This novel is her debut in long-form fiction.